"Admit it, that night in the hall was hot."

A muscle spasmed in Brad's jaw, the deep green of his eyes sharpening to a blade.

Digging a little deeper, Gabriella said, "And in the barn... Aren't you just a little bit curious as to what would've happened if we hadn't stopped?"

His arm around her waist squeezed a little tighter. "We know what would have happened. I can't get involved with you, Gabriella."

"I know you don't want to admit this, but—" she lowered her voice to a whisper and spoke directly into his ear "—we're already involved."

His Adam's apple moved up and down as he swallowed. And then, she swore he pulled her a little closer.

Dear Reader,

Thank you for picking up *In the Rancher's Footsteps,* the second book in my new North Star, Montana series. Saving the ranch is a bit of a romance novel cliché, but when something we love is threatened, we dig in our heels and fight. Ready and willing to do almost anything to protect what's ours.

How far would you go to protect the only home you've ever known? What would you do to keep a best friend's dream alive and flourishing? And what if getting what you wanted hurt people in ways you never dreamed of?

I hope you enjoy Brad and Gabriella's story. Be sure to pick up next month's release, *Christmas in Montana,* which features the third delicious McKenna brother—Chance. Also look for more North Star, Montana books soon.

For details on my books, blog, appearances, etc., please visit my website, KayStockham.com. I love to hear from my readers! I cannot tell you how much your comments and notes mean to me. To keep in touch, please "Like" my Kay Stockham Fan Page on Facebook and follow @KayStockham on Twitter.

God bless,

Kay Stockham

In the Rancher's Footsteps

Kay Stockham

™ **Harlequin**®

TORONTO NEW YORK LONDON
AMSTERDAM PARIS SYDNEY HAMBURG
STOCKHOLM ATHENS TOKYO MILAN MADRID
PRAGUE WARSAW BUDAPEST AUCKLAND

Recycling programs
for this product may
not exist in your area.

ISBN-13: 978-0-373-71734-7

IN THE RANCHER'S FOOTSTEPS

ABOUT THE AUTHOR

Kay Stockham has always wanted to be a writer, ever since she copied the pictures out of a Charlie Brown book and rewrote the story because she didn't like the plot. Formerly a secretary/office manager for a large commercial real estate development company, she's now a full-time writer and stay-at-home mom who firmly believes being a mom/wife/homemaker is the hardest job of all. Happily married for more than fifteen years and the somewhat frazzled mother of two, she has sold ten books to Harlequin Superromance. Her first release, *Montana Secrets,* hit the Waldenbooks bestseller list and was chosen as a Holt Medallion finalist for Best First Book. Kay has garnered praise from reviewers for her emotional, heart-wrenching stories and looks forward to a long career writing a genre she loves.

Books by Kay Stockham

As always this book is dedicated to my family.
Love to you all.

And for my BFs: you know who you are.
We've shed a lot of laughs,
tears and stories over the years.
Here's to a whole lot more!

CHAPTER ONE

"OOH. RIDE 'EM, COWBOY."

Gabriella Thompson paused in the act of writing a catalog item number to see what her assistant manager, Alicia, was talking about—or rather *who*.

She had to squint since she'd left her glasses in her office, but she was able to make out the very tall, very broad-shouldered man who had paused outside the doors of *Premiere Vue*.

He glanced at something in his large hand as though double-checking the address, then frowned into the interior of Gabriella's shop, even though she knew he couldn't see beyond the window displays.

"He's not Clint Eastwood but I'd tap that."

A former stuntwoman and current body builder, Alicia's muscles were only slightly less bulky than those straining the sleeves of the man's gray T-shirt.

Not bad, but he definitely wasn't Gabriella's type. "Down, girl. He's probably looking for something for his *boy*friend," Gabriella said, tossing the catalog aside and standing to go to her office.

She had calls to make, work to do. Two months of paperwork and orders to catch up on, contacts she needed to touch base with because the past two months had been spent taking care of her best friend Molly in the last weeks of her illness.

"Oh, he's coming in. How do the girls look?"

Gabriella shook her head at Alicia's behavior, knowing her assistant was trying to lighten the mood. Molly's death after a short but deadly bout with cancer had left Gabriella struggling to find her footing. "The girls are envy-worthy as always," she said, referring to Alicia's bountiful double-Ds. "Just remember store policy."

"I know, I know. Hands off the customer. So can I put other things on him?"

Alicia's quick return brought out the smile in Gabriella she'd worked so hard to achieve. "You are incorrigible." And Gabriella loved it. The guy walking in the door didn't stand a chance.

He wasn't the first pseudo-cowboy to cross the threshold of her business. There had been plenty of cowboys, aliens and vampires over the years.

Located a couple blocks from the many soundstages and sets in Burbank, California, *Premiere Vue*—or *First Blush*—saw more than its share of famous faces as well as extras, studio executives and Hollywood elite.

Gabriella didn't want to jinx herself, but *Premiere Vue* was fast becoming the rising star in high-end romantic gifts. No cheesy cards, porn or boxers with hearts on them here, only the best the world had to offer. Lingerie and perfume from Paris, lotions and soaps from London, chocolates from Belgium and Switzerland, flowers from all over the world.

Alicia looked tough but she designed some of the most feminine, sexy and unique-looking gift baskets to be had. In addition to their merchandise, they also planned hot-air balloon rides, sunset cruises and handled all the arrangements required when it came to everything from catering romantic dinners for two right up to full-blown wedding showers and anniversary parties. If it involved romance, *Premiere Vue* made it happen.

The electronic door chime did its thing and the cowboy stepped inside. He wore jeans and boots, and the dove-gray T-shirt that wasn't quite cowboyish but showed off the rock-hard muscles of his arms. No sense in hiding those guns.

The hat was the kicker, though. Apparently he played the good guy on whatever movie or soap opera he filmed. Didn't all good cowboys wear white hats?

When he stopped to peruse the latest arrivals from Paris—tiny black lace corsets with soft pink ribbons and matching panties—she found herself studying him as thoroughly as Alicia and wishing she had her glasses to sharpen the fuzzy edges.

Alicia approached him with an extra sway in her sashay. "Welcome. I'm Alicia. May I help you?"

The moment he heard Alicia speak the man pierced her with a surprisingly intense stare. "Maybe."

Alicia gave him her most flirtatious smile and indicated the shop in a graceful Vanna White wave. "We're the best in the business. Are you looking for something for your wife? A girlfriend?"

Instead of answering Alicia's question, the cowboy's gaze shifted to Gabriella and narrowed.

"You're not the woman I need to see."

A knot formed in Gabriella's stomach. Not the woman he needed to see? What did that mean?

Maintaining eye contact, he left the display of corsets and moved toward her. Gabriella straightened to her full height. She was five-eleven-and-a-half in her bare feet and presently wore four-inch heels, but this man was taller and definitely broader, and he moved with a careful pace, like a man stalking prey.

Or one intimidated by the contents of her store? "Gabriella?"

He knew her name. Up close she knew he hadn't come from a sound stage or recording session but was the real deal. Which could only mean— Surely not?

Despite the hat, crinkles fanned out from the man's eyes from too much time in the sun. His boots were well worn, layered with a coating of dust he hadn't picked up on any L.A. street. "Who's asking?"

"Braddock McKenna. We need to talk. Privately."

McKenna. A short huff of a laugh left her chest as awareness kicked in. Of course. A somewhat handsome cowboy walks into her shop and he was one of *them.* "I'm not interested."

She didn't care why her biological father's adopted son was there to see her. Molly had harped for years that Gabriella needed to ignore her mother's dictates and go to Montana, settle the issues between her and Zane McKenna face-to-face. But this close to Molly's death, Gabriella simply wasn't capable of making that leap. "As you can see, I'm busy."

Gabriella turned to walk away but two steps into her grand exit, Braddock caught her by the arm.

"Not so fast. I'm here about your father and I've come a hell of a long way to talk to you. The least you can do is hear me out."

"Of course it's about Zane. Why else would you be here? But whatever it is? I'm *not* interested. Why would I let you waste my time talking about a man who means nothing to me?"

Braddock's face turned to stone at her words but he didn't budge.

"Fine, what? Is he sick? Needs a kidney? A piece of my liver? What?" She knew she sounded mean but the man had cared less about her, why should she care about him?

"Zane died two weeks ago. His attorney has been trying to contact you but you haven't returned his calls."

Because of Molly. Because she'd slept on Molly's couch or even sometimes in Molly's hospital bed beside her so Molly wouldn't be alone, and she'd thought...

She wasn't sure what she'd thought the calls from the Montana attorney were about. She'd figured if it was important, the man would have left a message that wasn't merely a curt request to return his call.

"Honey, you need to take a step back and let go of Gabriella," Alicia ordered.

Gabriella hugged herself when Braddock did as ordered. In the three years Alicia had worked here, she had personally taken down two perverts, five shoplifters and a paparazzo who had snuck in when J-Lo was shopping post-pregnancy. No one messed with Alicia.

Braddock's gaze narrowed on Gabriella's face and she found herself wanting to squirm at the intensity.

"You almost seem sorry."

She was. Every life was important and should be mourned, even Zane McKenna's.

The phone rang. In response, Alicia pointed a finger at Braddock and waggled it in warning but moved to the desk to answer it.

"Thank you for letting me know. I won't keep you."

"Stop." His tone was brusk.

Gabriella didn't like being ordered around. Most business owners were people who didn't like being told what to do.

She lifted her chin, careful to keep her voice level. "Whatever this is about, leave me out of it."

Braddock's mouth flattened into a hard line. "That's

not a problem. All you have to do is sign." He pulled folded papers from his rear pocket.

"Wait a minute, what is she signing?" Alicia demanded, off the phone and moving close once again.

"Simply put," he said, never breaking eye contact with Gabriella, "you are agreeing to sell your inheritance to me and my brothers for the price Zane specified in his will."

"Inheritance?"

Braddock shifted, his lashes lowering over his eyes. "Zane left you one-fourth of the Circle M Ranch. The selling price is one hundred thousand dollars."

Gabriella gasped while Alicia whistled long and low. Why would Zane leave her a piece of his ranch? Why would he leave her anything at all when he'd ignored her nearly all of her life? "I see. I don't know what to say except I'm surprised. I'll have my attorney look over the paperwork."

She didn't think it possible but Braddock McKenna tensed even more. "We've put this off several weeks already due to you not responding to the calls or the notification letter. If it's all the same, I'd like to get this taken care of today. Now, preferably."

He waved a hand toward the contract Alicia had plucked from Gabriella's hands and was now reading.

"It's simple language and very straightforward. All you have to do is read and sign."

"Not so fast, cowboy. It says here her part of the land is worth an estimated one *million* dollars."

Shock bulleted through Gabriella. A million dollars? "Let me see that."

Alicia handed over the document and pointed out the paragraph. Gabriella read that portion then started at the top, her eyes skimming over the words as quickly as she could, mentally tallying up the points of interest.

"As you can read, there are conditions to be met before you'd ever get your hands on the property," Braddock said. "To be done with Zane, as you wanted, the price is a hundred thousand."

She ignored his statement and kept reading. One fourth of the ranch—worth an estimated one million—had indeed been left to her by her father. She had two options: sell immediately to Braddock and his adopted brothers for one hundred thousand. Or to obtain full legal rights she had to—

"I'd have to live there *three months?*" She reread the paragraph a second time but the details didn't alter. To be deeded the land, she had to spend three consecutive months on the ranch, living *in* the house. At the end of that time, she would be deeded the property and could do with it what she wanted.

Gabriella stared at Braddock. "What about you?"

"What about me?"

"What conditions do you and your brothers have?"

"None. We've already been deeded our portions."

Gabriella thought of a few choice words she didn't have to say aloud because Alicia was muttering them for her. "So let me get this straight. The man fathers me, abandons me, gives me an inheritance—but I can't have it unless I jump through hoops Zane's no longer even here to see me jump through?"

Carrying the document with her, Gabriella paced several steps away, her back to Braddock as she tried to take it all in.

"He didn't abandon you. Zane wouldn't do that."

"But he did," Gabriella argued. "Don't stand there and tell me he didn't when you weren't even around."

"Maybe I wasn't around when you were little but I've been there the past fifteen years. Where were you?"

Gabriella gasped but he didn't give her time to answer.

"I have a flight in a couple hours. Are you signing or not? I have a check for a hundred grand in my wallet ready for you."

"Why are you in such a hurry?" Gabriella demanded.

He removed the hat long enough to run his thick fingers through his dark brown hair. "Because I have a ranch to run. I didn't come here to argue with you but I do need a decision."

He obviously didn't think she could do it, or *would* do it. And he was right. She had no interest in Montana, visiting it or owning a piece of it. She would always associate the state with her father and the combination brought out enough baggage from her childhood to choke a horse. She couldn't do it, no matter how badly she wanted to wipe the knowing, you'd-never-make-it expression off Braddock's face.

He produced a folded square of paper—the check—and held it between two fingers. "You'll never have to think about Zane or Montana again. A hundred grand is nothing to sneeze at. What business can't use extra cash flow?"

Some businesses, maybe, but *Premiere Vue* was doing very, very well. Her clients had money to blow and people to impress, typically a new love interest every few weeks.

But that wasn't to say she didn't have improvements she wanted to make. She and Molly had always wanted to expand into a chain. They wanted to take what was a single-store boutique business and go global. But the website alone was estimated at approximately thirty grand. The check would cover it and then some, and she should be grateful for it.

Still, a part of her was tempted. With a million dollars, she could open that second location *and* have a website. A million would make their dream a reality.

"Gabriella, can I talk to you?" Alicia asked, tilting her head to step away from Braddock.

"Sure." Gabriella needed a few minutes to soak in this latest development. Couldn't anything ever be simple?

"We'll only be a minute. Why don't you look around for a while?" Alicia suggested to Braddock. Then under her breath, "Country boys like you could learn a thing or two in here."

Gabriella smirked at the slight, glad someone had gotten a shot in after his boorish behavior, and allowed the other woman to pull her behind the counter.

"Okay, I'll make this quick. I know this—" Alicia indicated the legal document "—is probably the last thing you want to think about right now, and I know I'm not the one who should be bringing this up but—*do it.*"

Gabriella blinked, taken aback. "What?"

"Do it. I've taken care of things for a while now, right? So you could be with Molly?"

Gabriella pressed her fingertips to her temple. A pounding headache loomed. "Alicia, it's three months when I've already been gone most of the past two months. Besides, it would never work. Me? On a ranch? What would I do?"

"Sleep. Eat. God knows you haven't done enough of that lately. You could rest and relax, pretend it's a working vacation."

A vacation? She hadn't had one in a couple years. Not even a day on the beach. "If you added up all the time Zane spent with me growing up it wouldn't *total* much more than three months. Why should I go there now?"

"Because not everybody gets a shot at a million dollars?" Alicia said with a coaxing smile.

"Yes, I know it's a great opportunity but it would be unprofessional of me to be away that long, especially since I've been away so much."

"Gabriella, no offense, but you look like you're ready to topple over. You need a break. Maybe this is it. If you don't stay the three months, you still get a hundred grand."

"But you'd be working seven days a week again."

Alicia took a deep breath that nearly made the girls pop out of her top. "And it'll be hard. It *was* hard. But Molly needed us to be there for her. Now you need this. And maybe you couldn't expect or trust your assistant manager to run the business for that long with you so far away, but you *could* expect your new partner to."

New partner?

Alicia raised both eyebrows high, a wary yet hopeful expression on her face that was at odds with her tough-girl appearance. "I know. I *know* my timing sucks but, come on. Like you and Molly didn't know I've always wanted to be a part of things? You think I'm busting my hump to be an assistant forever? Uh-uh. I was biding my time because you two kept talking about expanding, and two stores would eventually lead to three. Molly's death changed things but this place is still a gold rush waiting to happen and I'm a big part of why. You can't deny that."

"I wouldn't dream of denying it." Because it was true. Alicia's designs were *that* good. She'd been a great addition to the team and she was an event planner's dream.

"Okay, so even though the timing sucks and I wouldn't have brought it up for a while to let things settle, helping you pull this off so you get your inheritance and the money to expand is my ticket in. We can do this—for Molly."

Gabriella couldn't process information fast enough. Of all times for her brain to take a hiatus. "You'd do that? Work three straight months if necessary?"

"For a partnership? Yes. It's not a chain gang," Alicia said with a wry smile. "We bumped Todd's hours up while Molly was sick. With him taking care of deliveries and pitching in here, we could get that million."

Gabriella mulled that over, her mind spinning with all of the details. It was *so* tempting. "What if I can't stand it? What if I leave before the three months are up and I don't get the land to sell?"

"That would really suck, but I'd still get the partnership. No matter what."

It was only fair. But when Gabriella thought of how the next three months might play out, she shook her head. "I can't even picture it. And dealing with him—"

"Yeah, I know. But bad attitude or not, you've got to admit he's still hot."

"I'm going to pretend you didn't say that," Gabriella murmured. "That man is one of the reasons my father didn't want me."

Alicia's expression softened. "Look, Gabriella, I know it won't be easy but people have endured a lot worse things than living on a ranch for a *million* dollars. And if you need incentive, all you have to do is think about Molly. Remember how she talked about all the things she wanted to do? The plans you guys made?"

A wave of sadness overtook Gabriella despite her attempts to shrug it off. She and Molly had come up with the idea for *Premiere Vue* together, as part of their university marketing and business class project. They'd definitely made big plans, but only Gabriella remained to see their dream to fruition. "Yes."

What was the point of being in business if it didn't grow and prosper? Molly's life had been cut too short, but taking *Premiere Vue* to the next level would be the ultimate in honoring Molly's presence on earth.

"So let's make it happen. Get the land, sell it for its *full* price, get closure on all the daddy-dearest crap while you're there, and let's do this."

Gabriella wasn't sure what was scarier—the fact Alicia voiced the very thoughts running through her brain or that getting satisfaction appealed so much. Gabriella liked to live and let live and she'd tried for years to put her abandonment issues behind her.

But honestly? She'd be lying if she said she didn't feel as if Zane McKenna *owed* her. What was the price for child abandonment?

She turned to stare at Braddock where he looked over a display of lotions. As though sensing her perusal, he raised his head and their eyes locked.

And Braddock's look? His expression? That became her deciding factor.

Zane hadn't been there for her but Molly had, through thick and thin. Sacrificing three months of her life and putting up with Braddock was the least Gabriella could do for the *only* person who had ever shown her the meaning of unconditional love and friendship. Molly's dream would come true. "I'm not signing," she said to Braddock, ignoring Alicia's excited *yes*. "Keep your check. I'll see you in Montana."

CHAPTER TWO

KEEP YOUR CHECK. I'LL see you in Montana.

It took everything in Brad to get out the door without punching his fist into the wall.

Gabriella hadn't cared enough to return a phone call or attend her father's funeral, but she wasn't about to pass up the chance to get a million dollars from the sale of the land.

His land. His *home*.

The Circle M meant nothing to her but it was everything to him—which was why when Zane's attorney hadn't been able to get a response from Gabriella, Brad had emptied his bank account, borrowed from the ranch's operating account with his brothers' permission and got a bank loan against his deeded portion of the ranch to gather the hundred grand before he'd flown to California and tracked her down himself.

He and his brothers would be making the payments for quite a while but it was the only way to protect the Circle M. What if she went through with this plan? Stayed the three months? No, he couldn't consider it. She wouldn't last a week. Still...

Brad made sure no one was close after he walked around the corner, and then let loose a string of curses as he scraped his palms over his face. As if that would erase two weeks of sleepless nights and a mountain of worry.

When Gabriella hadn't appeared for his adoptive father's funeral, Brad had thought they were off the hook. All he had to do was come to California and settle up, once and for all.

Self-centered gold digger.

Brad walked for a while, his boots loud on the sidewalk, the check burning a hole in his pocket. How could he not feel betrayed? What was he going to do now?

His brothers had demanded he call as soon as Gabriella signed the papers, but Brad couldn't call—not when he'd failed them. He was the executor of Zane's estate, that's why he'd scrunched his too-large frame into a damned small seat and made the flight. Because he was the oldest and it was up to him to watch over the ranch and his brothers.

Spying a taxi at the end of the block, Brad picked up his pace and flagged it down the way he'd seen actors do in the movies, jogging the last few feet. He couldn't wait to get out of here. He didn't like concrete and noise, hated crowds, and he hated airports as much as he hated flying. God gave humans legs for a reason. There were ways to get around that didn't involve being thirty thousand feet in the air. He had to get to the Circle M as soon as possible and come up with a plan. Unfortunately, flying was the quickest way to do it.

"The airport, please."

"No problem. Meeting someone?" the cabbie asked.

"No. Going home."

"You're leaving sunny California? Why? It's beautiful here," the driver said with way too much enthusiasm. "The sun, the sand, the women. Ah, the *women*." He made a kissing motion with his hand, his accent thick. "So did you enjoy your visit?"

Brad's gaze landed on the identification card on the

back of the driver's seat and he barely repressed a shudder. Beside the card the cabbie had posted his résumé listing his acting credits, most of which were rated triple X. "No. It'll be a cold day in hell before I ever come back to this town."

The cabbie made a face in the rearview mirror as though mocking Brad's words but it was true. His plan of getting Gabriella's signature had backfired in the worst possible way. His brother Chance was the charmer in the family. Maybe Brad should have sent him.

Their future rested in the piece of land Gabriella stood to inherit. Land she wanted to possess, although he could only imagine why. He'd barely managed to scrape together the hundred grand. No way could they come up with the million or more it was worth on the real estate market if she decided to sell.

Lost in his thoughts, Brad had no idea how much time it took to get to the airport.

"Here you go. No more California for you. I drive fast so you can leave quicker, yes?"

The cabbie rolled the taxi to a stop outside Departures and Brad paid the man, adding a tip he could no longer afford. "Thanks. Appreciate it."

Inside the building, Brad spotted the signs telling him where he needed to be. He already had his ticket, and with no bags to check, he stalked straight to the security line, earning narrowed-eye looks from airport personnel who seemed to zero in on him due to his size.

Brad forced his shoulders down from around his ears. He didn't want any more hassle, and getting pulled out of the line for additional scanning and a weapons check was exactly what he needed to make his day spiral to the lowest of lows. Having a wand hovering over his privates and some dude patting him down was plain uncomfortable.

Gabriella's face popped into his head and Brad swore silently. No doubt she would find the irony hysterical if he wound up stuck here because he decked a too-friendly TSA agent while she had to stay in Montana to get her inheritance.

Brad stepped forward when the line moved, his thoughts focused entirely on Zane's daughter. His mind jumped from his impression of her business to Alicia to Gabriella again.

She'd taken after her daddy.

Tall and slim, she not only had Zane's height but also his white-blond hair and blue eyes. Where Zane's had been a lighter blue, Gabriella's eyes were a shade or two darker, the color of the lake after the spring thaw.

Regardless, the similarity was biological, whereas Brad and his two adoptive brothers carried the Mc-Kenna name simply because of a piece of paper. The fact they were fighting to keep Zane's legacy alive and thriving, while his own flesh and blood planned who knew what, tipped the scales of Brad's fury.

Gabriella *Thompson*. *Not* McKenna. Gabriella wouldn't even carry Zane's name but she had the ability to make or break the ranch. Of all the things Zane could have done, why this?

Zane had been a good man, a man of honor and integrity, wisdom and kindness. He'd been a mean card player, an avid reader and considered stone-cold crazy for adopting the three no-account teens who had torn up his ranch. He'd done it anyway, taken them in, taught them right from wrong. Zane didn't abandon children, he gave them a purpose, a future. A home. Brad knew from experience that Gabriella was wrong about Zane abandoning her.

And what was with her business? Some of those lingerie sets could set a block of ice on fire. And the lotions? He'd seen one that promised *burning heat and fiery passion.* A real man already knew how to get that response from a woman.

"Sir? Would you step over here, please? *Sir?*"

Brad snapped out of his thoughts and glanced toward the uniformed man. Ah, hell.

The security officer waved him out of line, and two more guards watched to see how Brad would respond.

Brad sighed and did as ordered. Nothing was going to keep him off that plane to Montana.

"How are you today, sir? Everything okay?"

"Yes, fine."

"That's good. Remove your hat please. Do you have any weapons on you, sir?"

Out came the wand.

Brad shook his head and gritted his teeth, feeling his ears get hot with embarrassment when other passengers stared.

"Spread your arms and legs wide, sir."

Oh, yeah. Hell would definitely freeze over before he'd put himself through this again.

GABRIELLA ARRIVED IN Montana the following Saturday.

She'd considered flying but she didn't want to be stranded for three months without a vehicle. And after talking to Zane's attorney, Gabriella figured the sooner she got there, the sooner the ordeal would be over.

The long trip was boring and uneventful, with lots of stops for coffee along the way. She buzzed through the tiny town of North Star to see what was available, then kept driving to the Circle M, unable to believe she was actually going through with this.

Three months? *Here?*

North Star didn't have a Starbucks, the movie theater looked like a throwback from the 1950s—and showed only two movies—and on the outskirts she'd had to stop and wait while someone herded cattle across the road and into the fenced field on the other side.

She stared out at the rolling terrain, everything green and beautiful but containing nothing more than rocks and grass and hills and mountains and livestock. Three months?

"Pretend you're on a reality-TV show," she said, continuing the pep talk she'd begun immediately following Braddock's departure. "Alicia's right. People do worse things for a million bucks. Staying here will be a cakewalk."

Following GPS directions, she crawled along the rutted road in her sports car, yet still managed to hit a pothole the size of a small country. Finally she arrived at the cluster of buildings surrounding the ranch house. The structure was two stories and plain, although the wraparound porch had a lot of potential.

Gabriella tensed when she realized instead of the house being closed up following Zane's death as she'd expected, there were a couple men standing *on* the porch. They had apparently been watching her progress up the drive.

Gabriella parked beside an oversize truck with a trailer of hay hitched behind it. She gripped the wheel, her sweaty palms squeaking against the leather now that she was here. *Don't let him get to you. You can do this. You've faced down size-twelve divas who were convinced they were a two. When Brangelina hit the news and the flowers were linked to* Premiere Vue, *you kept your cool. This will be over before you know it.*

Molly's voice filled Gabriella's head. *It's like a pelvic exam—you just gotta do it.* Gabriella smiled at the memory. Her BFF had been talking about getting a bikini wax but the sentiment applied here, as well.

Even with the pep talk, the questionable salad she'd forced down at lunch threatened to reappear if she made any sudden moves.

Surely the house was empty. The men were…checking on it? She couldn't be expected to live there *with* other people—right?

Gabriella ignored the intensity of the gazes shooting her way from those gathered on the porch, grabbed her purse and somehow managed to get out on her shaky legs without looking too much like a giraffe walking for the first time.

Deciding what to pack had been difficult. Her mother had always told her she had the shoulders of a linebacker but she didn't have to dress like one. Gabriella knew how to dress to best show off her assets while downplaying her flaws, and she had a tendency to wear dresses and skirts that emphasized her long, long legs.

But those weren't appropriate here. So she'd planned ahead as best she could, bringing mostly jeans and cargo pants, shorts, T-shirts, blouses and a few skirts and dresses just in case.

For her arrival at the ranch she had chosen snug jeans that emphasized her legs, heels because she refused to not meet Braddock at eye level—at least for this second meeting—and a designer tank that made her look as though she wasn't entirely flat-chested.

Not that it mattered now when nothing could ease her nervousness at meeting her…father's sons.

Gabriella swallowed the knot in her throat and used the excuse of fumbling with her bag to inhale another calming breath.

Settling for the hundred grand was looking better and better. *Get in, get the money, get gone,* her mind suggested.

You need incentive? Think of Molly. Alicia's argument came out of nowhere but it was the grit that forced Gabriella to find her courage. No matter what came of this adventure, whether she stayed one day or three months, it was worth it to know Molly would approve.

She tightened her grip on her oversize purse and looked up to see Braddock—accompanied by a few more people, including a woman and child—emerge from the house. Like the other guys, he had the sunburnished tan of an outdoorsman, but his eyes were so green they reminded her of the imported ferns in her store. Combined with his dark chestnut hair and rugged looks, he wasn't *bad*-looking. Too bad he was such a boor.

Gabriella focused her attention on him and purposefully ignored the others who followed him. "Hello."

Braddock didn't speak. Shifting uncomfortably, she noticed a little boy among the group. He held the woman's hand and had a blue cast on his arm.

When the men didn't say anything, the woman shot Gabriella a tight smile that appeared to be even more uncomfortable than Gabriella felt.

"Ignore them. Hi, you must be Gabriella." She went on to introduce herself as Carly Taggert and the boy, Riley Mays-soon-to-be-McKenna, then Braddock's brothers: Liam, who was Carly's fiancé, and Chance, who was obviously the heartbreaker of the three. There was also Charlie, Liam's father.

Wait a minute. Liam had been adopted by her father. She wondered how the Liam-Charlie dynamic worked but wasn't going to ask. Yet.

"Liam and I are taking Riley to the movies so we need to get going. I'm sorry we can't hang around to visit but I promised Riley this as a reward. I'll try to come by later this week."

An olive branch. Gabriella liked Carly Taggert already. "That would be nice. I look forward to it."

Carly's somewhat awkward friendliness was a welcome relief from the men's stoic and unwelcoming expressions.

Liam lifted the boy up and settled him onto his shoulders, then headed toward a nearby truck. As they passed, Liam gave her a nod but that was it.

"I'm, uh, I'm sorry for your loss," Carly said as she followed them, pausing when she reached Gabriella's side. "North Star won't be the same without Zane. It's been twenty years since he first donned the red suit for the Christmas program at the church. I remember sitting on his lap when I was a little girl. Of course I didn't know it was him then." She smiled. "I don't know who will replace him but it won't be the same."

Gabriella struggled to keep her thoughts off her face as she tried to imagine the man she'd known—the one she hadn't seen for nearly fifteen years—playing Santa to a slew of children. She couldn't do it.

Then again, so long as the child wasn't *her,* Zane apparently had more tolerance. What else explained him adopting *more* children instead of caring for his own?

Sons. He wanted sons. And even though you're as tall as most men, you weren't good enough.

That awareness was an issue she'd struggled with her entire life.

Gabriella shut down the negative thoughts and watched as Carly murmured one last goodbye and joined Liam and Riley.

Missing Gabriella's childhood was *Zane's* loss. And despite his absence, she'd grown up to be a strong, independent person. One she was proud of, whether he was or not.

"I've got to get going, too," Chance said, slapping Braddock on his back before sidling past her. "See you around, Gabriella. Brad, call me if you need anything."

Brad. That suited him so much better.

Chance climbed into the truck hauling the trailer of hay, and followed Liam and Carly down the driveway.

"Gonna go home myself," Charlie said. "Miss." He dipped his head at her before he ambled toward a barn.

"You're a piece of work, you know that?" Brad said, a bitter pinch to his mouth. "You haven't even made it through the door and you're putting Zane down."

She was taken aback by the accusation. "Excuse me? I didn't say a word."

"You didn't have to. Your expression said it all when Carly told you what a good man Zane was. Do yourself a favor. Don't disrespect him in front of the people who loved him."

Or *what?* Brad had the nerve to stand there and give her orders? She hadn't agreed with Carly but she'd kept her mouth shut out of politeness. Obviously that was a trait Brad had never learned. "Look, I know you're not happy about this but there are two sides to every situation. The past week gave me plenty of time to think about why Zane left me an inheritance. And the answer? *Guilt.*"

"Is that right?"

"Yes, that's right. I think it's obvious we'd both prefer if I had stayed in L.A. but I hope we can be adult enough to make the best of this for the time that I'm here."

"And how long will that be?"

You just got here. Don't let him drive you away. That's exactly what he wants to do. "Three months." No need to give him reason to think that with pushing on his part she'd leave, even if it was probably true.

"Your father loved this ranch. He worked too hard to keep it running for you to come here and put us under."

"You're forgetting *I* didn't set this scenario up. *He* did, and he obviously knew the risks. If you want to be angry with someone, be angry with him."

Brad scowled at the words, the expression unsettling on such a large man.

Gabriella crossed her arms and saw his gaze dip. Her shirt had seemed like an okay choice but now the neckline probably revealed more than she'd like. Flat-chested or not, she wasn't obtuse when it came to how some men looked at her. What surprised her was that Braddock was one of those men. Even more surprising was her body's awareness of him. The man was… *horrible.* "It was a long drive. I'd like to settle in."

He shoved his hat a little lower on his head. "The bedrooms are upstairs. You can use Liam's old room, first door on the right of the landing with the blue paint."

"Good. My bags are in the car."

He smirked. One thick eyebrow lifted high, and a rough huff of sound left his chest. "Then I guess you'd better get to work carrying them in."

CHAPTER THREE

BRAD STAYED AWAY FROM the house, finding plenty of chores to keep himself occupied because he couldn't stand the thought of having to spend time with Gabriella. Maybe he ought to move into the bunkhouse while she was here. To keep things simple.

No. That reeked of cowardice. He wouldn't put it past her to take his wanting distance as a sign of surrender, and he wasn't surrendering. He was looking out for Zane's interests and trying to keep the ranch going the way his adopted father would have wanted.

Zane's horse, Major, nickered softly and Brad patted the horse's rump, continuing to brush Major's flanks in long, smooth strokes. "I know, boy. My mood's pretty sour but don't you worry about it. You're going to be okay. I'll see to that."

But would the ranch survive? As much as he resented Gabriella's presence on the Circle M, he respected Zane too much to do anything underhanded enough to drive her away. That didn't mean he wanted her there, though.

Brad heard a motor outside the barn and poked his head out of the stall to see out the open double doors. Delmer Frank. Of all days for Delmer to arrive to get his gift from Zane, did it have to be today?

"You in here, Brad?" Delmer called, a hand shading his eyes as he peered into the recesses of the barn.

"Yeah, just finishing up." He set the brush aside and

let himself out of Major's stall, washing his hands with the hose. "How are you doing, Delmer?"

"Better than you, I'd say. Heard some rumors in town. That her car out front?"

Nothing moved faster in a small town than gossip. "Yeah. She pulled in an hour or so ago." It had taken her nine trips to carry in all the bags and boxes she'd brought with her. What could she possibly need with all that? Didn't she plan on doing laundry while she was here?

Brad looped the hose over the hook with a yank on the length. If she expected maid service he'd turn her over his knee and—

The image hit and he jerked back, pissed with himself. He was letting long legs and a hot body screw with his brain when he stood to lose everything to a woman who would rather stab him with her killer-spike heels than do the right thing.

"Something wrong?"

"She brought enough luggage to clothe the whole town," he said simply.

"Which means she doesn't plan on leaving anytime soon." Delmer shook his head slowly. "I can't believe the mess this is causing. She wouldn't take the check? What if you upped the amount a little? I can help you out some if you need it."

"No." Brad met the man's gaze, humbled by the offer. For a kid who'd once been considered a bane to the town, having Delmer extend a hand meant something. "Thanks for the offer but I can't accept it—and I seriously doubt she'd take it. She's got her sights set on getting the sale value no matter what she has to do to make it happen."

Delmer whistled. "Can you get that much?"

"A million dollars? Not without a miracle. I barely managed to get the hundred grand. It's a cash-only world at the moment. No way will a bank loan a rancher that kind of money."

"I don't think this is what Zane intended when he created that will. I think he wanted to entice her to visit is all, maybe have some money to help her out."

It had taken some soul searching but Brad understood that, hard as it was to grasp.

Like all ranches, the Circle M was land rich and cash poor. Paying out the $100,000 would leave them struggling to stay afloat for quite a while.

But if she would agree to take the money and run, he'd willingly cut another check to replace the one he'd shredded after his trip to California and hope he could manage long enough to get the ranch on its feet.

"You don't need this today. I'll come back another time."

Brad shook off the bad mood. He needed a solution. Getting caught up in his anger wasn't it. "No, it's fine. Come on in the house. We'll get that gun for you," he said, latching onto the excuse to go inside so he could see what Gabriella was up to while also having a reason to leave after he retrieved the gun Zane had left his longtime friend.

The kitchen was empty, the living room, too. In Zane's den, Brad unlocked the gun cabinet and retrieved the pricey weapon, holding it a long moment—Zane had been the last to touch it. "Why'd you do it?"

Brad wasn't aware he'd said the words loud enough for Delmer to hear until Delmer squeezed his shoulder.

"If you want to keep it, son, I understand."

Delmer was a good man, he'd been a good friend to Zane. To all of them. "No, the gun is yours. I meant—"

"I know what you meant. But maybe the gun ought to stay. You might want it later if—"

If they lost the ranch. That's what Delmer implied without actually saying the words. "Zane wanted you to have it. It's yours."

But even as Brad said the words, he had to acknowledge the truth of them in regard to Gabriella. "I know he loved her but— How could he do it?"

"Zane loved you boys. I've never seen a man so proud as the day he drove you into town and signed those adoption papers. As to why he did this, I can only guess. Zane trusted you boys with this ranch and I can't help but think he believed if anyone could get his daughter to see how special this place is, it would be the people who love it the most. Maybe you should try getting along with her, see how she responds."

Brad locked the door of the hand-carved cabinet. "That would be like petting a rattlesnake. It would never work. She's California through and through. All I can do is pray she changes her mind and doesn't stay. Women like that get bored, right?" He didn't give Delmer a chance to answer. "In fifteen years she's never called, never visited. Never even sent Zane so much as a postcard. Surely she'll get fed up of being stuck out here and leave."

"For all your sakes, I hope she does. But you have to be prepared to deal with things if she doesn't."

A soft thud sounded over their heads and Brad stiffened. That hadn't come from Liam's room.

"I'd best be going. Call me if you need anything," Delmer said.

"Thanks. I appreciate it."

Brad followed Delmer to the front door. The second it closed, Brad took the stairs two at a time.

At the top he headed toward the rear of the house where— "What the hell are you doing?"

Gabriella looked startled by his bellow. She had white cords running from her waist to her ears, and she pulled them out one at a time, giving him a glare.

"You startled me."

He scanned the room in an instant, noting she'd spread her clothes and shoes and bags and *crap* everywhere. "Get out."

"The blue room is too small."

"This is *Zane's* room," he said, gritting his teeth.

"I figured that out when I walked in."

"You're not using his room."

"Looks like I am."

Zane wasn't even cold in his grave and she was moving in? Taking over?

"You're really easy to read right now. You're standing there trying to figure out if I'm the heartless bitch you think I am."

He needed to work on his poker face. "You have no right to be here."

"And you do?"

Gabriella lifted her chin. A challenge if Brad ever saw one.

"Let's set the record straight, shall we? You will *not* make me feel guilty where Zane is concerned. The day I got the message from Zane's attorney that he needed to talk to me was the *same day* I buried my best friend. So that call, combined with the fact that I hadn't talked to Zane in years, was too much. And while I should probably be sorry I didn't call the attorney back and come to Zane's funeral…I'm not.

"Molly was there for me when my *father* wasn't. And you can make every excuse in the world for him, but you seem to be forgetting something here. I was a *child.* I didn't make the decisions but I had to abide by them. And by not contacting me, Zane made it very clear he didn't want me."

Brad's temper soared at Gabriella's choice of words. "Didn't *want* you?" he demanded, incredulous. "Did you look around the room before you started unpacking?"

"Of course I *see* them," she whispered, referring to the pictures of her Zane had scattered throughout the room. "I see them but I don't understand why they're here. I was the toy Zane put on the shelf when he got tired of playing with me. This doesn't make sense. If Zane cared for me, if he *loved* me, why did he treat me the way he did? And why did he do this?"

"Think about it. If he abandoned you as you say…"

She swallowed, shrugged, remaining stubborn despite the visible proof of Zane's love.

But the emotion behind her words packed a powerful punch Brad felt all the way to his soul. He didn't know what to say. What to feel or think, because judging by her expression Gabriella was as hurt and torn and angry over the situation as he was. There was too much feeling behind her questions for her not to believe Zane didn't love her.

What was the truth?

Delmer's comment repeated in Brad's head. Zane really expected Brad and his brothers to make things right with Gabriella. Was it possible?

"Forget it. I'll move into the blue room but I'm going to have to store some things in here or one of the other rooms."

"No. Stay." Because when it boiled down to it, Brad knew Zane would want her right where she was.

Somehow, some way, he and Gabriella had to come to a compromise on their living arrangement. Maybe this was a start? "I'll move Zane's clothes out of the closet."

"There aren't that many. You can leave them. I'll scoot them over, it's fine."

Frustrated and confused because she was such a complicated mix of attitude and vulnerable sensitivity, Brad nodded. "Suit yourself. But if you want them gone, let me do it."

"Fine. Brad...wait."

He paused in the doorway, his grip on the knob tight.

"Where is Zane buried?"

He supposed he had to give her credit for asking. "Your father is buried in the McKenna cemetery." When she stared at him blankly, he jerked his head toward the window. "On the knoll up from the barn. It's a private plot and he's buried beside his wife, Noelle."

"Thanks."

"No problem."

"Brad?"

Couldn't she ask all her questions at once? He wanted out of the room, away from her.

"Have you read your letter from him?" She referred to the handwritten letters Zane had left each of his four children.

"Not yet." He'd been too angry since receiving the letter to read it, too upset with Zane because of what he'd done. But now that she was here, Brad was going to read it. He had to. Maybe the letter would shed some light on things and answer the questions he had about Zane's motives. God knew Brad couldn't figure it out on his own.

"You're angry. But is it because of me or the will?"

He had to choose one? "How can I not be angry? You gave Zane's name away and yet you're here. It doesn't make sense to me."

Unable to stand it any longer, he walked toward the stairs. She followed him as far as the doorway.

"Would you like to know why I gave it away?"

He refused to ask, but, yeah, he wanted to know. He'd felt nothing but pride when Zane had adopted him. He couldn't imagine anyone denying the McKenna birthright only to lay claim to it after the fact.

"I gave it away because he gave *me* away."

She couldn't get any more blunt than that. Wrong though she was. "If you think that's true, why stay in his room? In his house? Why are you doing this?"

"Because it's the biggest, because I *have* to stay here according to the will," she said, answering his questions in order. "And because Zane owes me. That's why."

She stepped inside and closed the door, shutting him out of the room.

Out of the ranch?

CHAPTER FOUR

HALF AN HOUR LATER GABRIELLA sat on the stone bench in the well-kept family cemetery, her jumbled, rapid thoughts slowing after some time alone in the fresh air.

It was beautiful here. She had to admit that. Staring at the ranch house and outbuildings below, the sky stretched far and wide, everything was a lush, verdant green, and the sun warmed her face.

Brad's comments and attitude had cut her like fine glass, nothing too sharp or piercing but enough to scrape and make her feel raw and exposed. She wondered if they discussed the same man. How could Zane McKenna be such a saint to them, yet abandon her?

All the accolades and kind words made it that much harder to stomach that he'd been nothing—*nothing*—to her. While growing up, he'd been a man who mailed a check once a month to her mother, and who'd sent her a check once a year for her birthday and Christmas combined. Not even two checks but one with *buy yourself something pretty* in the memo section.

That sweet, respected, well-liked man?

She didn't know him. And she resented the fact that Brad and the rest of them obviously did and they'd benefited from it, too.

The sun slid lower in the sky while Gabriella remained on that bench, unable to make her feet move.

Since Molly's death, Gabriella had tried to keep moving, keep functioning, keep herself from thinking too much. Feeling too much. She knew she couldn't maintain the pace she'd set since the diagnosis, but she felt as if she needed to live for herself and Molly, too.

The envelope crackled in her hand and because it had to be done, Gabriella opened it, catching the faint hint of cigars that brought a surprising wave of emotion and more than a little sorrow.

She lifted the papers to her nose and inhaled, closed her eyes as the tangy scent brought back the memory of pressing her nose into her father's shirt when he…when he carried her to the car after a day spent at a carnival along the pier.

For one week every summer during her childhood Zane had come to see her. She'd stayed with him at a hotel and they swam and went places, explored. A couple times he'd come to the location of her mother's movie or play and they'd explored that city, calling themselves adventurers.

Images flickered through her brain like a child's fast-paced steps. Carnivals and ferry rides, hot dogs and movies, parks and kites and horse-drawn carriages. Riding atop her father's shoulders, a balloon tied to her wrist, her fingers gripping his hair tightly—probably too tightly.

For that one week, everything would be wonderful. Magical. The stuff little girls dreamed of. Zane, with his big hands and loud boots and the cowboy hat he would place on her head with a special smile. Memories that made her heart hurt because she never understood what she'd done wrong to make him simply…*stop*.

Gabriella took a deep breath and sighed. It didn't matter now. Didn't matter why.

Inhaling the scent of cigars one more time, she lowered the letter until the words came into focus.

My Ella-belle,

If you're reading this my time on earth is over. You have always been my little girl, Ella. Despite that paper you asked me to sign, I've never thought of you otherwise.

I suspect it was rough on a girl growing up with a father who came from dirt and work and what little education I had. I signed those papers and let you go because you and your mother made it clear that's what you wanted. But not a day went by that I didn't think of you, even though I never knew exactly what to do with you.

You stayed at the Circle M once. You were a curious little thing, all hair and legs and eyes. I loved seeing everything through you. It was like seeing it for the first time all over again. You snuck into the corral to ride Satan and to this day I can still see his hooves coming down right next to your head. I was too far away to help. All I could do was watch. Thank God old Barney stepped in. He saved you, but his leg was never the same. Guess that proved this ranch was no place for a little girl.

Gabriella, I wrote down some of my favorite things, places, a few chores. Stuff I always wanted us to do together when you were old enough to come back. I hope you'll do them, even though I'm not there to do them with you.

Come back? He'd *never* asked her back.
Gabriella scanned the list quickly, her mouth part-

ing in surprise when she read a few of them. Why on earth…?

> You don't owe me anything, I know that. But it's because I love you that I'm asking you to stay at the ranch and do these things. I missed out on most of your life. I let my cowardice get in the way of raising you. I let people convince me I couldn't do it, shouldn't do it. That was wrong and I accept full blame. By the time I figured it out, I wasn't sure how to fix the mistakes I'd made. Strange as it may sound, this is my way of saying I'm sorry.

Gabriella pressed her fingers to her mouth, the words on the page blurring from total disbelief. He was sorry? *Now* he was sorry? She'd considered her father a giant, and not only in a physical sense. He was…larger than life. Big and strong. A *cowboy*. So cool.

Not always. Not when you were old enough to understand why Crystal curled her nose and sneered when she talked about him. You went along with her.

Gabriella had. Almost a teenager, she'd had one thing on her mind—testing to see how much she could get away with, how much her father loved her. Hurt because he didn't come to see her for several years straight when Crystal worked out of the country.

He signed those papers because he thought it was what you *wanted. He gave you up because he thought it made* you *happy.*

But it hadn't. Not at all. She ran her hand through her short hair and glared at the gravestone so recently etched with Zane's name, her stomach in knots. What

did Zane mean he let people convince him he couldn't?
Meaning her mother?

Who else would it be?

I know you were upset about me adopting the
boys. Gabriella, you had your mother but those
boys had no one. They needed a father in a bad
way and even though I should've been more of a
father to you, deep down I know I did the right
thing by adopting them. All three of them are
good, decent men and they're your family, too.
You can trust them, depend on them. It comforts
me knowing the boys will look out for you, even
though they aren't going to be happy with my decision. Give them time. Work with them, get to
know them. More than anything, know I never
stopped loving you.

The waterfall was my favorite place and whenever I was there, I'd think of how much you'd
enjoy it. You always liked water and swimming,
and I always wanted to take you there. That's why
I left the falls to you. They are special to me, just
like you're special to me. I learned the hard way
that opportunities pass us by in the blink of an
eye. The longer I live, the more I regret not being
a better father to you. Forgive me. Everything
seemed so black and white back then, but as I
aged things changed and plenty of gray crept in.

Stay and do the things on the list. Maybe they'll
help you think of me with fondness rather than
disappointment.

Love always,
Your Daddy

Gabriella finished reading the long letter, numb by the end. It was the longest conversation, however one-sided, she could remember having with Zane since she was a child. That's why her stomach hurt and her chest felt tight and that spot between her shoulder blades *ached*. So much time gone, lost forever because of her stubborn pride and his silence.

Was what he said true?

Something wasn't right. The two sides weren't adding up. What she'd believed about Zane all these years, what her mother had perpetuated with every comment and sneer.

What had her mother said to Zane? Told him?

Crystal had never believed Zane was good enough, had always put him and his "little pile of dirt" down. Was that why Zane believed *Gabriella* felt the same way?

Shaking, she dug her cell phone out of her purse. She had to have answers and there was only one person who could clear up the confusion. Her mother would freak when she found out where Gabriella was but that couldn't be helped.

Phone pressed to her ear, Gabriella heard the rings.

If her mother had lied to Zane, said Gabriella didn't *want* to see him, didn't *want* to visit… No wonder he hadn't come to see her.

"Hello? Gabriella?"

"Hey, Mom. How's Europe?"

"Fabulous. We made it to Paris yesterday morning. I found the best little boutique today. They have this lotion you simply *must* get for your shop."

"I'll check into it," she said automatically. Her mother liked the success of *Premiere Vue,* liked that Gabriella worked so closely with Hollywood's brightest. "Mom…"

"Gabriella, is something wrong? Are you sick? Oh, I knew I shouldn't have left you. It was too soon after Molly's death."

"I'm fine."

"Oh, good. You're so quiet it scared me. Did you go to the beach house like I suggested? You know you're welcome. It's sitting there empty."

"I know it is but, Mom…I'm in Montana."

"*What?* Why?"

"Because he's dead. My— Zane's dead."

Silence. Not a comforting silence or shocked silence but a *guilty* one?

"I see. Oh, Gabriella, I'm sorry to hear that."

"Are you?"

"Yes, of course I am. Gabriella, I know he was your father but how many times do I have to tell you Zane McKenna was DNA and nothing else? We had a two-day fling in an airport hotel during a blizzard. But I *do* care, because you're hurting. Why are you putting yourself through this by going to that godforsaken place? I want you to get on a plane and go home—better yet, fly to Paris. We'll shop and eat and get massages and I'll help you forget all about…everything."

Did she really think that was possible?

Gabriella closed her eyes, the letter gripped tight in her hand. Zane had been more than DNA but she hadn't realized how much until now—or how his death would affect her. "Mom, did you tell Zane I shouldn't be with him? That I didn't want to see him or come here—that I didn't want him to be my father?"

"Gabriella…"

"*Did* you? Is that why he signed the papers authorizing my name change? Because you told him I was *embarrassed* of him?"

"Gabriella, do you remember how angry you were when Zane wouldn't fly to New Zealand to visit you? The things you said? I simply supported you."

"That wasn't the question. I was a disappointed little girl, but whatever you said convinced him he wasn't good enough. You played off his fears and made him go away, didn't you?"

"I did what any mother would do. I protected you from a man who would be a liability to you and all you've accomplished."

"Did he call? Want to see me? Did you tell him he couldn't?"

"It was so long ago, Gabriella. What does it matter now?"

"Did you lie to me? When I'd ask you if you'd heard from him, if he'd called, did you lie?"

"Gabriella…"

Hearing the answer in her mother's tone, Gabriella hit the button to end the conversation.

Her gaze fastened on Zane's headstone again.

Beloved husband and father.

A father to *them* maybe, but not to her.

She wasn't sure what to believe anymore. Who to believe.

At the moment, she wasn't even sure who to blame.

CHAPTER FIVE

BRAD NEEDED SOME SPACE after his talk with Gabriella so he drove to one of the pastures to check on a pregnant mare. He had the letter from Zane with him.

Parked on a hill, Brad read Zane's last words. He praised Brad's hard work, his dedication to the Circle M and the responsibility he shouldered, asking that he do everything in his power to keep the family, and the ranch, together and running strong. To carry on the McKenna legacy.

Zane asked for Brad's understanding and patience regarding Gabriella and the decision to give her that portion of land. Zane also asked for his forgiveness.

How could Brad be understanding and patient when she behaved the way she did? How could he protect the ranch when Gabriella, via Zane's decree, could control things Brad needed to control?

He sat in his truck for a while, brooding and coming to grips with the responsibility Zane placed on him. Whatever happened, he owed it to Zane to find a way. He'd given Brad a life, a home. Now he had to defend it. He just wished he knew *how*.

After seeing the signs that Pikipsi would deliver soon, he proceeded to calm the nervous mare then loaded her into the trailer to transport her closer so he could keep an eye on her.

In his distracted state, he didn't get the door fastened

quick enough and when Pikipsi stepped back her large butt shoved the door open, right into Brad's head.

He felt the trickle of blood sliding down his face from the scrape but he fastened the door securely before grabbing the tail of his shirt to stem the flow.

At the barn, Brad was happy to note the mare and Major hadn't been separated too long. The stallion welcomed Pikipsi with whinnies and tosses of his jet head.

After settling the mare into her stall, Brad checked the cut on the stallion's foreleg. It was mending nicely but it was best not to take any chances.

Brad stroked his hand over Major's long nose, and the horse's nostrils flared wide to get his scent. "I know, boy. I'm ready for a nice long ride, too. It won't be long. You be nice to your girl. Don't get her too riled up and we'll see what we can do to make that ride happen."

Brad lingered with the horse because Major had belonged to Zane.

Zane wasn't the bad guy—Brad knew that firsthand. But Gabriella had a point. Zane had been the parent, the adult. The one who should have made an effort in their relationship. The fact that he hadn't… Brad wasn't sure what to make of that.

Maybe Zane had felt guilty as Gabriella said, but how could Zane expect Brad and his brothers to welcome her when she could bring an end to the Circle M? Hadn't Zane given that some thought?

The cut on his head stung like crazy but he dreaded going into the house and having to deal with his unwanted guest. All he wanted was a shower and his bed. Maybe Gabriella was asleep by now. If she wasn't, it didn't matter. He wasn't going to play host. He had a hard day ahead of him with haying season approaching and he dared her to disturb him or his work.

Brad made his way to the house, his gaze on the ground in front of him. He didn't look up until he reached the steps. A curse slipped from his lips before he could stop it when he spied Gabriella there.

"I don't blame you," she said, her voice carrying on the night air. "I've muttered a few myself today."

Gabriella's white-blond hair gleamed in the light streaming from the house. At some point in time she'd obviously shed a few tears if her puffy eyes and raspy voice were any indication. He refused to let himself soften toward her.

"You're bleeding. What happened to you?"

He continued into the house, the smells of coffee and floor wax bringing him comfort the way it had for the past fifteen years. "Before I forget to tell you, a woman comes every two weeks to clean. She's due in Monday morning. Her name's Sally. Stay out of her way and don't be mean to her."

"Why would I be mean to her?"

"Because she won't like you and she'll probably let you know it. But she's the best housekeeper around and the only one willing to drive out here for a decent price. If I were you, I'd make sure all your stuff is organized and put away. Sally will be upset enough to see you in there."

"Why? If she's the housekeeper, what's the big deal?"

He slid Gabriella a glance over his shoulder. "I told you. Good housekeepers are hard to find and she's heartbroken. She doesn't need you upsetting her."

"You mean they were—"

"No. Sally and Zane were never more than friends but they *were* friends and that means something here. Sally's mourning Zane and you need to respect that." Brad tossed his keys onto the counter and left his hat on the hook by the door. He froze for a moment, only then realizing one of Zane's old work hats still hung there, the new one he favored for church or his trips to town buried with him.

Brad let his hand drift over the stained, aged material.

According to the state records, his biological father had died before he was born, his mother soon after by a semi driver who had fallen asleep at the wheel.

He'd never considered losing his parents before he'd even known them a blessing. Until now. Seeing Zane's hat, his books, the glasses he hated wearing— They were all reminders.

"I won't say anything to hurt her feelings. Why are you bleeding?"

"It's nothing."

"Your shirt is ruined—and your cheek is bruised. Were you in an accident?" She sniffed delicately. "Have you been drinking?"

Gabriella studied him with an intense and disapproving stare. He opened his mouth to comment that with her puffy eyes she didn't look any better, then closed it, too tired to begin an argument he couldn't finish by kicking her out.

Zane wanted her there.

Brad had to remember that, even if he had to say it a thousand times. He couldn't afford to antagonize her, not and live with her for the duration. Not when she would hold the ultimate prize if she managed to tough it out. "The trailer door caught me. It's fine."

"It's not fine. Where's your first-aid kit?"

"I'll take care of it."

She made a sound of frustration. "Okay, listen. Neither one of us wants me to be here right now. And right or wrong, I resent that Zane chose to be a father to you when he ignored me. But here I am, and I'm not leaving. It's going to be almost impossible for you to see the cut to treat it. Plus you work in dirt and grime, which could infect it. So stop being a baby and tell me where the first-aid kit is located."

A baby? He raised an eyebrow, his blood pressure rising and he hadn't been in the house a full five minutes. "Bathroom cabinet, upstairs."

Without a word she led the way and Brad couldn't help but notice the sway of her hips as the denim material cupped her behind—not that she had much of one. The woman was built like a stick with a few knotholes in strategic places to give her shape. He liked his women to be a bit more padded and curvy. Still, from this angle, he'd grudgingly admit the view wasn't bad.

He swallowed a groan, shaking his pounding head. If Zane had been there and caught Brad looking at his daughter's ass, his adoptive father would have hauled Brad outside by his ears for a talk about propriety.

"Sit," she ordered, once they'd made it to the bathroom.

Brad reluctantly lowered himself onto the closed toilet lid and waited while Gabriella searched the medicine cabinet for supplies. He took the opportunity to study her, and compared Gabriella now to the photos of a younger her Zane had stashed throughout the house.

The child with buckteeth and glasses was long gone, and in her place was a woman not beautiful but unique with her height and her hair and the delicate shape of her face.

"Ah, finally." She held up a bottle. "Antiseptic."

Brad opened the cabinet then handed her a clean washcloth.

Gabriella set to work and Brad locked his jaw when she stepped close and her scent reached him. She smelled like sunshine and warmth and some kind of perfume that probably cost more per ounce than his favorite pair of dress boots.

"Here we go."

The cut stung like a hundred yellow jackets zeroing in on the side of his head and, even though he didn't mean to let it happen, his breath hissed through his teeth.

"Sorry. That's got to hurt."

"It's nothing."

Aw, damn, did she press harder?

"It looks deep. You might need a stitch or two."

"It's fine. Clean it up and I'll put superglue on it."

"What?"

Brad shifted on the seat, his gaze widening slightly when he discovered the thrust of her breasts at eye-level. He'd noticed the snug tank top earlier, any man with eyes in his head would notice, but he hadn't noticed the semi-sheer material. Up close he had a clear view of her bra—something black and lacy. "We, uh, can't go to the hospital for every little cut. So long as it's clean and small, superglue seals the wound until it can heal."

Her mouth pursed in a disapproving line. "Next you'll want me to use duct tape."

"If that's what it takes." Ranching was hard, sometimes dangerous, work. Her response to a simple cut was yet another reason she shouldn't be there. "You read Zane's letter while I was gone?"

It wasn't smart to interrogate her now but it was either ask questions or stare at her chest, which wasn't acceptable. Pretty or not, if she stuck around, his world would most likely come to an end.

Brad forcibly blanked his thoughts. He couldn't think straight because she stood so close, even though she spouted off about how she resented him? Yeah, that made perfect sense.

Gabriella put some antibiotic cream on a cotton-tipped swab and dabbed it on next. "Yeah. I read it."

"And?" Positioned as she was, his breath blew across the fine, light hair on her arm and his gaze narrowed when he saw goose bumps appear.

"The letter was…enlightening."

He raised his eyebrows but winced when the cut pulled.

"Hold still."

"Why enlightening?"

"Because all this time I've believed certain things about my father."

"And now you don't believe them?" He was surprised by the admission.

"Some of them are still true. There's no changing or denying that."

"Debatable," he muttered.

"Whatever. Look, I get it that there was more to Zane than I grew up believing there to be, but you have to give me the benefit of the doubt. I didn't *know* any different. It's not like he showed that side of himself to me. Not that my mother would have let him."

There was too much vehemence to her words, too much pain and anger and confusion for her to be lying. "What's your mother got to do with things?"

A sad smile pulled at her lips. "I called her. She admitted to not telling me the whole truth about Zane."

Whoa. That *was* an admission. "The truth?" He felt like a mimic but wanted to prod Gabriella along.

She stepped back and leaned her hips against the sink. "Apparently he'd ask to talk to me and see me but she'd refuse. I thought Zane didn't call, ever, but turns out he did." A rough laugh left her chest. "Crystal had this rule about the housekeeper answering the phone. I always thought it was because of her ego but—" She sighed. "It was to keep me from talking to Zane. Every time Crystal calls me now she leaves a little bit more information on my voice mail, like little mini confessions."

"I'm sorry." That he meant. He'd imagine it was a lot to absorb in a single day.

"Me, too. I mean, I love my mom but how could she lie to me all these years? And why did Zane let her? Why didn't he try to contact me another way?"

Brad remained silent, not having the answers. Maybe a better question was why did Gabriella allow it to continue once she was older? When Gabriella was younger, maybe Crystal had more control, but what about later, during her teen years? As much as Gabriella might not admit it, she held some responsibility, too.

Brad wanted to broach the subject but given Gabriella's exhausted and confused expression he didn't have the heart to do it. There would be time to dig deeper later. Three months' time if Gabriella stayed that long.

"You received a letter from Zane, too," she said. "Did he ask you to do anything?"

"Zane mentioned that I needed to keep the family and the ranch together. Why?" he asked, watching her thoughts flicker over her features. "Did he mention you doing something specific in yours?"

Brad supposed Zane making a few requests wasn't

too surprising, but why ask now rather than when he was alive? It didn't make sense. But then nothing about this scenario did.

"Yeah. Actually there is a whole list of things. Some are simple and kind of silly but some— He wants me to go to his church and sit in his pew." Her blue eyes searched Brad's. "Why would he want me to do that?"

Knowing Zane, there were probably a million reasons. But only one stood out in his mind. "Zane liked going to church Sunday mornings."

"But that still doesn't make sense. He's not here, so why should I go?"

"He always liked to show you off. He'd pull your picture out of his wallet every chance he got. Maybe he wants everyone to finally meet you in person."

She stiffened at the statement.

"What?" Brad asked, confused by her reaction. And curious. He wouldn't mind reading her letter to see if it would give any insight as to why Zane had done this. "Come on, I gave in and let you play doctor. Tell me."

One side of her mouth lifted slightly. "It continues to hit home that nothing is what it seemed. If he'd fought harder to be a father, he could have taken the real thing instead of— No, you know what? Never mind. It's been a long day and I'm not in the mood for this. I can't take any more. Not tonight.

"It's all so crazy. The things Carly said today, were they *really* true? Did Zane *really* play Santa?"

He started to take offense in Zane's honor but the look on Gabriella's face wasn't one of sarcasm. It spoke of bewilderment and pain. She was asking because she couldn't believe it possible. Or that she'd missed out because that wasn't the father she'd known. Which reinforced her point.

How could the man Brad had known be the same man who had let his daughter grow up thinking the worst of him? "Yeah, he did. Why? Was there something your mother said?"

Gabriella began to put away the items she'd assembled to care for his wound.

"My mom always told me Zane stayed away from me for my own good, but when I think about what Carly said, what you said— That's not the kind of guy someone keeps their child away from."

"No. Zane wasn't that kind of guy. He liked kids. In fifteen years he never once made me or my brothers feel like we were the hired help or adopted, not even when we probably deserved to be treated that way. He always treated us like his sons."

Gabriella closed her eyes and squeezed them tight and Brad realized he'd hurt her without meaning to.

A rough laugh left her chest. "So it *was* just me."

He might not be good with people but everyone, everything, gave clues to what they were thinking if a person looked hard enough. The coiling of a snake before it struck, the bunching of muscles and flickering of ears before a horse reared. A woman busying herself to keep from feeling or thinking too much.

The image of the confident, ultracool and uncaring daughter Gabriella had presented earlier today was gone. Maybe if he saw that woman instead of the one in front of him, he wouldn't feel himself softening the way he always did when he came into contact with an injured animal.

One look said she was on edge like the rest of them, Zane's death affecting her in ways she hadn't expected. In ways Brad hadn't expected to matter to her.

Over the years he'd formed his own opinions on Zane's daughter but she'd obliterated one of them.

"When I told my mother where I was she went nuts. I was so angry I hung up on her midrant. She's called back eight times and left messages for me to call her but I can't. I don't want to talk to her right now."

Not news he wanted to hear. It had been a while since Crystal had called here, but he suspected she would only wait so long before she did in order to get ahold of her daughter.

Maybe Crystal would push Gabriella back to California? Urge her to return home?

He didn't like it but the sad truth was if Crystal called, Brad needed to answer, because he and Crystal were on the same side. They both wanted to convince Gabriella to take the hundred grand and leave as quickly as possible, regardless of the lies Crystal had told.

Brad stood, stopping in his tracks when he saw Gabriella merely look up rather than take a hurried step away. He was used to that reaction, used to people giving him room, or being afraid or thinking he was less than intelligent because of his size. That was something he and Zane had talked about a few times when Brad had first come to live at the ranch. How different a person could be from the way they were perceived. "Thanks for patching me up. I'll take it from here."

"You don't need help with the superglue?"

Brad waited, watching as Gabriella quickly glanced in the mirror above the sink and winced in response to her reflection.

She looked tired, worn out. Like a woman with a lot on her mind. After driving in from wherever she'd stayed last night, he was surprised she was still on her feet—especially in those ridiculous shoes. Even more surprising was that he actually felt sorry for her. "No, I can handle it. Good night, Gabriella."

"Good night. Brad, I'm...sorry for your loss."

He was sorry, too. More than she'd ever know.

CHAPTER SIX

BRAD GOT UP ON SUNDAY morning and packed himself a lunch, then rode to the area where Zane had taken Brad and his brothers to work off the damage they'd done to the ranch all those years ago. Brad stayed there all day, sat by the creek and watched the water flow by, grateful Zane had included that particular parcel in Brad's allotted tract.

Gabriella was in her—Zane's—bedroom when Brad returned so he fed the animals and went to bed, still at a loss as to how to handle the next twelve weeks.

With Monday morning's sunrise Brad was hard at work in the barn, trying to repair the old tractor. Sally arrived on schedule, the dogs barking as she parked.

Not long after she entered the house, Brad noticed Gabriella established a makeshift office on the porch. She alternately paced the expanse or sat with her computer on her lap, typing away.

He wondered what had been said between the two women but wasn't about to extend the effort to find out. So long as Gabriella wasn't bothering him or Sally, he didn't care what she did or where she did it.

The object of his thoughts again set the laptop aside to pace while she talked on that cell phone of hers. One hand waved and motioned in the air. Gabriella was dressed in snug jeans and a form-fitting shirt, this one with sparkles on the front. Every time she turned and faced the sun, the sparkles flashed, drawing his attention and distracting him from his chore.

"Take a break," Charlie, the Circle M's newest foreman, said. "It's not going anywhere and you've been at it since I left this morning. Missing a meal ain't going to make it start."

Brad complied without comment, beyond frustrated. The tractor hadn't been operable for a while. But Brad was determined—and hungry now that Charlie had reminded him of the time.

Brad tossed the wrench aside. "I suppose you're right. I'm going in for some lunch. You coming?"

Two days after the funeral, Charlie had moved into the small cabin Zane had deeded him in the will, but Charlie still ate with the ranch hands or joined Brad for lunch to go over the day or week's work schedule.

Brad liked the company. On the days he and Zane had been around at the same time they'd always eaten together. So it was nice when he didn't have to sit alone and mull things over too much. Especially Zane's empty chair.

"Not today. I'm taking a load of hay into town for Chance. Figured I'd stop by and check in with Liam afterward, if that's all right. See how much progress the boy's made," he said, referring to the addition Liam was hoping to complete on his house before Riley's adoption became final.

Liam and Carly had decided to live in her house in town, but the two bedrooms were cramped and they hoped to have kids of their own soon, in addition to the children Carly fostered.

His bachelor cabin was within sight of the ranch house, but once the marriage certificate was dry, Liam would be moving into town. The cabin would be used on weekends and days off when the little family came to the ranch.

The only problem with Charlie's intention was that Liam would probably send the old man packing instead of being thankful Charlie had decided to stick around. Maybe it was childish, but Brad would admit to being jealous of Liam. In the wake of Zane's death, Brad felt like a thirty-year-old orphan. Liam had a shot at a relationship with his father—he was just too stubborn to appreciate it.

"Tell Liam I'll be around to help as soon as I can."

"Will do. Thanks, boss, appreciate it," Charlie said.

Brad nodded but his curiosity got the best of him. "How are things going between you two?"

"Oh, you know how it is. Can't walk in another man's shoes, and Liam's taking Zane's death mighty hard. I think he blames himself some. He was there but couldn't save him."

Charlie shot Brad a look filled with regret. "No disrespect. All you boys are taking it hard and with good reason. Zane was a good man through and through."

"Yes, he was." And thanks to Zane, they now knew Charlie was a good man, too. But it was taking Liam too long to figure it out, which pissed Brad off.

He followed Charlie's gaze toward the porch.

"I still can't believe Zane left that particular piece of land to her," Charlie said.

Brad was trying hard to keep his mind off the fact that Gabriella's presence on the ranch would only lead to disaster. The land in question contained the water rights for the entire ranch—and if those rights fell into the wrong hands, the ranch would literally dry up. With each day she stayed, the chances increased that she would meet the terms of the will. "No one can. You and

I need to sit down later, go over the map of the wells and all the ditches."

"Think we're going to need to add more?"

"Probably so—and fast." But where was the money going to come from to build the new wells?

The best scenario he could hope for was that the bank would respond within a day or so. Times were hard and banks were leery of loaning money to anyone, but he'd received texts from both Liam and Chance this morning saying they would do whatever it took to secure the money needed to buy Gabriella out if she managed to stay all three months.

In other words, Chance and Liam were willing to use their allotted tracts of land as collateral. Combined with Brad's portion, maybe the bank would loan them the million dollars needed to buy Gabriella's inheritance from her privately before the land ever went public.

Brad didn't want to think of the monthly payments required to pay off a million-dollar debt, but at this stage he had to prepare for any possibility. And since the paperwork and red tape had to be handled, he and his brothers needed to act now to be prepared.

"Good luck with Liam. Don't let him give you too hard a time." Brad said goodbye to Charlie then ambled toward the steps knowing he couldn't avoid Gabriella any longer.

Thankfully the object of his thoughts wasn't on the porch. Maybe he could slip in unnoticed. He wasn't good around women, especially women like her with her fancy clothes and designer hair and nails. He liked his women curvy, soft and without a lot of makeup. He liked women who didn't spend three hours getting ready.

Through the screen door he saw Gabriella bent at

the waist, her head in the refrigerator, her behind right *there* for him to stare at.

He glanced away, knowing Zane wouldn't approve. He was pretty sure jonesing after her wasn't what Zane had in mind when he'd asked Brad to look out for her.

Brad noticed her laptop on the card table she'd dragged outside. Curious, he narrowed his gaze and stared in surprise when he saw the screen was filled with images of lingerie. That brought back memories of the outfit he'd seen in her shop—and the bra she had worn beneath her see-through shirt.

What she was wearing today?

"See anything you like?"

He started at her question. She stood at the screen door, a glass in her hand, a thin eyebrow raised high in feminine knowing.

She pushed the door open and he noticed she was barefoot, her feet long and slender and sexy because of a little ring of silver around one of her toes, the nails painted a bold pink.

From there his gaze rose, over her long legs, the curve of her hips. When he made it to her waist he zeroed in on the glass. "What *is* that?"

"A seaweed protein shake. Would you like to try one?"

He nearly gagged at the smell and she held it a good foot or so away. "No."

"It's good, and good for you."

She sounded like a commercial. No way did he want to eat green *sludge*. "I'll pass, thanks. You couldn't find anything to eat in the house?"

She wrinkled her nose. "I'm a lacto-ovo."

A *what-o-what-o?* "Excuse me?"

"It's a form of vegetarian." Gabriella tilted the glass

back and forth in her hand. "I do eat dairy and eggs, but no meat."

A vegetarian. Seriously? He'd never met one before. Especially not here in cattle country.

"So did you see anything you like? I could order something for your girlfriend."

He refused to look at the screen again. Yet somehow his gaze wound up there. "That shop. It's yours? You own an *adult* store?"

She laughed, her eyes sparkling up at him. "Not adult in the sense of anything triple X. We sell romance. The lingerie you saw, lotions, oils, some jewelry and high-end bags, flowers, gift baskets. A little bit of everything so long as it's romantic and unique."

Meaning expensive and out of his price range.

"I see something's caught your eye."

Brad felt the tips of his ears burn and he stalked toward the door, all because he couldn't stop thinking about hot lotions and skimpy underwear and Gabriella wearing both.

There had to be something wrong with him. No man in his position should be thinking of her that way. She was Zane's daughter, therefore off-limits. So why was he so intrigued?

"I saw you working." She followed him. "Did you get the tractor fixed?"

"No." The reminder ticked him off. He needed that tractor fixed now but because of having to sit on the hundred grand he'd scraped up—in case she bailed during the next three months—he couldn't afford to buy a part. He could only repair the broken one.

"Oh. Now is probably not a great time but I was wondering…"

He glanced over his shoulder and saw that glass of

green goo. The sight turned his stomach. He couldn't imagine getting a swallow of that down, much less a whole glass.

"Could you clarify a few things on Zane's list?"

Brad opened the fridge and grabbed the leftover ham, some lettuce, bread, mustard, baked beans and some kind of potato casserole, never more appreciative that some of the neighbor women continued to bring food. "Might not have the answers but you can ask."

"Great."

He piled the food onto a plate to heat up in the microwave while he constructed his sandwich. He was a big man with a big appetite.

"Where do I begin?" she asked, the papers practically pressed to her nose as she tried to read them.

"Do you need glasses?"

"Have some. Just don't like to wear them. They make me look old."

He laughed at the comment. Zane had hated wearing his glasses, too, and for the very same reason.

"Oh, forget this. Just read the list, if you don't mind. There are a few I know I'm not doing but I need more information."

He would have liked to read the entire letter Zane had left her but maybe Gabriella's list would be enough to shine the light on things.

The microwave *dinged* but he ignored it and set the sandwich aside. He read out loud from the list. "Go to church and sit in my pew, stay for dinner afterward. Plant something and watch it grow, see a foal take its first steps, learn to ride, drive my old stick-shift and explore the ranch, watch a sunrise, take eggs to Merrilee Brown, pitch in at the store and meet people, go out on a date with a local boy, see the falls—"

"*Now* do you get it? There are so many of them. And that one about going on a date with someone local? He was joking, right? Why would I want to do that?"

Brad could only guess Zane's hope was to get Gabriella involved enough in the community to want to stay. But that would never happen, not with her ties to California. She was temporary no matter how long she stayed.

"And what about Merrilee Brown? *Why* do I need to buy this woman eggs?"

Her query brought a reluctant smile. "Not *buy* her eggs, *take* her eggs. From the henhouse. Zane did it every week."

"You mean I'm supposed to steal the chickens' eggs?"

She couldn't be serious. "We own the chickens. You can't steal what you already own." He handed the list to her. "But, yeah, the eggs have to be gathered a couple times a day."

That earned him a glare that was meant to be a reproof but was sexy as hell.

Glaring is sexy?

He piled on the mustard with a silent mutter. Zane had clearly lost his mind when he'd made up that list.

"Don't they miss them?"

Brad finished constructing his sandwich and took an oversize bite before he said something he shouldn't—or laughed.

She *was* serious. He supposed he could remind her that humans were the superior race but some abandoned their babies without a second thought. Ask Liam. If his own mother didn't miss him, how could Gabriella expect a chicken with a brain the size of a pinky fingernail to miss eggs?

"Never mind. I eat them so I don't want to think about where they come from too much. The most important one is the waterfall so I should probably get it out of the way first. How do I get there? Do you have a map? My phone has GPS if you can give me the coordinates. I'll hike it."

Brad froze, the sandwich halfway to his mouth for another bite. Give her the coordinates? And then what, plan the search party? "The waterfall is a two-day *ride* from here."

"Ride?" She paled, then heat quickly rushed into her cheeks. "You mean that's why he wants me to—"

"Learn to ride a horse." He'd never imagined any child, adopted or otherwise, of Zane McKenna's could grow up not knowing how to ride. "Yeah, I imagine so. I take it you haven't ridden much."

"I don't ride *at all*. And I won't. I don't like horses and Zane knew it."

Whoa, not like horses? To him that was like saying she hated apple pie, his favorite. He couldn't find the words to respond.

"Whatever, it doesn't matter. I'll take one of those things. You have them. I've seen several of your men riding them."

"Those things?" He felt stupid repeating everything she said, but keeping up with her thought process took some doing, especially since he wasn't a mind reader and she left key components out—like the name of whatever she was talking about. "An ATV?"

She snapped her fingers. "Yes. I'll use one of those."

He tried to imagine her manicured nails on the grips. "Let's get this straight. While you're here, you're not to go anywhere alone."

"Excuse me? I'm a grown woman," she said. "You can't tell me where I can and can't go."

"I can when it means you could be hurt as a result. You get lost and it's my responsibility."

"Fine. *We* can use a couple of those ATV things to get us there."

We were not going to take her to the waterfall and lose nearly a week of work doing it. "Part of the trail isn't big enough for a four-wheeler and all the gear we'd—" how had he managed to include himself? "—need to pack. Plus Zane never wanted a trail leading up to the falls so no one would be tempted to trespass and destroy the area around it. To get there you *have* to ride a horse."

In that moment it dawned on him that he *was* going to be unlucky enough to have to take her there. Chance had to work McKenna Feed & Seed since his manager was out caring for his wife and newborn after a premature delivery, and Liam had enough to juggle walking around with a badge on his chest and trying to work out the details of his love life.

"Oh. I was hoping to see it."

And because she had to ride a horse she wasn't going to?

He couldn't imagine anyone being that afraid of horses. They weren't rattlesnakes or copperheads.

Gabriella frowned, her teeth sinking into her lower lip and drawing his attention there. Brad blinked at the sight and took another bite of his sandwich. Zane might have been a world-class rider but obviously Gabriella preferred Rodeo Drive over rodeos.

Gabriella's cell phone rang and she glanced at the screen. "I've been waiting for this call. I have to take it and check in with my assistant."

He had no intention of taking time out of his workday to help her with her list but he didn't want to spend his lunch arguing about it, either. She was on her own.

Then again, if she stayed the entire three months and was deeded the property, he needed her sympathetic to his cause as Delmer Frank had suggested. Talk about an impossible situation.

Brad pulled out a chair at the oak table and sat. He really didn't want to volunteer to help her with the list, but Delmer might have a point. Spending time with Gabriella, showing her the ranch, might be the only way to get her to see what those water rights meant to him and the surrounding ranches. If he pointed out certain things, made her aware of them…

But other than asking for the coordinates to the falls and an explanation for why she needed to take eggs to Merrilee, Gabriella hadn't really *asked* for help, even though they both knew she was in over her head.

As Gabriella talked, she made her way outside. Once the screen door shut behind her, Brad scraped his work-rough palms over his face.

He remembered a time when he hadn't had callouses on his hands and was headed down a path of self-destruction because no one had ever taught him the satisfaction of a hard day's work. Back then he hadn't cared for much of anything but a good time, more than a little aware that life was short so he had to live it fast.

Now that he thought about it, Gabriella's list was a good indication of Zane's thinking, his purpose clear.

She lived in the fast lane of L.A. and Hollywood. How many times had Zane remarked that he worried she was doing too much? Taking too much on, wearing herself down? She was always on the phone. Always pacing. Moving. Brad didn't doubt Zane's list was a way to get Gabriella to slow down. To realize what was important. Things such as people and family and community. Of working and watching something grow from the effort. Why else would Zane want her planting, visiting? Going to church?

Zane had known Gabriella would need help, which meant she'd have to spend time not only with Merrilee and the townspeople, but with all of them. Zane was attempting to blend his family, forge a bond, even though he wasn't here to see it.

But then what? It wasn't as though Gabriella would ever make North Star her home. But maybe she would feel comfortable enough to come visit. Maybe she wouldn't sell her part and ruin everything.

He finished his meal then put his plate in the sink, unable to imagine a future with Gabriella involved in the ranch. Maybe Zane had made a huge mistake in his treatment of Gabriella, but now Brad and his brothers were paying for it. He loved Zane, respected him, would have died for his adoptive father. But he was pissed, too.

Because Zane expected them to atone for his sins.

Brad grabbed his hat and headed back to work. He would keep the Circle M in one piece, which meant no matter his sympathy for Gabriella, Brad couldn't afford to let down his guard when it came to those water rights.

Not even for Zane.

CHAPTER SEVEN

"OKAY, WHAT IS UP WITH your mother?" Alicia said the moment Gabriella pressed the cell phone to her ear and said hello. "She's left a dozen messages with the service demanding to know if I've talked to you. Didn't you tell her you were leaving?"

"No, but she knows where I am now. She doesn't like it. We had an argument and I've been ignoring her. But I'll call her and tell her to leave you alone."

"No, that's okay. You don't have to. You know how much I love drama," Alicia teased.

Gabriella could envision Alicia rolling her eyes and gagging as she made the claim. And smirking all the while because she rubbed Crystal the wrong way for some reason. Probably because Alicia was young and gorgeous and could have stayed in the acting world to become more than a stunt double had she wanted to, whereas Crystal was slowly fading out due to her age.

"How are you holding up? Is the cowboy giving you a hard time?"

Gabriella rubbed her fingertips over her temple. Brad definitely wasn't the easiest person to get along with but after their talk… "He's been okay. Not exactly friendly but not a jerk, either."

"Well, *not a jerk* is an improvement. No wonder your mother's thong is in a knot. She's probably worried you'll stay."

"No chance of that happening."

"That bad, huh?"

Gabriella looked out at the land spread before her. "No, it's not bad at all—but it's not good, either."

"No chance of a vacation?"

"Not hardly," she said, explaining the list and her mother's twenty-year deception.

"Wow. That's some argument. Mommy Dearest really does have issues, doesn't she?"

"Apparently so." She was saddened by the fact her mother felt the need to be so deceptive and controlling she'd stolen Gabriella's childhood in a sense.

"I wish I knew what to say but I don't."

"You aren't the only one," Gabriella murmured, the surprise of her mother's behavior still sinking in. Maybe one day she would understand, but not yet. And while she knew she didn't want permanent distance to form between herself and Crystal, for now some breathing room would do. "But I will say I've been sleeping better. Must be the fresh air." Or exhaustion.

"So try to relax and enjoy. If you need anything, let me know and I'll send it with the sample packages."

Gabriella's gaze settled on the gravestone on the hill, visible from her position by the railing. "Thanks. I don't know what I would have done without you these past couple months. You know that, right?"

"Molly would be proud of you." Alicia's tone lost its enthusiasm. "She's probably up there with your dad, telling him all the adventures you two got into."

The thought brought a reluctant smile to Gabriella's lips. A part of her hoped so. But the other part?

How irrational was it to feel a twinge of jealousy at the thought of Molly—dear, sweet, wonderful, dead

Molly—spending time with her father when *she* hadn't been able to? Like with Zane and his *boys,* it wasn't fair.

It was dark and twisty, and Gabriella didn't like that part of herself that resented everyone who had known Zane while she hadn't. She also resented the fact there was nothing she could do about it.

"Anything else I need to know? How are those brothers of yours? Are they cute? Single? Do they look anything like the one that flew here?"

"What they are," Gabriella said, "is unhappy I decided to come. They don't want me here."

"They'll get over it. Zane did and that's what matters."

If only it were so simple. "Let's hope so. Oh, and before I forget, if my mother calls again, don't pick up. You don't have to listen to her rants."

Alicia sighed in her ear. "Have I told you lately how much I love you?"

"Hey, Brad, I was wondering— Oh, wow. Bad day?"

Brad looked up, his face dripping with water. Gabriella stood outside the bathroom in a strange replay of last night, only this time she wore a pair of slinky black shorts that ended below her knee and a matching lace-edged tank top that made her skin look even creamier.

The soap stung his eyes, reminding him that he was hunkered over the too-short sink simply staring at her.

He dipped his head and rinsed his face before trying to get the grease from his forearms and hands. "Not compared to others."

"Did you get the tractor working?"

Did she always have to ask that question? "No."

"Oh. That's too bad. I noticed there's another tractor in the field. Why don't you use it?"

He stared into the sink at the dark-colored bubbles circling the drain and wondered how he could explain the importance of getting the old tractor running to someone who only had an inkling of who Zane had really been. "I don't want to use it."

"Why not? It looks powerful and expensive, and it's obviously newer and in better condition."

He turned off the faucet with a flip of the knobs, struggling to control his frustration.

Jenkins from the bank had called. He said he'd do everything in his power to help Brad out but securing the full million was wishful thinking, even with three-fourths of the ranch as collateral. The real estate market was that unpredictable.

Why hadn't Zane made Gabriella stay for the hundred grand? Wasn't that enough for a daughter who never called?

"Your bandage is gone. Oh, and the cut is dirty. Sit down and I'll—"

"It's fine," he said, yanking the towel from the hanger. He dried his face with hard strokes.

When he tossed it aside he noticed she looked offended by his tone. A part of him didn't care but he also knew he wasn't doing himself any favors taking his anger out on her. He hated being in this position where the only decent thing to do was stay on her good side.

Gabriella's lips pressed into a prissy little line. "I'm a businesswoman. All I'm saying is that a company— and this ranch is a company—can't stall because of a broken piece of equipment. Why bother repairing that tractor when the other tractor is sitting idle?"

"Why bother?" He took a couple steps in her direction and intended to slam the door shut but stopped when Gabriella simply lifted her chin, her eyes daring him to respond rationally.

That expression, that inexplicable jab to cowboy up and not behave like an angry, bitter boy, was so *Zane,* Brad gripped the door frame tightly as a wave of mourning rolled through him.

"Use your words, boy. You might be big as a bull but that doesn't mean you get to act like one. You got a problem? Speak up, don't show yourself by stomping around and pawing at the ground"

Zane's voice filled his head. That conversation, the first of many, had been what had kept Brad from barreling out of control as a teen. Zane had been the voice of calm understanding layered with the steely strength Brad had needed. He'd been a bitter kid in the foster care system who farmers and ranchers wanted to work into the ground but no one wanted to feed or clothe for long. He'd taken his anger and frustration at being shipped around out on anything that pissed him off until Zane had taught him a better way of coping.

Hard work, time to breathe and calm down. A long ride on God's earth to realize that in the scheme of things, most things that anger a person aren't worth getting upset about.

"That tractor was the first piece of equipment Zane bought new. It meant something to him and it means something to me and I thought today would be a good day to fix it."

Gabriella blinked at him, her expression losing some of the challenge. As though she understood.

"That's very commendable, Brad, truly. But I thought I heard Charlie say something about needing tractors to repair a fence and for haying season. No offense to your foreman, but he doesn't appear to be in great physical shape. If he needs more than one tractor, why not use the one in the field?"

"He can if he wants. But I refuse to touch the tractor that rolled on Zane and killed him."

That said, Brad maneuvered around her and stalked toward the stairs.

GABRIELLA STOOD several seconds after Brad made the cryptic statement and left the second floor, seemingly trying to outrun her questions and his grief.

Even though she didn't think it entirely wise to follow him, she found herself doing that. She'd seen the flash of pain on his face before he'd masked it with anger and she hated that she'd been the cause.

Brad might be big and burly and strong but she'd glimpsed something vulnerable in him. Something she couldn't ignore. Because having talked with the grief counselors after Molly's death, she recognized that Brad was in the anger stage.

When she descended the stairs she expected to find Brad in the kitchen. He'd come into the house and washed up, obviously ready to eat. But he wasn't there, and the living room was empty. Zane's den?

Leave him alone. Whatever you say might make it worse.

Yeah, it might. But it could make things better. She might not be mourning Zane as a daughter should, but she was mourning the loss of her best friend. She and Brad had that in common. Maybe they could build on that. Find some common ground.

The den was empty as well but she walked to the desk and stared at the pictures there. Most were of her, but some were of Brad and his brothers.

She turned to leave but noticed the desk calendar

was several days behind. And because things like that bugged her, she flipped the three pages it took to be on the correct date only to pause.

Brad's birthday—30 was written in the neat handwriting she recognized as her father's.

His birthday. No wonder Brad was having such a hard time of it. Coming so soon on the heels of Zane's death, Brad's attempts to repair the tractor made sense.

Gabriella leaned against the desk, unsure of her next move. She felt guilty for her hand in the situation but the fact remained they were all in limbo. She and Brad had to find a way to coexist. Maybe their talk last night and the one they were about to have could bridge into a friendship they might enjoy while she was there?

You're planning to sell the land. It would be best to keep to yourself and stay away from them all.

But it was his birthday, and no one should have to spend a birthday alone. Brad had been out in the barn most of the day. He didn't need to brood out there over something that couldn't be changed.

Walking through the empty house, Gabriella spied a pair of calf-length waders by the door. She wrinkled her nose but put them on. Alicia would really get a kick if she could see this.

She grabbed a jacket from the hooks and wrapped her arms around her front, clumping her way to the barn.

Brad stood silent and still, head down, his hands spread across the fender above one of the tractor's giant wheels.

She opened her mouth then quickly closed it. No matter how she felt about her father's lack of parenting, she wouldn't become her mother, who had a tendency to ignore common decency to make a negative comment whenever and wherever she could.

What Brad felt was real and it was heartfelt. And at the moment, it was very, very visible.

Still, her resentment for him grew because she didn't feel that for Zane. Because her father hadn't let her know him well enough to feel anything but disappointment and anger.

"Did he ever tell you about us?" Brad asked softly, "How we came to be here?"

We. She knew Brad meant his brothers. "No, not really." She'd heard bits and pieces from her mother, of course, but how much of it was true rather than her mother's spin? Given the lies Crystal had told all these years, Gabriella wouldn't mind knowing the truth. No matter how much it hurt to hear it.

When she thought of her father caring for them, raising them, but not her— She knew it was juvenile and pathetic at her age. Water under the bridge, as the saying went. She was an adult in charge of a rapidly growing company, someone who'd been on her own since entering college. Her life was good—*great.*

That anger deep inside? That was hard to let go. She wondered if she would ever be able to let go of it completely even though she knew it was unhealthy to hold on to such negative emotions.

"We stole this tractor, hot-wired it for a joyride." He glanced at her but she didn't speak. "Then tore up the place. Zane caught us, but instead of calling the sheriff he made a deal with the head of the boys' home that we had to work off the damages."

"You must have been happy he didn't call the police."

A low, rough rumble emerged from his chest. "We were furious that he didn't. We knew if we had gone before the judge, we would've gotten a slap on the wrist and gone to juvenile detention for a couple months.

That would have been a piece of cake. Making us work wasn't part of the plan and we tried everything to change Zane's mind. Got in his face, told him off."

"So how did he get you to do it?"

Another smile. This one softened Brad's harsh, craggy features. "You don't mess with cowboys and ranchers, especially not men like Zane."

Gabriella found herself smiling even though she wasn't sure why. The image was enough to get a response, though. Zane had often told her he wasn't sure what to do with her sometimes. But seeing as how Brad and his brothers had messed with Zane's ranch, he'd obviously known what to do with them.

"Zane got his men to help load us up. They took us out into the middle of nowhere and dropped us. We had nowhere to go, no way to leave, and if we wanted to eat, we had to work. By the time we were done, we were too tired to cause anyone trouble."

She couldn't comprehend the process. Or what should have been the results of it. "I don't get it. How did you wind up staying with him? How did you not hate him?"

"We did at first," he said. "But after a while we figured out it was nice to have someone actually give a damn whether we lived or died. Zane did, even though he didn't have to."

Brad smoothed his hand over the metal, down a large scrape of yellow on the otherwise red paint. "Ol' Red quit running last year and Zane and I talked about fixing her but we never got around to it. It's not as big or powerful as the one out in the pasture but this one... this was the one we hot-wired, the one Zane liked the best."

And it was important to Brad because it represented the beginning with her father. That was sweet. And totally unexpected. "Why don't you hire a repairman? Someone who'll fix it for you so you'll have it in memory of Zane?"

The moment the words left her lips she noted Brad's reaction. A soft oath ripped through the quiet barn, filled with frustration. "That would be the easiest thing to do now, wouldn't it? Money fixes everything, right?"

What had she said wrong? Gabriella felt her own anger simmering in response to his. She was trying to be nice to him. To get along. Brad didn't have to be such a jerk about it. "I don't think that at all."

"Isn't that why you're staying here? Because you have your eyes set on the big prize of getting a cool million off Zane's death?" He shook his head in disgust. "Neither you nor your mama even care that he's dead."

His gaze narrowed in accusation but Gabriella refused to falter. He didn't know her, how could he understand her? How could he know what kind of person she was, why she'd come out here in the first place?

Brad was striking out in anger, but knowing that didn't remove the pain of the verbal blows. She'd been a child trying to cope with a situation her own *parents* couldn't handle. "I'm sorry you're struggling with the fall-out of Zane's decision, but you're right—I do want the *cool million*. And I'm honest enough to admit I'm not a bit sorry about that." She turned to go but paused long enough to send him a glance over her shoulder. "Happy birthday. I hope you get the tractor running."

CHAPTER EIGHT

BRAD WAS SO ANGRY HE couldn't sleep that night and the next morning his mind still circled the same paths.

How was it possible to find himself thinking about Gabriella as a woman, feel any sort of attraction for her, when she was as brutally honest as she'd been about wanting the money?

She had a valid point about the tractor and most ranchers in the area would shake their heads at his stand. The newer tractor had tipped, not through malfunction, but user error. Zane had miscalculated and paid the ultimate price because of it.

But Brad still didn't want to touch it, much less use the tractor again given the circumstances. Until he got Ol' Red running, he'd make do, have the ranch hands use the tractor that had crushed Zane.

But today was the last day he could let his mourning keep him from getting things done. He had to tackle what Zane had taught him to do—be a rancher.

He had culverts to dig out, fence lines to tighten, gates that had to be removed and rehung before the cattle were brought in for market in the fall. Hay that had to be cut in the next few days before the predicted storms rolled in and ruined it.

For now the sun was high in the sky, the birds sang in the trees and the culvert wasn't going to repair itself. He might not be able to fix the tractor, but he could use a shovel with the best of them. And having sent Charlie and the ranch hands out with their orders, Brad had saved digging and lifting the muck and debris for himself because it was an exhausting way to burn some of the anger pumping through his veins.

"Hey."

He turned to find Gabriella entering the field where he worked, via the gaping hole in the wood slat fence Liam had created when he'd driven through the fence trying to get to Zane the day of the accident. That was something else that had to be repaired, something else Brad had been putting off.

Brad kept digging, aware that Gabriella picked her way through the field, too aware of the running shorts and the tight top she had on. The sight of her long, lean body made it hard to swallow. She might not be the curvaceous type he preferred but she still had bumps in all the right places. The problem was every man on the ranch could see it, too.

Unable to stop himself, his gaze slid over her, noting that along with the snug, expensive-looking clothes, she wore sneakers that looked as though they belonged on a basketball court or in a gym, not on a dirt and gravel country road. And her legs… They stretched on forever.

"I'm busy."

"So I see. I won't keep you. Brad, I don't want to spend the next three months fighting with you."

He lowered his chin to his chest and inhaled. "I don't want to fight with you, either. You need to be careful out here. You could run into a surprise or two."

"Yeah, well, you can run into a surprise or two jogging the city streets, as well." Gabriella pulled the earphones from her ears and let them hang out the top of her shirt before tapping a small canister strapped to her inner wrist. "Don't worry about me. This will deter almost anything."

Pepper spray or whatever it was wouldn't stop a mountain lion—or men who didn't care about a little pain to get what they wanted. Hadn't she ever heard of Kari Swenson? "If you're going to run, be smart about it. Stick to the road between the house and Liam's cabin there on the rise. It's a half-mile with open visibility the entire way. Make a few loops if you have to. Things are pretty quiet here but we have our share of trouble."

"I'll be careful."

She was blowing him off, not taking him seriously, and he didn't like it. "I mean it, Gabriella. Women running alone on a stretch of deserted road are endangering themselves."

"Don't tell me you're the kind of guy who says women *ask for it*," she drawled, derisive.

Was she going to argue about every statement he made? "Of course not. But you're not used to being here, and even though it might sound like something from the Wild West, we get our share of outlaws and bad guys. Even an occasional bear or mountain lion. You need to stay on your guard."

Something in her expression changed, as though she was finally listening.

"Thank you for the warning. I'll stay on the road between our house and Liam's." Her reference to *our house* darkened his mood once more. It wasn't hers and, if he had his way, it never would be.

Brad tossed the shovel aside and climbed out of the ditch, heading for the truck. He reached into the cooler on the lowered tailgate and grabbed a bottle of water, glancing at Gabriella in time to see her jump the ditch in one smooth motion. Impressed despite not wanting to be, he handed her the bottle.

"Thanks. So, I was wondering if you needed the old truck by the barn for anything. That was Zane's, right?"

"Yeah. Why?" He sounded way too possessive but he couldn't help it.

"The list—driving a stick shift. Zane wanted me to learn."

Zane would have taught her in his old truck, too.

"If I'm going to see people the way Zane wanted, I'm going to have to use it or one of the other vehicles. My car is great but not on these back roads."

Back roads? There were a few ruts here and there but the roads were in good shape. Brad almost said no, then figured he could use some entertainment. Zane's truck was hard to start, hard to shift and hard to maneuver with no power steering. But if Gabriella was busy trying to figure out how to drive it, she wouldn't be in Brad's hair pestering him.

Or out running the roads alone. "Keys are on the hook by the door. Red tag."

"Thanks." She indicated the ditch with a wave of her hand. "I'll let you get back to work."

Brad sat on the edge of the truck bed and watched as she walked away, the water bottle popping in his hand when he realized what he was doing. He finished drinking and grabbed the shovel. Digging ditches ranked right up there with lifting cars when it came to expending energy. And thanks to those running shorts of Gabriella's, he now had plenty to burn.

SHE WASN'T GOING TO ask for help, Gabriella decided two hours later after she'd showered, changed into jeans and a T-shirt and smeared on a little makeup.

No, she flat-out *refused* to ask for help. And if she caught one more person smiling as they turned away because she couldn't get the stupid truck in the stupid gear without killing it, she was going to find a stick and take a swing at it. And considering she was a nonviolent person, that was a true indication of her frustration level. "Come on!" she said when it died with a sputter and cough for the tenth time in less than five minutes. "It's not that difficult. It can't be."

"Need some help?" Brad asked.

"No," she said loud enough for her voice to carry through the half-lowered window. The fresh breeze felt good on her anger-hot skin.

"You sure?"

He's trying to be nice.

So why did it seem like gloating? "I'm positive. Shouldn't you be working or something?"

"Time for lunch."

"Then go have some." She shoved in the clutch, put her foot on the brake and turned the key. The truck might be older than dirt but it had been taken care of, and in its own funky, old-fashioned way, it made a statement. "Wait, what kind of truck is this?"

"A 1953 F-100. Want to take a break and drink some of your sludge?"

She glared at Brad, noticing the way his eyes sparkled with amusement he couldn't hide. "Come on, don't look like that. Give the poor old thing a break. You're going to give her a complex."

Give the *truck* a complex? What about her? She'd graduated top of her class, owned her own very successful business—she didn't fail. "I can do this," she said around her gritted teeth.

"I don't doubt you can but stripping the clutch isn't the way to treat her nice."

"It's a truck, not a person."

Brad patted the shiny red metal. "But she's a pretty old gal and we'd like to keep her around for a while."

Gabriella hit the steering wheel with her palm. "She's the one being stubborn!" Unbelievable. She'd given in to calling the hunk of metal a *she*. "How long did it take you?" She didn't want to compare herself to Brad but sitting here in the stupid truck and not being able to get it to drive more than a few seconds after she began to ease out the clutch made a girl feel every one of her insecurities about not measuring up.

"What do you mean?"

Did she have to spell it out? "How long did it take for you to learn to drive it?"

Brad's gaze softened and that irked her more. "Gabriella—"

"How long?"

He shrugged. "Not long."

Meaning he hadn't had any trouble. Probably none of them had.

Her gaze locked on the photo wedged inside the dash, the one that had gotten her attention the moment she'd slid onto the old leather seat. Gabriella stared at her younger self—and Zane—and her anger built to an unimaginable level. If he'd wanted her to learn how to drive the stupid truck, why hadn't he shown her himself? Why had he taught them but not cared enough for her to *fight* to bring her back?

Why?

"Take a break and I'll teach you later, after supper."

A laugh bubbled out. She *must* be a sight if Brad was

volunteering to help her. He'd made it perfectly clear how he felt about her presence on the ranch.

She swallowed the lump in her throat, unable to look away from the photograph. It was one of…so many.

Everywhere she turned she found pictures of herself. They weren't only in Zane's bedroom but every room of the house, in books, beneath the protective glass on Zane's desk. Cabinets and drawers. She'd started opening things just to see if there was a picture inside. Even here, in Zane's truck.

"Gabriella?"

She grabbed the photo and turned it over.

She wasn't doing this for the list now. She would learn how to drive this truck because not learning was unacceptable. Because she didn't fail. "You go ahead," she said. "This is something I have to do myself."

A stranger at driver's ed had taught her how to drive. Not her father. Not her mother because she'd been at a casting call or audition, on location. A total stranger.

The truth was, Zane had helped make her the woman she was now by not being there for her. He'd forced her to grow up self-reliant, unable or unwilling—take your pick—to rely on other people for assistance. *Because the only person she could trust was herself—or Molly.*

"Suit yourself."

Brad walked away and Gabriella pulled her gaze from the back of the picture long enough to glare at Brad's long-legged stride and extraordinarily wide shoulders. A part of her wanted to call out, to accept his offer, but she couldn't. She could do this, figure it out, on her own.

She hadn't depended on Zane—and she certainly wouldn't start depending on one of *Zane's boys.*

CHAPTER NINE

THE NEXT DAY BRAD HAD returned to work on the roof of one of the buildings after lunch when he heard the truck rumbling. He looked up to find Gabriella hunched over the wheel, grinding the gears as she sped up enough to put it into second. He held his breath as she let off on the clutch. "Come on, come on."

She managed to keep the engine running and even across the distance he heard her cry of victory from within the cab. The sound brought out a smile and a chuckle he couldn't hold back. It was about time.

The old truck bumped along the road and Brad watched as Gabriella picked her way over the ruts. The grader was due tomorrow along with quite a few truck-loads of gravel. The state took care of the main roads but private roads were another matter.

Maintenance was a heavy expense the ranch couldn't afford but Zane had already arranged for the work to be done before his death and paid a down payment. Brad wasn't going to cancel the order and risk damaging equipment or the animals getting hurt moving them from pasture to pasture.

The truck jerked again as Gabriella approached the slope leading to Liam's cabin. Would she make it? Even as the thought formed he realized he cared, waiting to see what would happen—and that wouldn't do. But how could he not hover when she was so oblivious to the dangers of living here? Someone had to keep an eye on her, and like it or not, he was the only one he trusted enough to do it. He'd taken it upon himself to make a list of chores that kept him close to the house where he could keep an eye on her. For as long as she stayed, he'd tackle them one by one.

Gabriella made it to the top of the slope and turned into Liam's driveway. Brad grimaced, hearing the screech and grinding of the gears as she shoved the truck in Reverse. If she tore up the transmission, it would be a long time before he could afford to fix it.

She reversed but started rolling down the hill too fast, no doubt in neutral.

Brad eyed the undamaged portion of the fence and said a prayer he wouldn't have to add it to the list of what had to be repaired. "Turn, turn. Damn it, turn!"

At the last second the truck swung the other way and veered from side to side like a pinball machine as Gabriella struggled to maintain control and keep the truck centered in the one-lane road.

Shaking his head, he forced himself to look away and grab a strip of metal roofing. "It's gonna be another damn long day."

ONE DOWN, A DOZEN TO GO, Gabriella thought, sinking deeper into the steaming bathwater later that afternoon.

If she ever missed the comforts of home, it was now. The hot tub at her condo complex would have been heavenly but a good old-fashioned soaking was exactly what the aching muscles of her back, shoulders and arms needed. Her left thigh was sore, too, from shoving in the stupid clutch over and over again.

How did people drive vehicles like that? Power steering had to be one of the greatest inventions ever.

She closed her eyes and exhaled a deep breath, her body slowly relaxing in the sudsy water, the scent of lavender filling her nose. The next time someone ordered a spa basket she'd have to remember this mix of salts because the buoyant water and scent was heavenly.

Now…what to do next from her list?

A smile curled her lips because she'd done it. She'd driven the truck. "Didn't think I could do it, did you?" she murmured, intending the comment for Zane, for Brad. For anyone who had ever doubted her. "Ha."

BRAD FROZE COMING OUT of his bedroom, unable to believe his eyes.

One minute he'd been retrieving his wallet from his dresser and the next Gabriella was emerging from the bathroom wearing nothing but a towel.

She clutched the towel to her chest. "Oh, uh, sorry. I thought the house was empty. I forgot my clothes."

The towel was thin and damp and he tried not to notice the way her nipples pressed against the fabric.

He took in her long, long legs and noted how her toes curled into the carpet beneath her feet.

"Um, okay. So, I should go."

"Yeah. Me, too," he managed to say.

They stood there, a few feet between them.

Finally they both moved at once, both stopped—but doing so put them into closer proximity. The house was a hundred years old, the hallway narrow. "Go ahead," he murmured. "Ladies first."

Standing this close he could smell her skin, fresh and clean with something flowery but not overpowering. Wet tendrils framed her face and neck and, as he watched, a drop slid from her hair to land on her shoulder and drifted over her collarbone, lower, into the curve of her breasts.

His gaze met hers and his entire body went on full alert. "You go ahead," he said huskily, holding himself very still, barely breathing to keep from touching her.

She didn't move.

"Gabriella."

She lifted her face, her mouth, and he couldn't resist moving closer, telling himself he was going to walk on by but— She smelled *good*.

Holding her gaze he said, "Tell me no."

He would regret this. But when she stayed quiet and he fastened his lips over hers it sure didn't feel like something he'd regret anytime soon.

From the moment he'd walked into her store and saw her standing behind the counter so prim and proper and sexy, he'd wondered how she tasted, how she felt.

Now he knew.

Gabriella's lips parted and let him in. He wanted to take his time but the moment he touched his tongue to hers a jolt of lightning zipped through his insides and obliterated all sense of slowness because she *moaned*. A sound that set him on fire and made him want her fast and hard and now. Here.

He gathered her close, too aware she wore nothing but a towel with a knot rapidly coming undone between them. He nudged her the few inches it took for her back to hit the wall, pinning her there. One hand cupped her behind, sliding over the fabric until he felt warm, solid flesh, the other cupping her breast and squeezing gently.

Gabriella tore her mouth from his and gasped for air, the hot release blowing into his ear. She wound her arms around his neck and kissed him again, her lean body feeling soft and surprisingly fragile against his.

Brad kissed his way to her neck, the tender skin beneath her ear, and male satisfaction filled him at her shiver. She shifted her head to give him better access, the move knocking a picture from the wall.

It fell to the floor with a crash and Brad froze, his breathing harsh and loud in his ears. He shifted his hands to her waist and lifted her to safety.

Brad glanced at the broken frame and noticed the picture was one of him and Zane, taken at a rodeo not long after the adoption was final. "Were you cut?"

"No."

His heart still pounded like a race horse's hooves. "Go get dressed. I'll take care of this."

"Brad—"

"Go get dressed," he ordered, cursing himself for losing control like that.

With Zane's daughter.

What was Brad thinking? How could he disrespect Zane that way?

Even now Brad couldn't look at her. Not yet. Not without wanting to continue what they'd started. "Go."

Thankfully, Gabriella made a dash for her bedroom—but before the door closed he got a real good view of her backside.

THAT EVENING GABRIELLA drove into town to do some exploring. North Star wasn't big enough to hope for much by way of entertainment, but she needed some groceries, and, while she was out, she'd do some roaming since she needed to escape the house—and Brad—for a while. Apparently he felt the same because he was nowhere in sight as she left the Circle M.

What had possessed her to kiss him that way?

No immediate answer appeared and she entered the small store, frustrated with herself and her disturbing response to him. Distracted, she forced herself to focus on getting what she needed. The grocery was nothing like the one she frequented in California, but the produce was fresh and they had a small organic section.

Quite a few people stared as they passed by, pushing their carts and trying to be discreet but…not. She stuck to the perimeter, gathering fresh greens and vegetables, fruit, some milk and cheese. Her list complete, she headed toward the checkout.

"Haven't seen you before," a man said.

Gabriella looked up from her wallet and found a friendly looking older man watching her. He wore a button-down shirt and jeans, and had an air of authority about him. His name tag read Delmer but unlike the other staff, he didn't wear a red vest. "No, probably not."

"New in town?" he asked, waving away a cashier who approached to bag Gabriella's purchases.

The man began to sort and bag Gabriella's selection of fruits and vegetables himself, an act which drew raised eyebrows from the cashiers and extra-long looks of interest in her direction.

"You could say that." Call it instinct but she had a feeling the man knew good and well who she was and why she was there.

"You're Zane's daughter, right?"

Oh, yeah. He knew. "Yes, I am."

"I thought so. I'm Delmer Frank. I was a friend of Zane's."

Weren't they all, she mused.

"Your father loved this town," he said, stowing the last of her items then handing the three bags to her with a smile. "He loved you, too," Delmer added, his tone and expression softening. "I'm sorry for your loss."

"Thank you."

"You going to look around a few days before you head back to California?"

The question seemed innocent enough but she picked up on the intense undercurrent. "Yes," she said simply.

"Well, if there's anything you need while you're here, let us know."

"Thank you." She smiled at him, anxious to get out of there. While Delmer had been a friend of Zane's, she wasn't quite sure the man wanted to be a friend of hers. Possibly because he didn't think she belonged there any more than Brad did.

Brad kissed you. Maybe that's changed?

But why did he kiss her?

As Gabriella drove along Main Street, questions with no answers bounced around in her head.

She glared at the feed store bearing the McKenna name while she waited for the light to change so she could turn in the opposite direction. One of Zane's requests was that she spend some time there but taking a tour wasn't on her agenda today. Not when doing so would put her in direct contact with Chance. One run-in with a McKenna today was enough.

With her stomach growling she didn't think she could wait even the time it would take to drive to the ranch to eat. Besides, she was tired of her solitary meals. Brad's company might not be ideal but they'd yet to sit down to a meal together. And after the kiss?

Oh, this was going to be awkward.

Seeing the diner she'd noticed on her first trip through town, Gabriella saw an open parking spot ready for the taking and pulled in. Awkwardness avoided—for a little while at least.

She entered the diner, not realizing until she crossed the threshold exactly how busy the small establishment was or how much interest she'd draw from the crowd.

"Seat yourself," the waitress said from the counter. "I'll be with you as soon as I can."

"Thank you." But as Gabriella looked around she noted every table was occupied by at least one person.

"Gabriella, over here. Come sit with me," Carly called from Gabriella's left.

Not really seeing another option, Gabriella managed a smile as she headed toward the redheaded woman. "Hi, Carly, it's good to see you. I don't want to intrude—I stopped in for a salad and I can get it to go."

"Nonsense. Join me, please. Liam is going to be a while yet. That's the thing about being a cop, he's usually in high demand." She made a face. "I'd love the company. I hate eating alone."

Maybe if Carly hadn't said that… "Okay. Thanks." Gabriella dropped her purse onto the 1950s-style chair.

"How are things going at the ranch? Have you settled in? Sorry I haven't had a chance to stop by. Riley has baseball practice in the evenings, and with work—"

"Not a problem. What do you do?" Gabriella latched onto the subject as the way to make conversation with a virtual stranger. At least sitting as she was, her back was to the majority of the diner's occupants. Not that she couldn't feel their stares boring into her.

Carly explained how she rented out one-person offices and served as their secretary and receptionist, as well as their landlord.

"That's a unique concept. Very inventive," Gabriella said.

"Thanks. It suited our town and filled a need. I lucked into the building and my father helped rehab it."

"Not Liam?" she asked, hoping to keep Carly talking so she didn't have to reveal much about her own life since that discussion would likely wind up with her cataloguing the details of being Zane's daughter and yet...not.

"No, we weren't together then. So...everything going okay between you and Brad?"

The waitress delivered Carly's order and took Gabriella's for a salad and tea. When she was gone, Gabriella urged Carly to begin eating while her food was hot, and shrugged. "It's...going. I've been busy setting up an office and figuring out how to do everything long-distance. Good thing my cell service works there, otherwise the phone bills would be crazy high."

"Let me know if I can help."

"I will. Thanks."

"So what about Brad? What's it like being forced to live with a stranger?"

Gabriella laughed. "Weird—although I don't see Brad that much. He's usually gone by the time I come downstairs in the morning."

"What about in the evening?"

"He, uh, stays out in the barn or something most of the time. It's fine, though."

Carly looked surprised by the news—and then upset on Gabriella's behalf?

"Carly, it's fine. I think Brad is still dealing with his feelings about Zane's death and the decisions he made and— Did you know Monday was Brad's birthday?"

"What? No."

"It was on Zane's calendar in the den. I'm sure Brad didn't expect anyone to remember but I found it sad that he spent the day working on Zane's old tractor. He couldn't get it to start."

"That is sad. They all loved Zane but Brad and Zane were really close. Oh, I hate that we didn't acknowledge the day, though. We'll have to get together and do something." Carly paused as though forming plans to celebrate. "As to staying there, it's early yet. I'm sure Brad will come around. He's the quiet type but he's a nice guy. He's probably trying to give you some space."

Those words immediately brought the kiss to mind. Brad hadn't given Gabriella space then, that's for sure. Not that she was ready to share that info.

How long did it take to get a salad? Was she going to get the third degree the entire time?

"Can I ask you something?" Carly continued.

No. No, no, no. "Sure."

"*Do* you intend to sell your portion of the ranch once you inherit it?"

Gabriella was a bit taken aback by the bluntness and unsure of how Carly would react to her answer, given who she was engaged to. "Yes, I do. I'm sorry if that's upsetting but I need that money for my business." Seeing Carly's expression, Gabriella added, "Carly, it's not personal, it's business."

"Are you sure about that? I mean, you're not selling to get revenge on Zane or something?"

Inhaling, Gabriella decided to lay all her cards on the table. "I'd be lying if I said it hasn't crossed my mind. I'm angry about my childhood. But that's not why. I made a promise to someone very important to me and I intend to keep it. The only way I can do that is to sell."

The waitress brought Gabriella's salad and tea, then stayed long enough to refill Carly's water glass. Gabriella focused on mixing the salad up just so.

"Are you going to think me a total busybody if I ask who you made the promise to? What kind of promise it was? The ranch means everything to them."

"I understand that but Zane made the decision. Besides, they'll still have their portions."

"But yours is the key."

"What do you mean?" Gabriella asked, stuffing a bite into her mouth. The produce tasted fresh and absolutely wonderful.

"I mean the water rights. And the fact that it's not only the Circle M that depends on them."

"I'm afraid I'm not following."

"Okay, Ranching 101—not all ranches have ready access to water. The ones that don't rely on other ranches—like the Circle M—to water crops and livestock. If someone buys the land from you and cuts off the water supply or charges so much that the dependent ranches can't afford to pay…"

They dry up and go under. "I see," Gabriella said, confused all the more. *Why* had her father given her something so important to the Circle M's future? To the future of the surrounding area? That didn't make sense. "I had no idea."

"Now you do. So tell me about that promise."

Gabriella's appetite fled and she picked at the salad in front of her. "It was to my best friend, Molly. She was my business partner, too. She died not long ago. Actually, it was around the same time that Zane passed."

"You lost both of them close together?"

She nodded once.

"Gabriella, I'm so sorry."

"Anyway, that's why I'm here. Because of Molly." She appreciated Carly's sincerity, but wanted the conversation over with. "Without the money from the sale, I can't keep my promise, and that isn't acceptable to me."

"I can see why. No wonder you're so determined to see this through," Carly said softly.

The noise of the diner faded to the background. Gabriella could use an ally here, although wouldn't have expected it to be Carly, who appeared to understand, or at least sympathize with her predicament. "I'm not out to hurt anyone or destroy anything. But to me there is only one acceptable outcome and that is to get as much money as possible out of my inheritance."

"But a million dollars? Gabriella, Hollywood stars might have that kind of cash in their bank accounts but ranchers don't. Surely you can take less."

Silence descended and Gabriella knew she would ruin the tentative friendship with her next words. "No. I have to have the full asking price—more, if possible. It's the only way to make sure Molly gets her wish, and that is the only thing that matters to me."

CHAPTER TEN

OF ALL THE STUPID THINGS to do…

The next morning Brad heaved the freshly cut section of tree trunk out of his way with a grunt, still wrestling with the impact of kissing Gabriella.

He hadn't been able to think of anything but the way her skin had felt so soft, the feel of her breast in his hand, the earthy, husky little moans she'd released when he'd tasted her. Even the way she'd sat in Zane's old Ford wearing determined frowns flickered through his head and made him want her.

She'd been in Montana five days now and he was officially in hell.

With calving season over and branding completed, it was time to bring in the hay. They would start tomorrow in the larger fields to the west of the ranch.

While Charlie oversaw that, Brad tackled repairing the fence. There was a reason the term *bullheaded* existed. Once the animals got a notion to graze in a field fenced for haying, keeping them out took some doing. It meant regular repairs, not to mention herd checks to make sure the animals were where they should be and getting enough to eat so that when they sold in the fall market, they brought a good price.

But against those routine tasks he saw Gabriella.

For some reason operating her business remotely required the items Gabriella carried in her boutique to be sent here. Seemingly overnight she'd transformed the living room into a miniature mercantile.

There were wisps of barely there lingerie hanging from hooks and shelves, lotions on every surface, purses and bags on the floor.

He'd forgotten his thermos this morning and when he'd entered the kitchen to find it next to a box addressed to her, he'd been so annoyed he'd mentioned the mess in his aggravation.

According to her, before she agreed to sell something she had to touch it, taste it, wear it or see it first. If it didn't pass her inspection, she didn't pass it on.

That response had made him weak in the knees.

He not only had the kiss to contend with, but now he imagined her wearing the bits of nothing—or simply nothing.

"Hey."

Brad stiffened at the sound of Gabriella's call. He straightened, and found her on the other side of the fence heading toward him.

He lifted his hand in a reluctant greeting and kept working, hoping she'd get the hint. After he tossed another armload of brush onto the pile, he turned to find her leaning against the truck door, watching him.

"Need some help?"

"Help?" Was she kidding?

"Yeah, help," she repeated, sounding more than a little amused by his response. "I'm supposed to pitch in, remember? Besides, I'm missing my weight resistance exercises. Lifting the logs will help."

She was willing to perform manual labor for a workout?

She would be a hindrance but he was curious about how far she'd go.

Sure you're not thinking of that kiss? Wondering how far things would have gone had the picture not fallen?

He ignored the voice in his head. "There's an extra pair of gloves in the truck, front passenger side. You might want to put on a pair of coveralls, too. The branches will scratch you if you don't." Her impossibly long legs had to be covered up if he was going to be able to think straight.

Brad pulled off his hat and wiped his rolled sleeve over his forehead, watching as Gabriella opened the passenger door and dug around inside the cab. He was glad he hadn't pulled one of the guys from haying to help him. No one else needed to witness this.

A woman her height should look awkward and gangly but she moved with grace. Not that he was looking. He blamed the novelty of her presence for his preoccupation with her. That was all it was. He wasn't used to living with a woman, being around one 24/7.

Gabriella pulled on the lightweight coveralls—giving him a tantalizing view of her backside when she maneuvered them over her running shoes. During the process he got a gander at some strings sitting slightly above her waistband.

A thong?

"All gloved up." She zipped the coveralls, then smacked the gloves that she'd grabbed together and waving away the dust cloud that resulted. "Now what?"

He tried not to overthink her words—or the thong.

He didn't like whiners. The first time she complained that would be the end of whatever attraction he felt for her. "Now we see what you're made of."

An hour later Brad reluctantly had to give Gabriella credit. What she lacked in physical strength and know-how she made up for in determination and sheer will.

And that? That was a total turn-on.

Needing a break from watching Gabriella bend over, he said, "Let's take a breather."

Gabriella nodded, her cheek streaked with dirt and sweat. She'd talked until she'd finally gotten winded. Her comments about the beauty of the day, the lushness of the fields and the cloud-spotted sky dwindled to nothing but a few hard exhalations as she worked clearing the brush and trunk of the downed tree so that the fence could be repaired.

"It's hard to believe an area this large is fenced."

Brad had parked beneath the shade of the trees, beside the large pines that had fallen in the last big snowstorm in spring.

"This is only a small portion," he said, comfortable talking about what he knew best. As much as he wanted a wife and kids someday, he knew his faults. Being able to talk with women about something other than ranching was one of them. "The pasture will be used in late summer, when we herd the livestock in closer."

Brad lowered the tailgate then hoisted himself up to sit in the shade and Gabriella followed suit. He dug into the cooler. "You hungry? I don't have seaweed protein shakes but I do have a couple of apples and some trail mix. The sandwich has meat and cheese."

"An apple, please," she said, murmuring her thanks when he handed one over. "So I've been wondering. Is there a particular reason you don't come to the house to eat? Say…a certain kiss?"

Brad helped himself to some water and a handful of trail mix, the images from that afternoon resurrecting in his head. "Do you always say what's on your mind?"

"Usually."

"I don't always have the time to make it back for lunch. Sometimes it's easier to eat out here."

"I understand that. But you didn't come in for dinner last night, either, and I can't help but think it's because you're avoiding me."

Did she sound hurt? "Seems wise after what happened."

Gabriella took a drink, her lips moist afterward. Another thing he didn't notice.

"Brad, I know we have our own agendas but I don't want to run you out of your house. You're making a few kisses sound like something horrible."

"It was. I mean—" he grimaced "—it wasn't horrible. The kiss wasn't. It's—"

"I know what you mean. And maybe it wasn't *wise*," she admitted, "but I don't think it's anything to beat ourselves up about too much."

"I respected your father, Gabriella. He wouldn't want me or anyone else to take advantage of you."

Gabriella's laughter filled the air. "Wow."

"What?" He recognized when a woman made fun of him and he didn't like it. Guys never forgot that girl who shot them down in public, the girl who laughed and made a scene so all her friends could hear and get their kicks, too.

"It's nothing. Really. It was just that whole *take advantage* thing. It's very old-fashioned."

He lifted an eyebrow when he looked at her.

"Don't get me wrong. It suits you. I choose to look at things differently. Molly's death taught me a lot, like how I need to enjoy life more."

Meaning she'd enjoyed kissing him?

"So while getting involved with you is definitely

not on my list of things to do, I see what happened as a learning experience."

Not on her list of things to do? He didn't know whether to be grateful or insulted. "How so?"

"Back in L.A., I've worked longer hours than you. I don't get out that much. Molly and I busted our butts to make a name for ourselves. But Molly wasn't around long enough to enjoy our success. I need to make sure that doesn't happen for me. I need to enjoy life more."

Which meant since it wasn't wise to kiss him, she wanted to find another guy to kiss? To do more? He didn't like the sound of that. Not at all.

"I refuse to beat myself up about a kiss when I'm alive and healthy and—"

And? Brad waited.

"It's only natural that as two single members of the opposite sex we'd be curious. So, end of curiosity," she said briskly. "No more worrying about what happened in the hallway, okay? It's done. We know. End of story."

He would have preferred she finish the other sentence. He didn't look at her—couldn't for fear he'd reveal too much.

"Zane did stuff like this every day?"

Grateful for the change in topic, Brad nodded. "There's never a shortage of work on a ranch. Miles and miles of fence to check and repair, culverts and ditches to dig, wells to test, livestock that has to be cared for. When Zane bought the feed store we began harvesting more straw and hay to sell."

That reminded him to hurry to finish this job so he could check on Charlie's progress in the hay fields.

Despite the reminder, he didn't budge.

Gabriella gazed at the land spread before them and he tried to see it through her eyes, the lush pasture, towering trees, the beauty that Montana was. Not a day went by that he didn't thank God he'd found a home here. Zane had given Brad everything but Brad had never considered Zane might take it all away. And Brad resented the hell out of his adopted father for it.

"Where's the property line?"

That one question proved how little she knew about her father's life. "Everything you see is Circle M land."

They sat at the edge of the valley, the house and buildings, the rise of the pastures toward the mountains, all visible.

"Everything?"

"Yeah. There's more on the other side, too."

"Okay, so if my fourth is worth approximately a million, give or take in today's market," she mused, "what's the entire ranch worth?"

He spit out the water he'd sipped, unable to swallow after hearing the speculation. Calling himself a fool, he said, "Depends on who you ask. Personally, I don't believe you can put a price on a dream."

CHAPTER ELEVEN

"PERSONALLY, I DON'T *believe you can put a price on a* *dream.*"

Gabriella stared at the pasture that sloped into a hill that became a mountain. How many people *owned* mountains?

But Brad's statement had a point.

Zane had loved it here. More than anything. But what about her dream? Molly's dream?

This was a pretty view but she lived in reality and in her reality people had to take care of themselves. Why should she sacrifice her future for a man who had never sacrificed for her? Never fought for her?

"What are you thinking about?"

Her hand fisted over the apple. What was she thinking? "Nothing important now."

She'd seen all the pictures and knew Zane had wanted more of a relationship with her. But living in the past, living with regrets, would get her nowhere. She hadn't gone against her mother's dictates to see Zane and it was too late now.

"What was it like?" Her question emerged hoarse and low. She should probably be embarrassed but maybe Brad had the insight she needed.

"What?"

She couldn't look at Brad and ask the next question. "Living here? Growing up here?" When silence descended she glanced his way and found herself ensnared by his gaze. His eyes had softened. "You said after you came here you figured out how nice it was to have someone care—to have *Zane* care. How'd you get him to care enough to keep you? To fight for you?"

Maybe it was a childish question because rationally she knew no one could make another human feel an emotion they didn't want to feel but she'd spent the past fifteen years wondering what they had that she didn't.

"Gabriella…"

A rough laugh left her chest. The toe of her white running shoe was covered in dirt—dirt that was more valuable to Zane than fighting Crystal. Maybe instead of not knowing what to do with her, that's what Zane was really afraid of. Losing his ranch. Maybe it had been easier to let Crystal have her way rather than risk more.

You didn't make it easy, you know.

As a teen she'd pushed Zane away, yes. Still, while she'd argued and pouted, Zane was the adult. The parent. The one who should have known better. Every kid, especially teenagers, said things they didn't mean. They tested boundaries.

Zane was the one who should have forced her to visit—and proved he cared for her in the process. He'd brought Brad and the others here and made them work. Why not her? "I know it's a stupid question and a moot point. I just wonder, you know? *How* did you get him to want you when you were fighting him and trying to get sent away? How did you get him to care enough to not let you win? I would've liked him to care for me that way, to fight back a little." She thought of the times she'd acted out and been punished, tormented by the unknown reasons her father wanted them but not her. "I always wondered what I did wrong that he didn't like."

"You didn't do anything wrong. I don't think it was like that. Zane wasn't good with words, Gabriella. He probably didn't know what to say to you."

"Do you think that makes it better?"

"Of course not. But it's not Zane's fault that your mother said what she did. He wasn't a man who begged, and like it or not, everyone shares some of the blame."

Meaning Crystal.

And herself.

Was it so irrational to wish Zane had begged to be with her? *Why* had he given in to her mother's demands? Why had Crystal been so unreasonable? What was it about Zane that pushed her buttons?

One question after another. Gabriella was tired of the drama, the fighting. So tired of not having the family she'd always wanted. Tired of her mother's calls and all the messages she left—because Gabriella still wasn't ready to talk to Crystal.

Gabriella scooted off the truck and walked to one of the huge trees that had fallen. The tree trunk was as wide as a wheel at the base, branches spreading out like a fan. She put her foot on it and shoved but it didn't move. And she knew she could shove all she wanted but nothing would change. "No matter what I say, you're going to defend him, aren't you?"

"I'm telling you the truth, Gabriella."

"That's not a denial."

"Zane always defended me. It seems only right to return the favor, especially since the truth is different than what you think you know as fact."

"I know it was different. I get that, but he already had a child. A responsibility. He let my mother have her way and then turned around and adopted you. How is that right? How can anyone defend *that?*"

"He didn't abandon you. He called once a week, Gabriella, right up until the day you moved out of your mother's house. Not talking to you didn't stop him."

A caustic laugh bubbled out of her throat. "Maybe he did, maybe he didn't. How do you know?"

"Because after he hung up he'd be in a bear of a mood. Then he'd get quiet and…"

"And?"

"Try to work himself into oblivion until it was time for the *next* call. He'd do anything to take his mind off it, off you. That wasn't a man who didn't care, that was a man trying to cope with a mist—"

She knew what he'd been about to say. "A mistake."

"I didn't mean you. I meant your mother."

She shook her head. "You meant me. In your eyes we're one and the same, aren't we?"

His face revealed his thoughts. *Okay,* then. Brad didn't even try to deny that. "Zane could've come to see me. If he was really interested in knowing me, he could have fought my mother and *made* her let me talk to him. He had rights but he didn't exercise them. If he was such a great father, why didn't he?"

"Is that what you wanted? For a man you barely knew to force you to leave everything familiar to come live with him?"

Did Brad have to make sense? She needed to vent, she needed sympathy. She didn't need rationale, she needed—she needed Molly. Molly, who would have let her whine and complain for a while, then told her to suck it up. "I know I sound like a jealous shrew and maybe I am. Because he was always *here.* First he loved this place and then he loved you but he didn't love *me.*"

"That's your mother talking. Gabriella. Surely you realize that doubt was instilled by Crystal."

Brad looked way too smug and knowing and disgusted at her lack of belief. Her lack of faith in a man she barely knew but shared genes with. "Actions speak louder than words."

"There are always two sides. What did you want from Zane? You removed his *name* from yours. What about your part in how things worked out between you?"

"Don't blame me. I only asked he do that because I was angry. I *wanted* him to say no. One word would have proved to me he loved me. I was upset because he wouldn't come see me that summer. *Again.* He refused to come see me. But he didn't think twice about signing those papers."

"He thought that was what you wanted."

Because she'd asked it of him.

"You're a grown woman now, not a child. Look around you. Think about the things you now know, what your mother said. Why did he really refuse, Gabriella?"

Because of her mother. Because he would have had to travel to her mother's movie location in New Zealand or New York or Mexico.

The summer after changing her name, Gabriella had gone to camp and ignored her father's requests to see her. Then…Zane adopted the boys and her mother made it clear Gabriella was not allowed to spend a single night under the same roof as *them.*

At the time Gabriella hadn't cared because she'd hated them. All of them. Like dominoes, one thing after another had happened, furthering the distance between her and her father and she'd used all of them to arm herself with a shield of hatred.

"Maybe Zane wasn't around as much as you wanted him to be but did you ever lack for anything?"

Now who was the one thinking money fixed everything? "Anyone can write a check."

"But a lot of men don't. They abandon their kids completely and never think twice about it. Zane didn't do that. He loved you. I know it as sure as I know that tree is lying right there. I know it," he said, his tone growing darker, "because Zane left you the most precious piece of the most valuable thing he owned."

A piece of dirt attached to more dirt—that belonged to Brad and the others. They resented her for that almost as much as she resented them for her childhood.

So where was that resentment when she'd found herself pressed to the wall? Was being with Brad disrespectful of Zane? She didn't care, but Brad did. Whatever. "He left me a *thing,* and a list of chores to do when all I ever wanted was him. Great inheritance." She ran her hands through her short hair, too frustrated by what Brad said to give an inch.

She'd wanted to pitch in and get a good workout, to move beyond the awkwardness of the kiss. She hadn't wanted to debate Zane or her attraction for Brad or anything else. Talk about dysfunctional. She had issues. Sue her. How would Brad feel if he discovered his life had been a lie?

"Gabriella." Brad moved toward her. "Maybe Zane wasn't the father a young girl dreams of but he *was* proud of you. He was as proud as any father could be."

Maybe that truth was sinking in but that didn't make it any easier to accept. In fact, it hurt a little more. "All those years are gone. Now *he's* gone. I made one mistake and he never brought me back here to visit again."

"What do you mean? You were here?"

The apple hung forgotten in her hand and a bee buzzed by in determined interest. "Once."

"How old were you? When?" Brad took the apple and tossed it into the open cooler on the truck bed.

"Four or five. I don't remember a lot about the trip except I wanted to ride a horse like my dad. I picked the wrong horse and it tried to kill me." She glanced at Brad in time to catch his wince. "Someone got hurt saving me and the very next day Zane flew me home. From then on I got a week of his time. One week out of fifty-two. And then, I got nothing at all."

"He couldn't leave the ranch for long stretches."

"That's an excuse. I can't leave my business but here I am."

You have incentive. What was Zane's? Listening to Crystal complain and trying to make conversation with a kid who wouldn't talk to him?

"You're all about Zane not doing more for you, but what about you? Maybe as a kid you had to mind your mama, but what about since then? When you were old enough to come on your own?"

He sounded like Molly. She had always turned the questions, the responsibility, back on Gabriella. There had come a point in their friendship when Molly had warned about not taking what Crystal said at face value, to get blunt and talk to Zane about their relationship. Gabriella hadn't. And having Brad point out her flaws wasn't easy to accept. "He wasn't a good father. Not to me," she said. "I was a toy he put on a shelf and didn't want after the novelty wore off."

Brad grimaced but didn't respond verbally.

Gabriella walked to where they'd been working, far enough away that she couldn't see the confusing intensity of his gaze.

He represented everything her father had held dear. His boys, his precious ranch. He was a younger version of Zane, a rancher who lived and breathed dirt and sky and pride.

She should go back to L.A. Forget all about the stupid list and the million-dollar selling price. Putting herself through this…was it *worth* a million dollars?

Molly's worth it.

Gabriella could argue all she liked but she knew Brad was right. She could have hopped a plane on her own.

And now despite everything, she wanted to know Zane. Wanted to see and do the things he'd done. She wanted to feel a connection because she'd waited too long and a part of her *hated* that Brad was right.

She was so lost in thought she didn't hear him approach until his hand landed on her shoulder. He squeezed gently.

"He talked about you," Brad said, his voice low, soft, but clear. Purposeful, even though his discomfort with the topic was also audible. "We'd walk into a room and catch him holding one of your pictures with this look in his eyes…. He mourned not being with you. He'd tell us what you'd done, a big smile on his face. He'd puff up with pride—like a man who lived and breathed for his baby girl. Not a man who didn't love his daughter."

Brad let go and walked to where they'd been working. He grabbed the chainsaw by the handle, lifting it with ease. "We knew every time you made a good grade or went on a trip, every time you broke up with a boyfriend." He shot her a long stare. "Samuel was an idiot, by the way."

"How do you know about Sam?"

Sam had been her first real love, the guy she'd planned to marry after college—until finding out he'd used her Hollywood connections to try to further his acting career. Secretly dating a porn star while dating Gabriella didn't help, either.

"How do you think? Zane kept track. He might not have been there with you but he watched over you."

She shook her head. "That's impossible."

"Is it? Look closely at some of those photographs. He had a P.I. watching you, giving him periodic updates. We knew every time you and Molly got caught doing something you shouldn't have been doing. The fake ID and underage drinking? You streaking across the college campus on a dare? He cared, Gabriella. He didn't trust Crystal to tell him everything so he made a point of finding out for himself. Because he loved you. He just wasn't the best at showing it."

Her heart stilled before it began to pump in hard, thumping strikes against her ribs. Like the photos that filled the house, learning Zane had kept tabs on her left her feeling dazed. There were so many of them she hadn't remembered being taken but she'd passed it off as youthful ignorance.

Before she could demand further explanation, Brad started the chainsaw.

His words had blown more holes in her opinion of Zane and left her floundering between her reality and the one her parents had created to hide the truth.

She'd come to see Brad hoping to forge a truce between them but now she was more than happy to keep her distance. Brad would always side with Zane—and she'd always begrudge it.

CHAPTER TWELVE

"Gabriella?"

Gabriella bolted upright in bed, totally confused as to what had awakened her. The room was dark and cool, without the slightest hint of the sun outside the curtains.

"Gabriella? Did you hear me?"

It was Brad. "No, what? Is something wrong?" She felt groggy from waking so abruptly.

"You asked me about your list. Come with me and you can cross off a couple items."

What time was— Oh, no way. She'd kill him. It was five-thirty *in the morning!*

And she'd stayed up until three using her rusty French trying to straighten out a messed-up order. She'd attempted to handle it earlier but wound up playing phone tag with the designer.

Brad knocked twice. "Hey, you awake?"

"No," she said, feeling every one of the sleepless hours she'd had in the time since Molly's diagnosis.

"Meet me downstairs in fifteen minutes."

Rubbing her face, she finally woke up enough to realize he was talking about Zane's list. The stupid list she wasn't even sure she wanted to complete. And why was Brad suddenly agreeable? Wanting to help her?

Whatever his reasons, they didn't matter. It was too early.

Gabriella pulled a pillow over her head, grumbling

about being so rudely wakened. Brad's plans could wait—she needed far more sleep before her mother started her daily onslaught of calls.

End the torture. Just talk to her.

She couldn't. Not yet. A few more days…then she'd swallow her anger and call her mother. She'd already lost one parent. And Molly. Gabriella didn't want to be one of those people who held a grudge forever and ended up alone.

"Better hurry it up!" Brad called.

"Only a freaking cowboy gets up before dawn." But snuggled in the big bed, her eyes drifted open. She was one of those people that once she was awake, she was *awake.* "You've got to be kidding me."

She squirmed to get more comfortable and wound up with the sheet tangled around her waist. By the time she got it untangled, she was mad at the world and wouldn't be able to go back to sleep if her life depended on it. Finally she tossed the hand-stitched blanket aside. "He's going to pay for this."

Thirty minutes passed before she was showered, dressed and on her way downstairs. The moment she entered the kitchen, Brad stood from the table, looking handsome in jeans and a long-sleeved white shirt rolled at the cuffs. "Let's go."

"Can't I have breakfast?"

"No, we're late."

Late? "Are you kidding me? Where are we going?"

"You'll see."

They walked out and around the side of the house. The structure was pretty in its simplicity. Large and rectangular, it had several dormered windows and long porches along the two sides that faced the barns and outbuildings. It lacked a woman's touch, though. Even in the predawn light the porches looked empty, the dormers dark-shadowed eyes staring out at the land.

Gabriella stumbled over a root or a hole but Brad never broke stride. "What are we *doing?*" she asked in a whisper, feeling strange because of the eerie darkness. "I feel like we're on a secret mission."

"We are in a way."

"Huh?"

He chuckled and she decided then and there she hated him. There were morning people, and then there were *morning people.*

The smell reached her first. She'd quickly discovered there were a lot of smells on a ranch that weren't in L.A. but this was a new one. Then she heard the sound of clucking. "Chickens?"

"Yup. Stick your hand in here."

"I beg your pardon?" She saw the flash of his teeth before he snagged her hand and shoved it into an opening beneath the small, hinged door he'd lifted.

"Feel an egg? That's your treasure."

Standing so close to him she caught a whiff of his aftershave. He smelled good. Much better than the chickens. No wonder the coop was so far from the house.

Her fingers encountered a smooth oblong object and she couldn't help but get excited. "There is one!"

His laugh ruffled her hair. It didn't bother her that he laughed at her because her competitive drive was satisfied—she'd found the prize.

"Grab it and let's keep moving."

They moved down the line and checked each nesting box for eggs. Nearly all held one egg—some two—and she placed them in the egg crate Brad carried.

"Won't the chickens miss their babies?" she asked when they had finished.

"They're not babies. They haven't been fertilized."

She frowned, wondering what else she didn't know. She'd thought all eggs eventually turned into animals.

"Looks like it's going to be a pretty one."

"What?" She pulled her gaze from the container. The air was crisp and cool, the stars still shining above, sparkling on a fading blanket of purple.

"Over there." He pointed behind her.

She turned and gasped.

"Not a bad sight for first thing in the morning, is it?"

It was *glorious*. The sun was breaking over the horizon, sending out streaks of red and gold. She glanced at him; he looked big and broad and strong. Her heart picked up a beat or two, surprising her. He was *so* not her type.

They headed back to the house.

"So what's next? I hope you don't expect me to milk cows or anything."

"No, no cows to milk. Had one once but she proved to be more trouble than she was worth."

"But you said we'd mark off a couple things."

"We are. We're going visiting. Then into town."

"Visiting?" Right. Zane had wanted her to take eggs to Merrilee Brown. "It's too early."

Brad grasped her elbow in his hand and tugged her toward his truck. He even played a gentleman and opened the door for her. When she climbed inside, he placed the eggs on her lap. "It's not too early, Gabriella. You have to remember you're not in L.A. anymore."

THE DRIVE TO THE BROWNS' house took about thirty minutes. Brad knew the way, though it had been a while since his last visit. This task was something Zane had reserved for himself and one of the many Brad had avoided since his death.

Along the way he noticed Gabriella watching the sun rise higher, her thoughts flickering across her face because her guard was down.

He'd had a hard time sleeping last night, well able to hear through the walls as Gabriella talked to someone in what he thought was French. He didn't know another language. He knew ranching. But listening to her converse had reminded him how wrong his unwanted attraction to Gabriella was. They were worlds apart.

When he'd finally managed to tune her out, he still hadn't been able to shut his mind to her accusations that Zane had put her on a shelf. Not asking her to visit.

Why had Zane let things happen that way when it was so obvious Gabriella meant enough to Zane that he'd risk losing a ranch that had been in the family for generations.

Why *hadn't* Zane asked her to come back?

The only answer Brad could come up with had to do with him and his brothers. By the time Gabriella was at an age when she would know better than to hop in a paddock with a stallion or any other thing that could hurt her, Zane had adopted Brad and his brothers.

Were they to blame? God knows when they'd first come to the ranch they'd been half wild and nothing but trouble. Surely Zane hadn't thought they'd hurt her.

Then again, any decent father would protect his daughter from thugs. Zane would have been a fool to trust them, especially when they'd been hell-raisers. But why choose them instead of his own flesh and blood?

The last turn was ahead and Brad slowed, doing the math in his head of when she said Zane had abandoned her and when he'd adopted them. It gelled. Zane had caught them messing with the tractor the year before Gabriella's thirteenth birthday, after which she'd asked to legally change her name.

An oath left him before he could stop it.

"Something wrong?"

He kept his gaze on the road. "Remembered something is all."

They rolled to a stop outside the Browns' house, ending the conversation. A light was on in the kitchen, and smoke curled from the chimney.

"Do you know why Zane wanted me to do this?"

Brad opened his door. "They're nice people to know—and they're his wife's parents. I don't doubt they would've taken you in as their granddaughter had you been around."

As he walked around the truck, he noted the worn appearance of the small house. He would have to take a day or two to help Barney.

With Gabriella beside him, Brad knocked twice and saw Merrilee peeking out the window at them. She waved once she recognized him then opened the door.

"Come in. Brad, honey, I haven't seen you for a while. How are you? You holding up?"

Merrilee enveloped him in a hug the size of Texas, which was ridiculous since Merrilee's head barely reached halfway up his chest. "We're doing all right. How are you and Barney?"

"Fine. Sad about things, but that's life I suppose. Just got to have faith."

"That's what Zane always said, too." Brad searched the kitchen and what he could see of the small living room. "Barney's not sick, is he?"

"No, no, he's okay. Takes him a while to get moving some mornings."

Merrilee's gaze fastened on Gabriella and tears immediately flooded her eyes. She pressed her gnarled fingers to her mouth and stared like a proud mama.

"Oh. Oh, it's you, *Ella*."

Merrilee didn't give Gabriella time to respond. The eighty-something woman shuffled forward and Brad barely had time to retrieve the box of eggs before Merrilee wrapped Gabriella in a hug.

Gabriella slowly slid her arms around the very emotional Merrilee, patting her back.

He'd brought Gabriella here to honor Zane's request but he'd honestly thought the entire experience would be a mistake. She was Hollywood, designer clothes and expensive bags, not tired paint, cracked linoleum and polish-scented air.

Still, Gabriella treated Merrilee with kindness and respect, not shrugging off the embrace but holding on and making no move to step away until Merrilee released her.

"What's wrong?" he asked, noting the curious expression on Gabriella's face.

"I remember her—you," Gabriella said. "Your perfume. I remember you. You made cookies and bread, and you let me have jam and you blew bubbles on the porch and I chased them."

Merrilee pulled a tissue from her pocket and wiped her eyes, nodding. "I looked after you the summer you came to visit. You've grown to be so beautiful, child."

A door opened and Barney joined them, the man's limping amble an exaggerated swagger as he swung his permanently injured leg to the side.

What little color Gabriella had seeped from her face.

"Look, Barney. Look who's come for breakfast."

"So I see. Nice to see you, Brad." Barney nodded, a shy, humble grin on his face. "Who's your lady friend?"

"I think Merrilee considers Gabriella the guest, Barney, not me." Brad said.

"That's because you're family. You're both family," Merrilee added. "I'm just so glad you're here."

"Barney, this is Gabriella," Brad said, deliberately leaving off Gabriella's last name. "Zane's daughter."

Barney winked at Gabriella. "I see some resemblance now that you say it. Might be the hair."

Brad waited for Gabriella to respond but she didn't. "Gabriella?"

"I—I'm sorry," she whispered, her lower lip trembling. "I'm sorry you were hurt because of me."

"Aw, now, that was years ago," Barney said, his face turning a ruddy shade.

"It's my fault."

"You were a young'un who didn't know no better. And your daddy took care of the hospital bills and the like. He always watched out for us. No need for you to be frettin' about it."

Brad followed the conversation, wondering if the surprises would ever stop.

He knew Barney had been injured by a rearing horse but he'd never heard how it had happened. Added to what Gabriella had told him about picking a horse that had tried to kill her....

"I wish there was something I could do to help you."

"You did." Barney moved to pat his wife on the shoulder in a clumsy but affectionate way. "Merrilee always hoped you'd come one day and visit. She wanted to see you all grown up. And here you are."

It was such a simple request. One Zane had no doubt heard over the years.

Gabriella met Brad's gaze and he could practically hear her thoughts. She was in Montana only for the chance to reap a reward. She wasn't there out of any sense of caring or tenderness for her father. But now she realized there were other people involved, genuine people with no ulterior motive who wanted to know her. And while that reason might not matter to some, Gabriella's shame showed on her face.

It was the first time Brad had seen her react to something there other than with anger or stubbornness.

"Sit down. I'll get two more plates for breakfast. There's plenty made."

"Merri makes enough to feed an army sometimes. Got used to cooking for the ranch hands and can't get used to cooking for two," Barney explained.

"We'd be happy to join you," Brad said, knowing that being fed was part of visiting Merrilee.

"I've got eggs and bacon, some ham, potatoes, fried apples and hominy."

"Merrilee." He pulled out a chair at the table. "Gabriella doesn't eat—"

"That sounds lovely." Gabriella shot Brad a quelling glare. "I'd love some eggs and potatoes. What's hominy?"

"Corn."

"Ah, sounds delicious."

Brad sat, liking the way Gabriella bustled about the tiny kitchen with her big feet, ducking every time she set something on the table because the light hung low. Maybe there was a little more of Zane in her than he'd first thought. And maybe since it was partly his fault Zane wasn't always around for Gabriella, Brad owed her more than he or his brothers wanted to think about.

Two hours later Brad sat on the stool behind the cash

register in McKenna Feed and watched Gabriella as she meandered from aisle to aisle.

"Thanks for bringing that grain in. Saved me a trip," Chance said. "Here. Fresh pot." He handed over a mug filled with steaming coffee.

"No problem."

"How goes it with Gabriella?" Chance asked in a low tone. "You convince her to sell to us yet?"

Brad shook his head.

"But you've tried, right? Talked to her?"

"Some. I don't want to come on too strong. If she knows we're angling for a better deal, she'll shut us down fast. I think she needs to get to know us better first." He remembered his earlier revelation. "Did you know she visited when she was little?"

"No. When?"

"Not sure but she came close to getting killed and Zane began going to her after that, until she was older."

"What are you getting at?"

"Zane stopped going to see her. Didn't bring her to the ranch. You think it was because of us?"

Chance's eyebrows shot up on his forehead. "I'd say it had more to do with her legally dropping his name. That hit him hard."

Brad checked to see where she was in the store. As tall as she was, he easily spotted her in the sports aisle. That had been Chance's idea. Most of the store consisted of tack and feed, ranching supplies, but when the Second Chance Ranch began to attract more tourists to the area, Chance had insisted on carrying an inventory of fishing rods and tackle, climbing equipment and rafting supplies.

"Yeah, I think there's more to it. Think about the timing of our adoption," Brad said. "Added to some of her comments, it makes me wonder if maybe we're not to blame for Zane not bringing her to the ranch. He had us in the house."

Chance seemed to consider this before he finally shook his head in disagreement. "I get what you're saying but he knew we wouldn't hurt her."

"Would you bet on that? We didn't make it easy on him those first few years, which is when she changed her name. After that she was out of the country and they weren't speaking. Maybe that's why he brought her now."

If there was any truth to Brad's suspicion, it put a whole new slant on things. Meant they had to make an even greater effort to resolve the situation in a mutually agreeable manner because it was the right thing to do.

"You can't let some sort of misplaced guilt skew the truth," Chance murmured. "If Zane wanted her to visit, he would've sent for her. Period."

"He's right," Gabriella said.

Brad and Chance straightened. Gabriella stood at the end of the aisle, staring at them with an unreadable expression.

"Even if that were true, our visit with Merrilee today proved Zane could have had me stay with them. I would have been perfectly fine there. As much as I might like to blame you, it's very obvious that I can't. Not entirely. Zane had his own reasons."

Maybe so but the look on Gabriella's face stated loud and clear that she carried a hurt bigger than any inheritance could fix.

"Are you ready to go? I have work I need to do. The sooner I do it, the better."

Brad nodded and adjusted his hat. "After you." They said goodbye to Chance and headed outside.

They chatted about the town as they drove down Main Street. Once they hit the outskirts, Brad turned on the radio and kept his mouth shut. It was after noon when they arrived at the ranch to find a strange car parked by the steps.

A woman strolled to the railing of the wraparound porch. Dressed in high heels, a blinding white pantsuit that had no business on a ranch, a scarf around her neck and big, fancy sunglasses, she reeked money.

"No," Gabriella said softly. "No, no, no, no."

"What? Do you know who that is?"

"I'm afraid I do. That's my *mother.*"

CHAPTER THIRTEEN

GABRIELLA'S STOMACH TWISTED and squeezed as she slid out of the truck. She was aware of Brad watching her, taking his time exiting the vehicle while she headed up the porch steps. No matter how much work awaited Gabriella, Crystal had to be dealt with. "Mom, what are you doing here?"

Crystal moved forward, her arms outstretched to envelop Gabriella in a hug that smelled of Dolce. "I came for you, of course. I couldn't bear the thought of you staying here alone. I told Uri I had to see for myself that you're all right. We need to talk, Gabriella."

Crystal stepped back and Gabriella watched her mother's gaze narrow on Brad with shrewd intensity.

"Crystal Thompson-Salvatore, meet Brad McKenna. Brad, my mother." Gabriella mentally crossed her fingers that Crystal would not attack Brad.

"Ma'am." He tipped the brim of his hat.

Her mother did not like to be called *ma'am*—ever—especially by a good-looking man. Gabriella stepped in before Crystal could express her displeasure. "Mom, you shouldn't have come. Everything is fine. I just need some time to come to grips with things."

"Gabriella, really. Do we have to discuss this on the porch—and in front of *him?*"

"Don't mind me. I have work to do. Excuse me, ladies." Brad climbed the porch steps, the treads creaking beneath his weight. He unlocked the door and disappeared inside.

"How rude," Crystal said.

Gabriella rolled her eyes. "Yes, you were."

She reluctantly held the door for her mother, wishing she could start the morning over so she could stop at the part where she and Brad were getting along and the morning was going well.

"I can't believe the nerve. Gabriella, why are you still here? I can see how you might want to visit your father's grave but enough. It's time to go home."

Gabriella saw the house through her mother's eyes. The wood floors, painted cabinets and worn furnishings. The decor was totally different from Gabriella's trendy apartment and her mother's Hollywood Hills mansion with Uri, but she thought Zane's house was warm and inviting, not so stiff. It was blatantly obvious Crystal didn't belong. "You shouldn't have come."

"I wouldn't have if you'd come to your senses. What was I supposed to do when you wouldn't return my calls?"

"Continue your vacation? You've still got two more weeks left."

"I couldn't. Not when you're upset with me. You deserve the truth and I intended to tell you, but you refused to call."

"With good reason. I'm struggling with the concept that you know how to *tell* the truth."

"That's unfair. How many times do I have to say it? Zane and I did what we thought was best for you."

"How can never seeing a parent be best? What kind of choice was that? It's not like he was a drunk or an addict or a pedophile."

Her cell phone rang upstairs where she'd left it charging. "I have to get that."

"It can wait, Gabriella. Pack your things. We're catching the first flight home."

"No," Gabriella said, debating whether to inform her mother of the terms of Zane's will. Deciding to be done with it, she explained in as few words as possible.

"Gabriella, you can't stay here."

She didn't have time to watch Storm Crystal brew. "I have to check my phone. I'll be right back."

Gabriella hurried upstairs. She needed a quick breather, and work provided the perfect excuse. She shook off the sadness so quick to appear at the thought of not having Molly as her sounding board—for business and personal. She needed someone to talk to while she was here. Someone impartial and unbiased.

She could easily keep the peace by going home and giving up her right to inherit the land. Crystal would be happy, Brad and the others, too. But Gabriella couldn't. Not only because of her inheritance but also this morning with Merrilee, and the way the Browns had treated Gabriella like a long-lost granddaughter rather than the person responsible for permanently injuring Barney.

Phone in hand, Gabriella checked the missed calls list as she left her bedroom. At the same time Brad's door opened and he walked out. Gabriella looked up and froze. It was so hard not to ogle.

Brad had apparently come upstairs to change into a work shirt. Distantly, she found it sweet he'd dressed up for the visit with the Browns, as though he wanted to make a good impression. The aged cotton shirt he'd most recently donned was unbuttoned, revealing a chest honed by hard work rather than gym equipment.

Her fingers itched to explore. His chest was firm

and muscled, his skin tanned but slightly lighter than that of his hands and face. A triangle of dark hair covered his pecs and grew thinner as it trailed beneath the waistband of his jeans.

She'd seen plenty of male chests living in California—the land of models, actors and miles and miles of beach. Most of them were waxed but Brad's chest?

Not too little, not too much, but just *right*.

"You okay?" The question was a clear reference to her mother's sudden arrival.

Gabriella blinked to awareness, amazed to notice his ears looking a little red. Was he actually blushing? Was he that shy that her perusal embarrassed him?

Something tugged inside Gabriella. She'd always found shy men endearing. Molly said it was because Gabriella liked the idea of corrupting them. Not that she had enough experience to corrupt anyone. But after reading the product descriptions of some of the items she carried in her store, she had to admit she'd lost some of her innocence.

Unfortunately there wasn't time to contemplate Brad, not with Crystal downstairs alone—probably snooping.

"I will be," she answered his question. "Once she's gone. Thanks for asking, though."

Driving home from McKenna Feed earlier Brad had tried to engage her in conversation, but she'd been distracted by the statement she'd overheard Brad make to his brother. She wasn't sure what conversation had come before it but Chance had hit the nail on the head when he'd said Zane would have brought her to Montana to visit if he'd wanted her there. As much as she'd resented the adopted brothers growing up, as an adult she had to acknowledge the fact they'd had little influence in her parents' decisions.

"I'd best get to work." He grabbed the ends of his shirt with his big fingers and began buttoning it with surprisingly efficient motions. She bit back a smile, wondering what he'd do if she helped him because he'd missed a button at the top and was going to be lopsided when he got to the bottom.

"Yeah, me, too." She waved the phone in her hand. "I need to call Molly and—" She winced, a rough laugh emerging. "I mean *Alicia.* I need to call Alicia, not Molly. I guess Crystal showing up has unnerved me more than I thought."

"Understandable in the circumstances. I don't think I told you but I am sorry for your loss, Gabriella. You and Molly were close."

"Yeah, we were. Zane knew?"

Brad nodded.

She shrugged, not sure how she felt—she mourned Molly while Zane… She still wasn't sure what to make of his loss. Or her mother's part in keeping Zane from her. "It's fine. I'll be fine."

He made it to the bottom of his shirt, saw the error and tried to hide the mistake by shoving the front of his shirt in his jeans. She started to say something teasing but Brad stopped her.

"I don't doubt you will be. You and Crystal always land on your feet."

The comparison to her mother—and cats—ended all impulse for humor. "Don't compare me to my mother," she said roughly, unable to let the comment slide because, even though she loved her mother dearly, her eyes were open to Crystal's flaws. "You don't know my mother, or me for that matter."

"I meant—"

"I know exactly what you meant." She turned on her heel and stalked toward the stairs.

Her mother waited at the bottom, staring up at Gabriella and Brad, watching them too closely as he followed. Crystal was a visual reminder of how screwed up things could get when physical attraction outweighed common sense. Gabriella refused to let a fleeting attraction to Brad distract her from following her dream. She did not want to be like her parents who, thanks to her birth, had to deal with the lifelong consequences of an impulsive decision made in an airport hotel's bar.

With a silent nod Brad left the house like it was on fire. Gabriella squirmed beneath her mother's stare following the screen door's gentle slam.

"Gabriella, *what* is going on here?"

Gabriella stared at his broad form moving down the steps with a fluidity she envied, her mother's question echoing in her head. "I told you, I have to stay for my inheritance," she said. "I have to call Alicia—she left a couple of messages while I was out."

"Alicia can wait."

She sidestepped her mother and moved across the kitchen, putting some much-needed distance between them. She didn't want to have this conversation, this confrontation, now. Or ever.

"Gabriella, I had to protect you."

"From what?"

"A man I barely knew."

"You had plenty of time to get to know Zane. *Years.* How does lying to me count as protecting me? You told Zane I didn't want to see him. Didn't want to talk to him. What else did you say to him?"

"Let me explain."

"No. Save it."

"Gabriella—"

"I can't stand here and listen to you right now. I can't. I'm too angry and hurt and upset. That's why I didn't return the *twenty-two* messages you left me, Mom. I don't want to say something I may regret, so the best thing you can do right now is leave me alone."

Crystal stiffened. "You hate me that much?"

Gabriella leaned against the cabinet, welcoming the support it gave. Crystal meant well. She always meant well. That was the thing with her mother. Crystal didn't lack caring or compassion. It would have been easier if that were true. But Gabriella knew her mother loved her and that's why this was so hard. "No. I don't hate you. That's just it." She struggled to get the words out. "It's because I love you that this whole mess hurts so much. I can't believe you'd lie to me like that. That you kept me from knowing my *father*." She closed her eyes and inhaled. "You need to leave."

"Gabriella, if this is about the money, I will loan you the money. If I don't have enough, I'm sure Uri will—"

"I don't want your money. It's not even about that anymore."

"What do you mean? What is it about, then?" Crystal demanded. "Gabriella, you don't belong here. You didn't then and you don't now."

According to her. "Do you know," Gabriella said, "what it was like wondering why he didn't love me?"

Crystal wrapped her arms around her waist. Her shoulders squared and she stared at Gabriella from her ridiculous heels. Who wore white heels to a ranch? A white suit?

"He loved you. But even Zane knew you didn't belong here."

"And you fed that misconception, didn't you? You

reinforced every doubt he had when it came to raising a girl."

"How could I not? What mother would let her beautiful daughter stay with three out-of-control teenage boys under the same roof? Do you know where those boys came from? Their background?"

"They weren't always here. What about before they came, Mom?" Gabriella looked away from her mother, her gaze fastening on the corkboard by the phone. Yet another picture was tucked into the bottom of the frame. She looked to be about fifteen in that one, her racquet high over her head as she prepared to slam a tennis ball across the net. "The only reason you're here now is to do damage control."

"That's not true. I'm here because I love you. Please, let me take you home and we'll talk all of this out."

Crystal had always been demanding and self-centered, even self-absorbed at times. But Gabriella had never doubted her mother's love and now was no different, despite the underhandedness of Crystal's actions. Misguided though they'd been, they were born of love.

But Gabriella had to something to accomplish here. "I'm staying. Zane never asked anything of me. The least I can do is get to know him a little better by finishing the items on his list."

"And then? How long will this list take?"

"I don't know."

"Gabriella—"

"I don't know."

Crystal sighed, her gaze taking in the kitchen with no small measure of distaste. "I guess it can't be helped."

"What?"

"If you're staying, I'm staying. I'm not leaving you

alone with that Neanderthal," she said, waving a hand to indicate the door Brad had used.

"You can't be serious." Stay? Here? With them? *For three months?*

"I am quite serious. You are my daughter and while you might not agree with my past decisions, it's a mother's duty to protect her child. I did it then and I'll do it now. You either stop this nonsense, pack your things and come back to California with me, or I stay. It's up to you."

"You've always referred to Zane's ranch as a pile of dirt. You'll *hate* it here."

"Yes, I will. And you will hear how much I hate it every day I am required to stay. What'll it be, Gabriella?"

Tension coiled in Gabriella's stomach. "You're bluffing. You won't be able to handle it."

Her mother smoothed her hands over her jacket. "I think you underestimate how much I love you. Now, I'd like to settle in and freshen up. Which room is mine?"

CHAPTER FOURTEEN

BRAD SPENT THE REMAINDER of the day checking on the haying progress and repairing fences. He'd been so leery of the situation he'd find at the house that he'd skipped lunch and settled for a snack of water, protein bars and trail mix, grateful for Merrilee's hearty breakfast. He didn't want to see the hurt on Gabriella's face because of that stupid comment he'd made, or run into Crystal again. Logic told him she'd stick around for at least the night.

He could only imagine how Gabriella felt seeing her mother face-to-face for the first time since discovering the deceptions.

This morning when Merrilee had mentioned how much Zane loved having *Ella* at the house, Brad had seen the confusion and out-and-out pain on Gabriella's face because she truly believed Zane had abandoned her. That expression, combined with the way she'd looked at him upstairs in the hall, *had* made him momentarily forget the true reason Gabriella was here.

Brad loaded the chainsaw and the few other tools he'd used before climbing behind the wheel. Instead of starting the engine, though, he replayed the hallway scene in his head. Not today's, but the one when she'd emerged from her bath.

His hands tightened on the steering wheel, the

thoughts in his head going to places no "brother" would go out of sheer perfidy.

What was wrong with him? How could he look at Gabriella that way? How could he want to do…more? Zane would skin him alive if he laid a hand on her.

So would Crystal. The woman's glares broadcast her opinion of Brad quite evidently. He wasn't worthy enough to dirty their shoes.

If any good were to come from Crystal's appearance, it was that she could talk Gabriella into returning to California. Then they could all breathe easier.

He'd hoped for a phone call to send Gabriella home but Crystal's presence would have even more impact. And if it meant staying clear of the house so that Gabriella had to play host, so be it.

LATER THAT EVENING Gabriella was sitting in the swing when Brad approached from the barn. "Hi." He shot a glance toward the door.

"Hi, yourself." She indicated the lemonade. "Would you like some?"

"Yeah, thanks."

She couldn't quite hide her smile. He couldn't carry her luggage but he wanted her to wait on him? Yeah, right. "It's right there. Help yourself."

To soften the blow, she scooted over on the swing. The only other chairs on the wraparound porch were closer to the steps.

Brad hesitated a split second then poured himself a drink and waited until she slowed the back-and-forth motion enough for him to settle beside her.

"Where's Crystal?"

"In bed. She has this thing about age and sleep. I,

uh, wasn't sure what to do with her so I put her in the blue room. She says she's staying to chaperone."

"Chaperone?"

"Yeah. Don't take it personally. Trust me, she won't last. She'll go home soon."

He stayed quiet a long moment. "She can stay. It's fine by me."

"Seriously?" Was she imagining things? She would have bet a lot of money that Brad would be furious at the news. How could Crystal staying be all right with him?

"I don't spend much time in the house," he said simply. "You're the one who has to deal with her."

As if Gabriella didn't have enough to deal with without adding her mother to the mix. Running a business from a laptop computer and cell phone wasn't easy. "Well, I'm banking on her hating it here and leaving soon. I give her a day. Two, tops."

She almost missed Brad's grimace. "What?"

It dawned on her that Brad had thought the same thing about her, and she was still here. "Ha. Funny."

"I didn't say a word."

"You didn't have to. I know you want me gone, too."

Brad shifted on the swing. "It's not that. Zane made us family so there will always be a place for you here. But if you'd consider accepting the hundred grand—"

"No. I need more."

"You won't consider a lesser amount?"

"No," she said bluntly. "Look, Brad, I haven't been here a month yet. Am I leaving? Not unless I can't help it. But right now the biggest concern we both have is putting up with my mother."

The swing squeaked as they rocked, and neither spoke for several minutes. "So, you make progress out there today without me there slowing you down?" she quipped, aiming for a neutral subject.

They were adults. They should be able to hold a reasonable conversation that had nothing to do with inheritances or land or money.

"Yeah. That section is cleared, fence repaired. Only the far side is left but it'll wait for now."

"Why not do it while you're working in that area?" she asked. "Then be done with it."

"I'm not ready yet." He wiped a hand over his face. "The last section is where Liam drove through to get to Zane the day he— That day."

"Oh." No wonder he wasn't ready yet. Brad was obviously still grieving heavily. The tractor, the fence. If the ranch held so many hard memories for him, why was Brad so against her getting a portion of it?

"You had an early start this morning. Ready to call it a night?"

And there he was, trying to get rid of her again. "So did you."

"I'm used to it. And I wasn't up all hours of the night pacing and working."

She frowned. The comment seemed intended to run her off but something about Brad's expression suggested a hint of concern. "Sorry if I disturbed you."

"You always work so much?"

"Sometimes."

"Might be able to handle things even better if you were well rested. Don't you have some kind of schedule you're supposed to stick to?"

Ah, so that's what it was. "You know I have insomnia sometimes. It was in the—"

"Report. Yeah. I know. It's worse when you're stressed."

She was beginning to wonder if there was anything they *didn't* know. "Where are these reports?"

"Don't get huffy about it."

She had never been huffy in her life. Well, mostly only where Crystal was concerned. "Wouldn't you be angry at the invasion of privacy? From the sound of it, you know the name of the first guy I slept with."

Brad's mouth tilted down at the corners. "Zane certainly cursed it enough."

"How utterly humiliating."

"I haven't read the reports if that's what you're thinking. Just gathered bits from what Zane mentioned over the years. I do know you're supposed to keep to a strict sleep schedule, though. Stay in the habit."

"I get tired of staring up at the ceiling." In the dark, her mind whirled, going over everything she needed to do, products, problems.

"Last night when I heard you working I thought about that list of yours," Brad said. "You need to put in some saddle time to work up to the ride to the falls. It's exercise yet relaxing, too. Might help you sleep."

"I'm not riding anywhere. I told you that." She lowered the glass to her lap and felt the moisture pooling on the sides soak into her jeans until a ring darkened the material. "The last horse I was on tried to kill me. They're large and wild and they *smell*. Machines don't have tempers. If we can take an ATV, I'll go. But I'm not riding a horse."

"An ATV can't find its own way out if a rider gets into trouble. A good horse knows the way home. If it shows up with an empty saddle, people know to search for you."

"That's why GPS was invented. It's not going to work, Brad. I'm not getting on one of those beasts just to see a lousy waterfall." She could tell she'd insulted him. "Look, I would like to see it, but there has to be another way. Could I charter a helicopter? I saw one flying overhead yesterday."

"Rissa Taggert flies charter but she can't get you close enough. You'd have to walk the distance and you couldn't carry enough supplies. There isn't another way."

Gabriella rose and walked to one of the posts beside the steps. "Then I won't do that one. There, decision made."

"Of all the things on your list, that's the one you need to do most. You need to see it to appreciate it."

So that was it. He wanted her to appreciate the falls so she wouldn't sell it. She should have known Brad had an angle.

"Anyone can learn to ride, Gabriella. The Rowlands at the Second Chance teach people with disabilities to ride, young and old alike. Surely an able-bodied woman like yourself can do what a handicapped kid can do?"

She shuddered at the mere thought of it, her mind flashing to that day on the ground staring up at a massive horse about to stomp her into goo. She might not remember much about that summer but she remembered that. Thinking about it left her shaking.

No, no, she didn't want to go anywhere that she had to ride. She felt this way for a reason and Brad needed to respect that.

Gabriella leaned her shoulder against the post and stared at the ranch and the sky above. Despite Brad trying to convince her to do something she knew she couldn't and a mother she'd spent most of the afternoon trying to get rid of, it was peaceful here. The kind of peace that simply did not exist in Hollywood.

Very few lights, the sound of crickets and frogs loud in her ears, the whimsical sound of the wind in the trees.

"We'd take it slow," Brad murmured. "I'll even take you to the Second Chance and set you up with lessons if you like. Zane wouldn't mind who taught you so long as you learned."

Of course Zane wouldn't mind. He was *dead*. "It's not going to happen. Why on earth would I climb atop one of those hairy beasts and bounce up and down a mountain?"

It was getting late. They were both tired. But when an oh-so-sexy and decidedly ornery smile spread across his face, it didn't take a genius to figure out what he was thinking about.

But—on a *horse?* "You've got to be kidding. You mean you've actually…" Her mouth dropped in shock. She was the one who owned a shop dedicated to all things sensual and romantic and yet he had experiences she'd never even contemplated.

Until now.

Their post-bath kiss flitted through her head and left tangible images. Heat, tongue, the feel of Brad's hands.

On a horse?

He stood, his teeth flashing white in the dusky light as he moved toward her. The sight of him, all big and broad and tall, sent her heart skittering against her ribs.

"Don't knock it unless you've tried it." He tipped her mouth closed with a finger beneath her chin. "Looks to me like those California boys Alicia mentioned could use a few lessons from us Montana *men*." His low, husky chuckle filled the cool night air. "Lock up when you stop thinking about it and come in for the night."

CHAPTER FIFTEEN

"GABRIELLA, ARE YOU listening to me?"

Impossible not to, considering her mother's loud and persistent tone. "Yes, Mom, I hear you," she said, never taking her gaze from the computer. "Will you calm down, please? If you don't, I'm going to be deaf."

"Well, *have* you contacted a real estate broker? You don't want just anyone."

Oh, for the love of— Gabriella pulled her glasses from her nose and stared at her mother. Crystal wore a pink designer suit with pearls and looked ready to appear as a grand dame on a soap opera. Overkill.

Crystal's preference for dramatic show clothes had led Gabriella to her own understated style. Given her height, the last thing she needed was to stand out even more because of what she wore. "Mom, I have fifteen minutes to get this order placed or Alicia won't receive shipment for two weeks. *Drop it*. Please."

"I'm trying to help."

"I'm trying to work." She pinched the bridge of her nose and tossed the glasses aside.

One day. Her mother had been there one day and she was driving Gabriella up the wall. So much so she was willing to toss her mother a bone by way of stating facts that did indeed factor into her long-term plans because she hadn't thought of them before leaving L.A. "Why would I bother wasting a real estate agent's time when

I'm not sure I can even stay three months? You want to hear me say it? There, I did."

"So you realize staying here three months is out of the question?"

"No, I'm being realistic and plan to take it a day at a time. Now, can I please place this order?"

"But if you do stay, you'll need to be prepared to sell the moment you inherit."

"Yes. And if you let me place this order," Gabriella said, "I'll have time to research the market."

"Why bother researching it at all? Simply make the call. That's how agents earn their commissions. Let them do the work."

And that, Gabriella knew, was why her mother had a host of men in her life—to take care of such mundane things as details.

But not her. Gabriella preferred to do her own research because it gave her a sense of security to be armed with her own information. She could hold an intelligent conversation and had the sense of mind to know whether or not she was being taken advantage of. "I want to do it myself. If I inherit, there are tax consequences, inheritance fees and the like that have to be checked into. With the market so bad right now, who knows how long it could take to sell? I need to know what I'm facing."

"I know the perfect person to help you. He's an agent in Malibu."

"Thanks, but I'm not there yet. I might have to hold on to the property in order to get the money I need. Stop adding pressure to an already loaded situation."

Crystal's expression softened to one of concern. "I'm not trying to pressure you. Okay, maybe I am. A little.

I'm worried that you're staying here, doing this, only because you're still angry with me."

Growing up, Gabriella always wondered how every conversation would end up being about her mother. Good to know nothing had changed. Up next: the guilt card. If Gabriella *loved her mother,* she'd do as Crystal wanted because otherwise Gabriella was punishing her mother, aging her by adding to her worry. Every wrinkle on her face was born of Gabriella's antics.

Yet no matter how self-centered her mother was, she was also loving and caring, in her own it's-all-about-me way. Over the years Gabriella had learned to accept people as they are—and that included her mother. Crystal simply took a little more effort. "What do you expect me to say, Mom? It's not okay that you lied, but I'm doing my best to move beyond the issue. Let's not rehash this again when there's nothing new to say."

She finally found the two items she was looking for and added them to the order, saving and printing before hitting send. Deadline met. Just in time, too. No easy feat with Crystal harping at her.

Gabriella looked out the window to see the sun hanging low in the sky. She'd planned to go for a run earlier but handling one call or email after another had eaten up a whole day.

Brad wouldn't want her jogging this late, and no matter how much her muscles called out to her, she wasn't stupid. Leaning back in her chair, she stretched the muscles in her back and strove for calm. "Mom, I'm doing this for a lot of reasons that have *nothing* to do with you. I need you to understand that and back off."

"But why do you have to figure things out here?"

"The list—"

"Oh, that mundane list. It is ridiculous. You're really going to waste your time on something so silly?"

"You were in my room, weren't you?"

Crystal settled her hands on her hips, her oversize rings sparkling beneath the glare of the fading sun. "Zane's letter was on top of your dresser. I didn't snoop through your things."

Yeah. As though going into someone's room—into what used to be *Zane's* room—wasn't snooping.

Now you know why Brad was so upset that you barged into Zane's bedroom and made it your own.

"Gabriella, forgive me so we can go *home*. I love you. I never meant to hurt you. How many times must I say I'm sorry? You have to see women like us have nothing in common with men like your father. And raising a child together? Zane was chemistry and hormones and convenience. I protected you by keeping you away from him and this horrid place."

She couldn't simply drop it, could she?

Gabriella closed the laptop. No way would she get any more work done. "I understand the laws of attraction, but who made you judge and jury? Who decided you knew best when it came to raising me? You used to feed me popcorn for breakfast if you were late for an audition."

Her mother made an exasperated sound. "Where is this coming from? What has that man done to poison you against me?"

Gabriella's eyes burned with fatigue. She'd made no late phone calls last night but after Brad's comment on the porch, her insomnia had left her staring at the ceiling of her bedroom contemplating the logistics of... *that.* "Leave Brad out of this."

"Brad? I was talking about Zane. What does Brad have to do with this?"

Oops. "Nothing. All I'm saying is that you did your share of poisoning by convincing Zane I didn't belong here, and that was wrong."

The silence that followed her statement was so very revealing. Crystal knew she was in the wrong, but she didn't regret anything. That was the hardest to bear.

Gabriella *was* angry about losing the father she'd looked up to so much as a young child. She was hurt and more than a little embittered. Crystal was the only parent she had left, and while it might take nerves of steel to put up with some of her mood swings, at the end of the day she was still *Mom.* "You know, as angry as I am, I could've asked Brad to show you off the property yesterday when you arrived. He would have happily done it, because he knows you lied to me and Zane."

"This is between us, Gabriella. No one else should be involved."

"Well, they are. And every time you defend your actions, I think about what I *missed*…and I get angry all over again. I have a *right* to be angry, Mom."

Gabriella stood, moved restlessly until she stopped in front of the screened door. "Were you surprised? When you got here and realized Zane's *pile of dirt* is so beautiful?"

Crystal didn't answer.

"I like the peacefulness of this place, this house. The sooner you accept that I'm staying and *stop talking,* the better."

"I can't help but think you're making these rash decisions because of Molly. Is that it?"

Molly. Zane. Crystal.

Given time she could list a slew of reasons.

"Oh, Gabriella. You did everything you could to make Molly's last days comfortable. I think you're reeling so badly from losing her that you would've agreed to a trip to the moon to get away if you could. I know it's been hard for you but that's no reason to stay and put yourself through this. Why are you punishing yourself? You can deal with her death at home just as well."

Leave it to her mother to come up with that one. Gabriella opened her mouth to deny the accusation but no words came.

Maybe it was self-inflicted punishment. Maybe it wasn't. She honestly wasn't sure. Something so simple had gotten very complicated.

"Would Molly want you to do this? Put yourself through this only to expand a business?"

Molly would never want her to do something that hurt her. At the same time, Molly would have readily approved of Gabriella checking off the items on Zane's list. And Molly definitely would have approved of Gabriella getting to know her father. "Yeah, actually, I think she would. I know she would."

Crystal wasn't pleased by the news. Her features pinched as much as they could, but seeing as how they were loaded with Botox, the response was faint.

"I disagree. I think Molly would see the stress you're under and order you to go home. What is the point of wasting your time learning to do those things?"

"I have no idea. That's one of the things I need to figure out."

"What am I going to tell Uri? How long is this list going to take?"

"I don't know. That's why *you* should go home. You should be with your husband, not babysitting a grown woman."

"Gabriella, you're not just any woman. I'm angry *for* you. Can't you see that? I've had to stand by and watch this man impact your life over and over again. It infuriates me. How dare Zane leave those men *any-thing* when you're his only flesh and blood? All of this should have been yours and it should have been gifted with no strings attached."

When she'd first heard the news, Gabriella would have agreed. Wholeheartedly. But after seeing Brad's reaction to Zane's death she no longer felt that way. She knew who the imposter was here, and it wasn't Brad or his brothers.

Shouldn't the people who mourn receive all? To be honest, she mourned what could have been. She mourned a little girl's idealistic dream of her cowboy father. "I do not want to have this discussion again. Not another word, Mom. Stay, go, do whatever you want. But if you remain here, stay out of my hair and let me do what I came here to do—or I will ask Brad to make you leave."

Crystal wrung her hands. "I do not understand you."

Yeah, well, the feeling was mutual on most counts. "Guess maybe I'm more like Zane than you want me to be."

By bringing her here Zane had given her a chance to take a step back. Reevaluate. Mourn. And for that, she was grateful.

Gabriella pushed open the screen door, needing some air and distance.

"Gabriella?" Her mother trailed behind her to the porch like a little girl lost. "I'm sorry. I am," Crystal whispered, her tone full of raw emotion. "For a moment, put yourself in my shoes. Zane's phone calls... They upset you. You'd cry to talk to him, cry when he had to hang up, cry yourself to sleep. *Cry* when you got up in the morning. I didn't know what to do. You focused on him with such intensity after he visited you and it wasn't *good* for you."

Gabriella stopped on the steps and turned to look at her mother. Crystal's eyes sparkled with tears and she squinted against the sun, the lines on her face showing despite her fierce battle to stop them.

"I couldn't become his wife. Not even for you. We would have been divorced before the ink dried on the marriage certificate. As an adult you understand the meaning of *incompatibility* but as a child you didn't. What else could I do but separate us from him so that you could be happy."

"And that meant removing him from my life completely?"

"Yes."

Oh, Moll, do you believe this?

"Well, you must be happy now. Other than the list I have no way of getting to know my father, which means you no longer have any competition for my affection and love."

Crystal let the waterworks flow, though Gabriella had to admit the tears looked real.

Shaking her head, Gabriella turned and quickly left, knowing Crystal wouldn't risk her Jimmy Choo pumps. But two steps into her exit, she paused again. "You want to know the worst thing? You let me believe Zane didn't care for me. I thought he didn't *love me* and *you* reinforced that with every word you uttered. I thought I wasn't good enough. What kind of mother does that?"

Her mother's sniffles filled the air. "One who is afraid of losing the only thing that mattered. Every tear you shed for him made me afraid that you'd like him more. Love him more. That you'd leave me. Yes, I'm that selfish, Gabriella. Because I couldn't bear the thought of losing you to someone who lived twelve hundred miles away. Zane had his ranch and those boys but you... You were *all* I had."

Without a word Gabriella moved farther away, inexplicably drawn to the light shining from the barn.

"Where are you going?"

She didn't answer. She kept walking until she entered the structure to see Brad shaking an oversize bottle, the muscles of his arms moving with every thrust. He turned when he heard her approach and the moment he got a good look at her, his gaze sharpened.

"You okay?"

Okay? No, definitely not. "Peachy." Gabriella forced a smile. "You're smart to avoid the house."

"Lots of work to do."

And quite a few employees to do it from what she'd seen. Brad was obviously the hands-on type of boss, a trait they shared. At this moment she appreciated that he seemed to sense her tumultuous emotions and tried to spare her the truth. No doubt it was hard enough for him to deal with her—add in Crystal and he had a nightmare on his hands. Yet he was...gentlemanly, when he could have been such a jerk.

"Want to do something to make you feel better?"

"Definitely."

He handed her the big bottle then led the way to a stall where a calf was lying on a bed of straw.

"Oh. He's so *tiny*."

"She. And yeah, she is. Her mama rejected her and won't let any of the others nurse her. Now it's up to us."

"Poor thing. Mothers are overrated, aren't they?" Gabriella laughed weakly, her hand slamming over her mouth when Brad shot her a questioning look. She couldn't help it, though. Because her mind compared Crystal to the cow and Gabriella could only imagine her mother's outrage at the comparison.

Crystal hadn't rejected her, but her mother had rejected Zane. And Gabriella couldn't separate herself from that because she was so like her father. Her height, her hair and eyes. Her personality? She certainly didn't share Crystal's shallowness.

Gabriella dropped to her knees in the fresh straw, identifying with the calf lying weak and dazed by life. "Why did the mother reject her?"

"Don't know. It happens sometimes."

Brad knelt on the straw beside her, angling the calf's head. He covered Gabriella's hand with his and nudged the tip of the bottle toward the calf's mouth. Together they got the newborn eating.

Gabriella was torn between laughter because of the vigorous way the calf drank once she got the hang of it, and amazement that she was feeding it herself.

"Anytime you want to escape the house you can come out here and feed her."

She looked up, only then realizing that Brad watched her, his gaze warm on her face. "Really?"

"You'd be doing me a favor. She needs to eat every few hours. Even if you only fed her once a day it would help. I'll leave a sheet outside the stall. Just mark the day and time you feed her."

This was one of the things she'd missed out on doing as a child kept away from Zane and this ranch. Zane would have shown her how to care for the animals, gather eggs. Talk to the people here.

Suddenly, the items on the list made a little more sense because it felt good to help the calf. The way it had felt good to visit Barney and Merrilee, who had wanted nothing from Gabriella but her company. How many people in her acquaintance could she say the same about?

Her mother wanted her forgiveness and a measure of control over Gabriella's life. Alicia, the partnership. Her friends in California wanted discounts on items from her store. Everyone wanted something. Even Brad and the others wanted her portion of the ranch.

But the calf?

What would the calf miss out on, not being nurtured by its mother? Would the stigma of being rejected stay with the calf after it was returned to the others? Maybe it was silly but she wanted to feed the baby so it would be big and strong and…able to handle itself when the time came for it to face the ones who'd rejected it. Give the calf its own way of saying, *ha*.

"You interested?" Brad asked.

Crystal definitely wouldn't look for her in the barn. "I'd love to."

CHAPTER SIXTEEN

"THIS IS NICE. YOU TRY any of it on yet?" Chance asked on Saturday afternoon.

Brad looked up to see Chance fingering the lace edge of a negligee dangling by a hanger from a large picture frame and glared while Chance barely managed to keep a straight face. "You're a barrel of laughs, you know that?"

"Just trying to lighten the mood."

"You're supposed to be concentrating on finding us some more cash." Brad pointed to the computer. "Get to it."

He barely knew how to turn the computer on, which was why Chance had been searching through their accounts for the past twenty minutes, looking for places where they might be able to cut back. Every last penny had to be squeezed to have enough to buy Gabriella out should she actually stay long enough to inherit.

She had surprised him when she'd agreed to feed the calf. She'd probably agreed more to get away from Crystal than because she cared for the calf, but he wasn't about to complain. Although he admitted to himself that every few hours he listened for the bark of the dogs to signal Gabriella on her way to the barn.

"Can we afford to sell more of the hay?" Liam asked from his seat in front of the window. He examined one of the old-fashioned account books.

Zane had been a stickler about that. Chance could use accounting software as much as he liked, but he had to keep an up-to-date, physical copy at all times.

"No," Chance and Brad replied in unison.

"A long winter or a wet spring and we're looking at forty grand or more to buy enough to see us through," Chance added.

"And if we go by the almanac, spring will be late next year," Brad said. He wasn't one of those hard-core farmers who lived by the book but they had to be prepared for unpredictable weather. There had to be some other way to collect more money.

"You could try not being as accommodating."

Brad lifted his head from the account ledger in his lap and frowned at Liam. "What do you mean?"

"You think Zane would let his daughter hang her nighties in his den? She's taking over the house. If you want rid of her, give her a hard time about it."

"I have work to do that doesn't involve staying inside babysitting her. You want to keep tabs on her and give her a hard time, you watch her all day. Besides, you're the last one who can give advice on relationships."

"What's that supposed to mean? Carly and I are doing great."

"But you were told to be nicer to Charlie."

The statement earned a dark scowl from Liam. "Stay out of it."

Brad should. But he was frustrated and tired and Liam needed a good knock upside the head. "Zane told you to let Charlie make things right."

"And I said stay out of it. You don't know what it's like having a stranger show up saying he's your daddy."

"No, I don't. But I do know what it's like to bury the

only one I had before I was ready to. You're getting a second chance—don't screw it up."

"Words of wisdom," Chance murmured under his breath.

"I'm doing my best. Now can we get back to the subject?" Liam asked.

"I'd rather talk about the new decor," Chance said with a grin. "What are our chances at keeping some of this stuff? I wouldn't mind finding someone to model that corset over there. That one is enough to drive a man over the edge. How much do you think Gabriella makes a year selling this stuff?"

"Are you kidding?" Liam pointed a finger on the ledger to hold his place and looked up. "She caters to the stars. How much do you *think* she makes?"

Brad rubbed the pounding ache in his temple. This was getting them nowhere.

"Might be a lot but she's got expenses the same as we do. Can you imagine the property taxes there?" Chance countered.

Liam tossed the open ledger onto the desk. "You realize we're the last ones on a sinking ship, don't you? If she's not making seven figures it's probably close to it, while we're sitting here searching for nickels and dimes that will never add up to enough to buy her out. What are we going to do? There has to be some way of getting rid of her."

"You could arrest her," Chance said. "If she spends the night in jail, she voids the terms of the will."

Brad couldn't believe his eyes because it actually appeared as though Liam was considering the suggestion. "You can't arrest her," he said, wishing he didn't always have to be the voice of reason because truth be told, it wasn't a *bad* idea. "Both of you stop messing around and think up an alternative solution."

The boards creaked above their heads and seconds later Brad heard someone descending the stairs. He'd learned the sound of Gabriella's tread. Not quite light or heavy, her footsteps were…firm. Confident.

They were followed by the sharp click of Crystal's ever-present heels.

"Mom, drop it," Gabriella said.

Her rapid descent echoed through the house, and because she'd headed down the hallway toward the den, her voice grew louder as she approached.

"You don't want to go? Don't. You can stay here," Gabriella said, "but I don't know how long I'll be gone. According to Carly there is a dinner afterward."

Gone? Dinner afterward?

Brad straightened in his chair, his foot sliding off his knee toward the floor. Surely they weren't talking about—

"I can't believe you'd take off and leave me here," Crystal said.

Brad noticed all three of them turned toward the door as it opened.

"I told you it's on the list and I have to— Oh, hi. Sorry," Gabriella said with a forced smile. "I didn't mean to interrupt."

Zane's old chair squeaked as Chance scooted away from the hand-tooled cherry desk and stood.

"We haven't met," he said to Crystal.

Brad watched as Chance turned on the charm and Gabriella's mother ate it up. Gabriella performed the introductions but once that was done Crystal glanced toward Brad, making him abruptly aware he was the only one still seated. And because Zane had drilled manners into their heads, Brad closed the ledger on his lap and slowly got to his feet. His delayed reaction seemed to increase Crystal's dislike of him even more.

He felt heat rushing up his neck and into his ears, and hated the response. Growing up he'd always been the big doofus. Too big, too clumsy. Always trying to hide an oversize body that couldn't be hidden. People used to look at him and assume he was older. Then they'd treated him as stupid or incompetent. Big as he was though, few teased unless they had a good escape route.

Until he'd come to work for Zane, become a rancher, Brad hadn't felt good at much of anything. Zane had given all three of his boys a safe place, but he'd given Brad more. Zane had taught him how to be comfortable with himself without giving in to stereotypical big-and-stupid reactions—like the ones Crystal made him feel because she was so freakishly tiny yet irritating.

"Couldn't help but overhear," Chance said. "You're going somewhere?"

"Church tomorrow morning. It's on Zane's list."

"We're going, too," Brad heard himself say abruptly.

Liam and Chance's heads swung toward him but Brad nodded to confirm his words. When Zane had first adopted them, church attendance was mandatory. No exceptions. Not only that, they were the only high school boys there in dress shirts and ties; Zane had insisted. Brad had gone. Listened and learned. He would even say he believed. The outdoors he loved so much couldn't have come about by accident.

But like people often do, they'd all drifted out of the habit of going to church. In recent years their attendance was sporadic at best, marked by special occasions like Christmas and Easter. Liam often worked, Chance traveled and Brad…he preferred to say his prayers to sky than to four walls and a steeple. But if Gabriella was going, Zane would want them all there with her. No exceptions.

"You are? That's nice," Gabriella said, looking as though she meant it. "I didn't really want to go alone. I'll admit to being a little nervous."

"You'll be fine," Chance said, giving Gabriella a smile Brad wanted to wipe off his face.

"Any advice for fitting in?" Gabriella asked.

"Yeah, don't call yourself Thompson," Brad said, blurting out the words before he remembered honey was better than vinegar at attracting. "I mean, you might want to use *McKenna* when you introduce yourself."

"What?" Crystal glared at him. "No, absolutely not."

Gabriella was a McKenna. One glance at her made that quite clear. "Suit yourself," Brad said, careful to keep his gaze solely on Gabriella. "But if you don't, you'll only cause more talk."

"I'll…take it under consideration."

"Gabriella, I cannot believe you'd lower yourself that way."

"Lower herself?" Brad could not let that pass. "The McKenna name is something to be proud of."

"Maybe it is when you don't have a name of your own—"

"I *said* I'd take it under consideration," Gabriella repeated, her tone making it clear she wanted the argument dropped.

"Fine, but I've changed my mind, darling. If everyone is going, I'll go, too," Crystal said, sliding him a cold yet practiced smile. "You'll need my support."

Maybe it was uncharitable of him but Brad imagined Crystal had spent less time in church than he had.

But what bothered him most was that after being so angry with her mother, here Gabriella was allowing Crystal to have her say because Gabriella wanted to keep peace. Peacekeeping was an admirable trait, but not when it meant shutting down how she really felt. Could that be the source of her sleeplessness?

He'd love to see Gabriella take Crystal on, stand up to her, and he refused to examine why he felt it was so important. Especially since Crystal's annoying attitude and demands could go in his favor.

"I wouldn't mind having everyone's support," Gabriella said.

Such a politically correct answer. Brad wiped a hand over his face to ease the tension making his eyelid twitch. Crystal attending church had nothing to do with support. No doubt her intention was to make an appearance as a star and to stick it to Zane one last time by sitting in his pew and broadcasting Gabriella's last name to all who'd listen.

He wasn't sure what they could do about that, but if he had his way not a negative word would be said against Zane. Even if it meant clamping his hand over Crystal's mouth to keep her quiet.

"Then it's settled. I didn't mean to interrupt. I just needed to get something," Gabriella said, moving toward the bookcase where she'd stacked three-ring binders. "I'll be out of your hair in a second."

"What are you doing all huddled up in here?" Crystal asked, her gaze moving about the room.

"That is none of our business," Gabriella said.

"Or is it?" Crystal asked.

Gabriella turned and Brad watched as her focus shifted to the ledger in his hand. Wary guilt flickered briefly over her face before it was replaced with deter-

mined resignation. Almost as though she didn't want
to put the ranch in a bind financially but she was compelled to follow through on her plan.

But more surprising was the fact that he couldn't
blame her. Not really. As much as he hated the thought,
Gabriella had been given an opportunity to succeed.
Wasn't he trying to do the same?

"We're going over some things," Chance murmured,
flashing both the women his infamous grin. That grin
had won more women and broken more hearts than
Brad had fingers to count.

Like a charm Crystal responded, practically melting where she stood. Brad blinked at the sight, not for
the first time wishing he had a bit of Chance's finesse.
There were times—like now—when he and Crystal
needed to be working together instead of grating on
each other's last nerve.

"Well," Gabriella said, moving toward the door, "go
back to your meeting. Mom?"

The moment the door closed behind them, Liam and
Chance pinned Brad with glares.

"Church?" Chance said. "You ever stop to think
maybe I had plans?"

"I have to be at the station," Liam said.

"Zane would want us there and you know it," he said
to Chance. To Liam he added, "And you already said
you have tomorrow off. You can attend the service and
be out in plenty of time to make the sheriff's meeting.
You both know how Zane felt about going to church
Sunday mornings. We've all slacked off over the years."

"So why go now?" Chance asked.

Brad felt Liam studying him, knowing that his
brothers looked to him for answers he didn't have.

Why go? He wasn't even sure himself. "Because we

need the community behind us, especially if Gabriella inherits and sells to the highest bidder." Very slowly, he held up the ledger in his hand. "More than anything we need a miracle and I'd better see you both tomorrow morning in Zane's pew ready to pray for one."

CHAPTER SEVENTEEN

As THEY MADE THEIR WAY along the sidewalk leading to the First Christian Church, Gabriella found herself being tugged along by Brad's gentle but firm grip on her arm. He slowed his stride to accommodate her four-inch heels, but that wasn't the reason for dragging her feet and letting her mother stay ahead of them.

Crystal lived for attention. Why not let her get it so that maybe—hopefully—Gabriella's presence would go unnoticed? Was it possible?

Now that they were actually here, her nerves were kicking in. She didn't know why Zane had placed such emphasis on attending his church. Or maybe she did know deep down and she wasn't sure she was prepared for it. What would she say when people asked if she planned to sell her inheritance?

She couldn't lie in church. But with the information Carly had given her... Would they recognize it as a business move? Not take it as a personal attack against their community?

As they topped the steps of the church she realized something else, too. She'd made a huge error in dressing for the service. As much as she didn't want to stick out, she did. She'd worn her plainest dress but none of the flats she'd brought with her matched and her heels put her head and shoulders above most of the other women—many of whom wore pants.

But in addition to being taller, she and Crystal gave the impression they had stepped off a fashion runway in comparison to the plain, somewhat dated clothing of the other women.

Her mother wouldn't dream of wearing anything but the latest fashions, but Gabriella didn't want Zane's friends thinking her a snob because she was dressed up.

"I'm overdressed," she whispered, her panic clear in her voice.

"You're fine," Brad said, keeping his voice as low. "Your mother needs to lose that hat, though. I was hoping when I rolled down the window in the truck it would blow out."

A giggle burst out of her at his comment and she glanced at Brad to find him watching her. Her heart already pounded hard in her chest but it picked up speed.

"That's better. Take a deep breath. You'll be fine. Carly and Liam are here. There's his truck." Brad pointed toward a big red Dodge. "Chance will be here, too. He always races in after the singing is done but before the outer doors are closed."

"Good to know." She couldn't help but wonder, were Brad and his brothers here to see the crowd's reaction to Zane's long-lost daughter showing up or— "Any particular reason why you're showing a united front? I noticed you, um, didn't attend last Sunday."

Whatever response Brad might have made was cut off by the sight of Crystal stepping before the minister.

"Ah, newcomers," the man stated with a welcoming smile. He was balding, dressed in a suit and wore a pin of praying hands. "And one I believe I recognize."

"Oh," Crystal said, pretending humility by lowering her head. The pleased grin gave her away, though.

That was a total Scarlett O'Hara move. "You've probably seen me onscreen."

The minister smiled and nodded but managed to extract his hand and extend it to Gabriella. "Actually, I meant you," he said, his gaze narrowing. "You're Zane's daughter, aren't you?" He held his Bible close to his chest, a genuinely pleased expression on his face.

"Yes." She placed her palm in his, aware that everyone surrounding them had stopped talking the moment they heard the man's question.

Crystal stood less than a foot away, her expression pinched but picture-perfect.

"You look a lot like Zane. I'm so sorry for your loss. May God give you comfort and ease your pain."

"Thank you." Gabriella's voice sounded weak, her pulse surging past her ears but not loud enough to drown out the speculation she heard as word spread that Zane's daughter was in attendance.

"I'm Stuart Sampson, the minister at First Christian."

Gabriella glanced around at all the faces staring at her, sweat breaking out on her forehead because there were so many bodies pressing forward and more waiting to come up the steps behind them. And they all looked at her like the freak in a circus sideshow. "Gabriella Thom—ah, McKenna," she said, remembering Brad's advice at the very last second. Given the many ears listening, what could she do but heed it—and glare her mother into silence? "Nice to meet you. This is my mother Crystal Thompson-Salvatore."

Onstage once more, Crystal flashed a movie-worthy smile. Gabriella knew without a doubt she'd pay for the name switch the moment her mother got her alone.

Three hours later Gabriella couldn't take it anymore. She'd sat through the service and singing, enjoying the sermon and drawing peace from the minister's words. She'd even managed to pretend her every move wasn't being watched.

Her mother had sat on her left, Brad to her right, with the rest of the McKenna clan filling in the pew. Carly and Liam's soon-to-be-adopted son knelt on the floor, using the padded bench seat as a solid surface for his coloring book and plastic toy trucks. More than once she and Brad had exchanged an amused glance as Riley fussed over picking the right color or else made funny faces as he soundlessly drove the trucks, the hymnals standing in as mountains.

From the sanctuary they'd gone to the fellowship hall for lunch but when she'd carried in her lasagna dish and set it down, people practically fell over themselves avoiding it.

You shouldn't have told them it was meatless. You should have let them eat it and decide for themselves.

But she had, and it was like giving a child the choice between an ice cream cone or a shot in the hip.

Head down, she let herself into a bathroom stall and sank onto the closed lid, burying her face in her hands. Thank goodness her mother had covered her boredom with a feigned headache and asked Chance to drive her to the ranch as soon as the service was over.

It doesn't matter now. She's not here. Isn't that the most important thing?

The outer bathroom door opened and closed and water ran in the sink. A few minutes passed and the room was filled with the obvious sounds of the woman drying her hands and freshening her makeup.

"Gabriella? Are you okay?"

Carly. "I'm fine."

"It's all a bit overwhelming, isn't it?"

That was like saying a cat wouldn't claw if you tried to hold it underwater. She had been nearly six feet tall in grade school but she'd never felt so conspicuous in her life as she had sitting on Zane's pew. "Have they stopped talking about me yet?"

Carly's laughter bounced off the walls. "No, not yet. The last time I remember this much gossip about someone was when Skylar moved to town."

"Skylar?"

"My stepsister. Back then she was really into Goth and everyone was freaking out about it, afraid she'd corrupt their kids or drag them into a cult."

Gabriella laughed out loud but in her mind she wasn't. Those same people considered her the devil's spawn now. And after her mother's snooty behavior and quick departure, and Gabriella purposefully avoiding answering the question of her inheritance, no wonder.

It was only a select few. Most of them were kind.

"Brad's looking for you."

"Would you mind telling him I'll be out in a few minutes?"

"Sure but— Gabriella, I know it's not easy. Liam and Brad and Chance idolized Zane, but I understand why you're having such a hard time with this."

"You do?"

Gabriella hesitated but then opened the stall door and ventured out of her hiding place. She was too old to hide but every now and then a girl needed a quiet moment to get a grip.

"Yeah, I do. My mom left me and my dad when I was young. She never came back, never called, never had any contact."

Gabriella exhaled slowly. "You really do understand."

Carly flashed a wry smile. "Yeah, I do. And if my mom were to suddenly walk in that door or request I come see her, I honestly don't know how I'd react. All things considered, I think you're doing really well."

"I'm hiding in the bathroom."

Carly laughed again. "Not for long. I'm here to drag you out." Carly gave a wag of her eyebrows. "Oh, come on, are we that bad?"

"You? No, not at all. You've been wonderful. But all the fairy-tale stories everyone feels compelled to tell me about how great Zane was are starting to make my stomach turn."

"Laying it on a little thick, huh?"

"Totally."

"And you don't identify with that man? Not at all?"

Gabriella thought the question over, saddened by the fact her warm memories of Zane could be counted off on her fingers. "When I was a kid, really young, we had some fun times together but…after that? No. And combined with my mother's version of things, it gets really weird." But given Carly's mother issues, maybe she could help sort things out.

"I can imagine. Although I'm sure it's perfectly normal to feel the way we do. The thing is, we have to form our own opinions. As my dad says, look at the facts. If you weed out everyone else's opinion of Zane and you focus only on what you remember of him and the fact he remembered you in his will, what do you have left?"

"I have…a mess of emotions," Gabriella said honestly. "It's impossible for me to separate facts from my feelings."

Carly leaned against the sink, her expression sympathetic. "Gabriella, Zane *was* a good man. That's a fact.

But even my mom was a good mom—when she was here," she said. "People can say and do whatever they like. That's out of your control. But how you react to it? That's the key to everything. And here your reactions and responses matter more than they do in Hollywood."

"I understand that but I get so angry when people tell me how Zane was such a father figure to them. I resent it."

"I would, too. Honestly, when I think of my mom abandoning us I get totally ticked off, but what good does it do? One of the best pieces of advice Skylar ever gave me was to tell me not to let other people get to me because I let them take my power. I *had* to decide to forgive my mom and put it behind me for *my sake.* Until you do the same for Zane, you're always going to be on the defensive whenever anyone mentions him. Wouldn't it be nice to be able to listen to the story and enjoy it for what it is?"

Yes, it would. And if she held on to the anger and resentment, she'd wind up behaving like Crystal. "Why do you think Zane wanted me to come here? To his church?"

"I think you know why," Carly said, urging Gabriella toward the door and out into the deserted hallway leading to the Sunday school classrooms. "And maybe Zane hoped hearing nice things from his friends might change how you think of him."

Gabriella paused again, unable to face the group. Hearing the stories definitely had her pondering things. And reminded her that given the circumstances of her conception and her mother's personality, plus the accident with the horse when she was almost trampled, maybe Zane really had believed he was doing what was best for her. "Since I was thirteen I've told myself I didn't care what Zane or anyone thought. And I don't. But today brought back all of those overwrought childhood emotions and it made me realize that if things had been different, I wouldn't feel as though I'm an outcast who doesn't belong here."

"Do you want to belong?" Carly asked.

Did she? For what purpose? Wouldn't that make it harder when she had to leave? "Yes but—no. Why would I when I know how things are going to end?"

"Nothing's written in stone yet, Gabriella. If you want to change the end of the story, do it."

But at what cost? Molly's dream? Her future? Why should she sacrifice that when she'd already sacrificed her childhood? How much was enough?

She shook her head slowly. "It's too late. Zane and Crystal made the decision fifteen years ago but today confirmed that it was the right one. I don't belong here. I shouldn't *be* here. And if there wasn't a million-dollar piece of land at stake, I wouldn't be. The moment the three months are done, I'm putting the property up for sale and I'm leaving."

Gabriella stopped talking when she realized Carly's attention had focused on something else, something behind her. She followed Carly's gaze and found Brad leaning against the wall. Waiting for them?

"You were in there so long I thought you were sick. Glad to see you're okay."

He'd heard what she'd said. And even though the statement wasn't anything new, saying it aloud, in this building, felt wrong. Almost like a…betrayal of Zane.

"I'm leaving," Brad said in a hard tone, straightening from his slouched position. "Liam and Carly can give you a ride home."

"WHERE'S GABRIELLA?" Crystal asked the moment Brad's foot landed on the porch stair.

He'd known coming into the house to change after church was a mistake. He'd gambled that Crystal would be sleeping or in her room but obviously that wasn't the case. Instead, she stood in front of the door. "Liam and Carly are bringing her home."

He took another step only to hesitate when Crystal didn't budge. Big as he was, her hundred-pound frame kept him rooted. "I have work to do."

"I won't take much of your time."

Not what he wanted to hear. Not with Gabriella's remark about not belonging ringing in his ears. He was angry with himself because, for a split second, he'd wondered if he could change her mind. But change it to what? He wanted a woman who wanted to be a wife, a mother, a companion. How could Gabriella be any of those things if she wasn't staying?

Knowing that, however, didn't change the fact he couldn't think straight when she was around.

"She's thinner," Crystal said. "Thinner than she was at Molly's funeral. You know who Molly was, right?"

He bit back his immediate response to her tone and nodded. Not only did he know, he cared and he hated that Gabriella was taking her best friend's death so hard.

"I don't believe Gabriella's sleeping any better, either."

Brad wanted to suggest Crystal might know for sure how her daughter was sleeping if she herself wasn't always conked out on sleeping pills, but he could almost hear Zane reminding him to keep a civil tongue. "She holds things in," he said instead. "She'd sleep better if she had someone she could talk to. Is that all you wanted to discuss?"

She crossed her arms. "No, it's not. You and I need come to terms."

"About what?"

"What do you think? You don't want Gabriella here any more than I do. Perhaps if we work together we can get what we want."

A devil's pact. There was no other name for it. Even though he was tempted, he knew that wasn't what Zane would want. "Not interested. Excuse me."

This time Crystal moved out of his way but she followed him.

"You think you're being loyal to Zane but how loyal was he to you?" she called. "Every day that passes Gabriella gets closer to owning the property."

He turned to look at her, surprised. "I admire a bold woman but I'd think a mother would be more supportive of her daughter."

"I support anything that's good for Gabriella. I love her more than you can imagine. But this place isn't good for her. She doesn't belong here."

There was that sentence again. Second time today.

And he hated it as much now as he had at the church. "She's Zane's daughter. That's enough proof for me that she does."

"Even if it means your downfall?"

Brad hesitated again. "Even then."

CHAPTER EIGHTEEN

THAT SAME EVENING GABRIELLA took a break from her afternoon of researching inheritance taxes, land transfer fees and sales of Montana land in recent years, and left the house.

The real estate market was down drastically from a few years ago. Everyone knew that. But it also meant her only hope for a relatively quick sale was to list the land once she owned it with a California-based agent who had connections to people with cash. Otherwise, a sale could take years, and in the meantime she'd be responsible for the property taxes, which would be a huge financial strain on top of Alicia's new salary as partner.

The air was fresh and cooling rapidly with the setting sun as she picked her way along the path toward the barns and outbuildings. The ranch had been fairly quiet since Friday evening when the ranch hands had left for their weekend fun, but in the past hour she'd heard the rumble of vehicles returning.

Deciding to check on the calf, she made her way to the barn. The sound of male voices and ornery laughter reached her and she followed it into the building where a handful of men, Brad included, sat around an old table, cards in their hands. "Sunday night poker?" she asked. "So this is what cowboys do in a barn."

Everyone laughed except Brad, who folded and tossed his cards facedown.

"Zane had a rule." Charlie indicated the pennies in the middle of the table. "This is for fun. Biggest pot is usually a dollar at most."

"I'm done. Not my night for sure." Brad stood.

She hadn't seen Brad after he'd left her at church in Liam and Carly's care. And from the look of things, he still hadn't gotten over his anger.

She couldn't blame him under the circumstances. But she didn't have the words to set his mind at ease, either. At the moment she couldn't set her own mind at ease because she wasn't sure what was going to happen. She was not a person who dealt well with living in limbo. "Mind if I take Brad's place?" she asked, hoping for a distraction.

The men exchanged a glance and shrugged their agreement.

"Have a seat," Charlie said.

Brad played the gentleman and pulled out the chair he'd vacated but the moment she stepped toward him, he backed away. "You can use what's left of my pile."

"She's going to take it all anyway, eh, Brad?" one of the younger men said.

The men grew quiet and Gabriella felt every second of the awkward moment. Brad didn't seem the type to gossip but everyone knew why she was there.

"I'm going to go check on Pikipsi." Without another word, Brad's long strides carried him deeper into the large structure.

Gabriella played several hands, winning three but losing two—to the tune of eighty-seven cents. The game took her mind off her research and her mother's hovering presence in the house.

She could only imagine what her mother would think if she could see her sitting on a dirty chair in a dirty barn playing cards with men who labored for a living.

"I'm done. Time to call it a night, boys," Charlie said, tossing his cards down. "Early day tomorrow."

The other men quickly did the same, with the winner raking in a whopping forty cents.

"Night, ma'am." Charlie dipped his head toward her and got to his feet, the others following suit.

"Good night, Charlie. Gentlemen." She gathered the cards and stacked them neatly in the center of the table in readiness for the next game. She'd spent her share of sleepless nights playing computer solitaire and she'd forgotten how good it felt to have the cards in her hands. Like books, sometimes the electronic versions didn't feel as good as paper.

Hearing Brad's low murmur, she headed in that direction, the smell of hay and hard-packed dirt strong.

Spot—her name for the calf—was curled up on the floor of her stall, her impossibly long eyelashes low.

Gabriella continued to where Brad stood in a stall on the left. On the right, a monster of a horse blew air out its nostrils, seeming like it was pawing the ground ready to burst out and mow her down.

Pikipsi's head jerked back at Gabriella's approach, then backed up and sidestepped, pinning Brad to the wall.

"Whoa, girl. Easy."

Gabriella took another step, gaping when the horse retreated still more and Brad's breath left his lungs in a rush while the dark giant across the aisle whinnied so loud Gabriella felt goose bumps break out on her skin.

"Easy, girl. Shh."

"Brad, get out!" She was transported to being a little

girl, on the ground dazed and scared, opening her eyes to see the horse rearing on two legs ready to pounce. "Brad!"

"Stop screaming. You're scaring her."

Despite being pinned to the wall, Brad remained calm and spoke softly to the horse.

"Easy. Thatta girl, that's right. She don't mean no harm. Move over." He put his hands on the horse's side and pushed but nothing happened. "Come on, a little breathing room is all I need."

The big horse kicked the stall and Gabriella clasped her hands together, her knuckles pressed against her mouth so she wouldn't scream again while she watched Brad maneuver himself out from Pikipsi's weight.

Finally Pikipsi shifted and swung her large behind the other way, and he moved to stand at the horse's head.

"Are you okay?" Gabriella wasn't aware of doing it but somewhere in the past few seconds she'd opened the stall door so Brad could make his escape. For someone terrified of horses the way she was, it was a major step.

Brad turned his head and pierced her with a steady stare. "You owe me for that."

He was angry. Again. Could she do nothing right today? "I'm sorry. I didn't mean to scare her. Are you all right?"

"Come here. Now."

She shook her head. "You come out. Get *out* of there."

Some of her fear for him must have registered with him because she thought she saw his expression soften, just a tad.

"Gabriella, come here. Leave the stall door open if you like, but get your butt in here."

"Brad—"

"Do what I say so you don't put me or any of my men in danger again."

She swallowed audibly, her heart pounding in her ears. *Face your fear. You can do this.*

Gabriella took a tentative step toward them. Another, inching closer, until she stood behind Brad, her hands clenched in the material of his shirt.

"Good. Now give me your hand."

"No." Was he crazy?

"Don't be a chicken."

"Don't taunt me like a schoolboy bully. I'm too old for that."

He made a clucking sound that made the horse's ears twitch.

"Stop it. You'll scare her and she'll trample us both."

"Not Pikipsi. She's a good girl. Horses are one of man's best friends."

"You're confusing them with dogs." The ranch had at least half a dozen herd dogs. She liked them, not the thousand-pound monster that kept shifting and moving despite the way Brad held the bridle or harness or whatever it was that latched around the horse's head.

"To each his own. Come on, Gabriella. Give me your hand."

"I can't. Please, let's just leave."

"Don't be afraid. Trust me. I won't let anything happen to you. Let me help you. Do you want to be afraid forever?"

That wasn't fair. Seeing Brad get pinned had scared her. Unearthed her nightmare of horses, of being trampled. The horse could take both of them out.

"Tamed horses are a prize," Brad murmured, scratching the horse's jaw. "And way more trustworthy than humans."

"Is that a shot at me? You'd let her eat me if she wanted to," Gabriella said, not caring what Brad thought of her whine.

"She's a vegetarian, too. That's another reason you should like her," Brad said. "Give me your hand and I'll introduce you."

Gabriella pulled her gaze from the massive horse long enough to glance at Brad and found herself trapped by his gaze, held captive by the strength and trust he instilled.

Brad's will, his determination to help her, was written in his expression. They were opposite sides when it came to the terms of the will but in this, Brad was on her side and…she liked it.

Gabriella loosened her grip on his shirt. She hated that her hand trembled so badly but he didn't seem to notice.

He tugged her closer, bringing her front into contact with his back. Brad guided her fingers down the silky texture of the horse's long nose. Once, then again.

"See, Pik? Not bad, eh, girl? Gabriella, this is Pikipsi. She's gonna be a mama real soon so she's a little more skittish than normal."

"She's going to have a baby?" Oh, she was so *soft.* Gabriella hadn't expected that.

She extended her arm a little more to better reach the horse, careful to keep Brad's bulk between them even as she tried to ignore his smell—wood smoke and after-shave. Her heart was gradually slowing its frantic pace and the scent of his shirt drew her so much she fought the urge to bury her nose against the cloth.

"Maybe if you can get over your fear you could name the colt. We generally don't name our cattle but horses are different."

His words made her think of Spot and she smiled inwardly. How weird was it to have grown up and lived her adult life without a pet but here she was, surrounded by them.

Maybe it was her hormones and emotions talking but she felt a kinship with her surroundings, one strong enough to ease the horrendous ache she'd felt ever since losing Molly—at least distract her from it. Wasn't that one of her goals for coming?

Molly had wanted kids. She'd never wavered in that wish, whereas Gabriella had always questioned her desire for them. Seeing Brad's patience with the animal made her wonder if she'd be a good parent, have the required patience. She knew she was a strong woman but everyone had fears about the unknown and, with her childhood, she was no different. How much did she actually know about raising a family? What if she screwed the kid up? She couldn't consider herself entirely sane at times.

He shifted his hold to open her fingers a little, until the velvety softness of Pikipsi's head could really register.

"Not so scary now, is she?"

"No. She's…amazing." This entire experience was due to Brad's determination she overcome her fear. Brad, who hated her presence on the ranch because she threatened to take it away.

"Zane wouldn't want you to be afraid, Gabriella. He wanted you here because he wanted you to care about this place, the people and animals on it."

She focused on petting the pregnant mare while wondering if she'd ever understand men.

Brad was angry with her—but being nice. He'd left

her at the church because he was upset at her being there for her inheritance and nothing else.

In this moment all she was aware of were the sounds in the barn, of Brad's masculine scent and the hard warmth of his body. Standing the way she was, with him smoothing her hand over the horse, it was hard to remember he wanted something from her. He'd made no bones about wanting her to take the hundred thousand so that the Circle M would remain intact. Was this his way of getting on her good side?

Brad turned to look at her and she studied his features up close. The five-o'clock stubble shadowing his jaw, the lean line of his mouth. Strong nose. Thick eyebrows. Sexy little lines around his beautiful eyes.

A sharp ripple ran through her, the kind she'd heard talked about but had never experienced. Brad was… rough. Big. A man who made a woman, even a woman as tall as her, feel small and feminine.

The hand holding her in place curled around hers, tightening, while he angled and lowered his head. Brad's nose brushed her cheek as their mouths met in a soft, barely there kiss that parted lips and touched tongues but couldn't go deeper due to their awkward position.

The kiss was light, the mere brushing of lips, enough for the taste of each other to register. An exploratory kiss guaranteed to titillate. But the question in her head couldn't be silenced. "Why are you kissing me?"

"A man usually doesn't kiss a woman unless he wants to."

Okay, that was acceptable but… "Because you want me—or the land?"

Brad muttered a curse and released her hand.

"It's a reasonable question." And one she felt compelled to ask, much as she didn't want to.

"If you have to ask it, kissing you was obviously a mistake. Go back to the house, Gabriella."

Maybe if he'd hesitated before ordering her to leave, she could have chalked the experience up to attraction and acting on desire. Maybe if he'd come right out and said yes or no, she could have let the matter drop. But she couldn't.

After Samuel's betrayal, Molly had often accused her of being cynical, because Gabriella always wondered why men asked her out, kissed her, whatever. But where Brad was concerned, she had every reason to be cynical. In fact, she had a million of them.

She lifted her chin to the haughty angle she'd watched her mother practice in the mirror, and stepped back.

A part of her wanted to run like an embarrassed, humiliated, awkward girl, but she was all too aware of the massive horse right there, afraid any sudden move would startle it again.

"I don't know why I keep—" Another curse. "I apologize," he said.

"I don't want an apology. And I'm getting really tired of people referring to me as their mistake. Once again, let's chalk this up to curiosity. But it's nothing dating one of the local boys wouldn't fix."

She was proud of herself for saying it without any inflection. She even managed a small, quirky smirk. Maybe sitting in on her mother's acting classes all those years would prove useful after all.

Gabriella took measured steps to exit the stall. Once clear of the opening and safe from trampling hooves, she tossed an extra swing in her stride as a silent kiss off to his boorish behavior.

Her mother had made one point about Zane abundantly clear over the years. Regardless of how wonderful the weekend they'd spent in bed was, she'd had plans, dreams she had no intention of letting him—or anyone else—disrupt.

The same was true for Gabriella. A few sappy thoughts about baby animals and a kiss or two from a handsome cowboy were not going to derail her plans. She owed it to Molly and Alicia and, most importantly, to herself.

At the house, Gabriella let herself into the kitchen only to come face-to-face with Crystal. Her gaze sharpened on Gabriella, who knew when she was busted.

"Where were you?"

"I went for a walk."

"With Brad? Gabriella, please tell me you're not—"

"I'm not." She was not in the mood for this rant. "Trust me, Mom. I'm not."

She spent a sleepless night pacing her room and wandering the lower level in the dark once she knew everyone else was asleep. She dozed a bit on the couch in Zane's den but woke early, realizing it had been a few days since she'd last delivered eggs. Merrilee had been so open and welcoming. Why not go see her again?

A sudden smile broke over Gabriella's face and a sense of adventure filled her. Maybe she ought to feel strange about making the trip to Barney and Merrilee's alone, but as the sun rose higher over the horizon, her dark cloud of worries lifted a little.

She wrote a brief note on the table stating she wouldn't be home until the afternoon and addressed it to her mother but left it in the open where Brad would see.

Twenty minutes after that, Gabriella had the eggs crated and tucked on the truck's floorboard for safekeeping. Driving her car would have been quicker and definitely easier, but she liked the old truck.

Fifty-five minutes later—because she couldn't make the trip without making at least one wrong turn, could she?—she rolled to a stop outside the Browns' small house.

"Good morning, Ella," Merrilee said, opening the door and stepping out onto the porch while Gabriella grabbed the eggs. "I'm so happy you came for another visit. Brad's not with you?"

It was a struggle to keep her smile in place. "Not today." *He doesn't want anything to do with a mistake.*

"I made plenty of potatoes. Barney already ate. He's out back in the garden trying to beat the heat. Supposed to be a hot one today."

Gabriella ate and talked, then helped clean up the kitchen. Merrilee asked if Gabriella wanted to see the garden the couple were so proud of.

"You've done all of this already this year?" Gabriella stared in wonder at the large plot.

Merrilee smiled. "Zane built us a small greenhouse one year for Christmas. We start the plants early and move things here as soon as we can."

Yet another kind act. How many kindnesses had her father performed in his life? "That's still a lot of work."

Merrilee laughed, her wrinkled face lighting up. "Oh, we've downsized *a lot* from our younger years. People have to make ends meet, though. I can or freeze most everything we eat, and sell some to pay for odds and ends. Do you like to garden?"

"I don't know. I've never had one," she said, thinking of Zane's list once more. She lifted a shoulder in a shrug. "My mom traveled a lot when I was younger and then she married and… It's never really come up."

"Some of my favorite memories are of being on my knees in the dirt beside my father." Merrilee's expression grew distant as though she had traveled to another place, another time. "We'd tell stories and sing, and talk about everything."

A sudden longing filled Gabriella. "That sounds nice." Like something a family should do.

"I have a few more tomato plants to set. Would you like to help?"

"I'd love to."

"After that, I'll show you the way to a good man's heart. Brad loves my apple tarts."

Gabriella wasn't sure what to make of Merrilee's comment but Brad's image immediately appeared in her mind, the way he'd looked at her in the barn before he'd kissed her.

He did appear to be a good man. But was he also desperate enough to use their mutual attraction to gain her cooperation?

Could she truly be angry with him when being attracted to Brad was a complication she hadn't planned on while she was here?

He was obviously experiencing the same confusion. "Brad and I aren't— Things are too complicated for that."

"I see."

"My home is in California." And it always would be. She might not be quite the city girl her mother was, but California *was* home.

"Home is where you make it. Sounds like you're compiling a list of excuses."

"It's all true."

"I see a lot of Zane in Brad. Your father didn't know quite how to handle you and I imagine Brad feels much the same. Men have a tendency to stick their feet in their mouths a lot when that's the case. We have to overlook them when that happens."

Getting a headache rather than any answers, Gabriella squatted beside the surprisingly agile Merrilee and shoved her French manicure into the dirt, imagining her mother's expression if she could see this.

Then she began to laugh. "You're better than therapy, Merrilee, you know that?"

Instead of the smile she'd expected to receive, Merrilee frowned. "What's Brad done to send you here today all alone?"

"How do you know it's about Brad?"

"I knew the first time you came here with him. I could tell by the way he watched you."

"Yeah, well, he's watching me because he wants the land Zane left me. Brad will do anything to keep control of the water rights."

"I imagine it's hard to find trust when that worry is flittin' through your mind. But has Brad given you reason not to trust him? Are you sure you're not holding your feelings toward Zane against Brad?"

When Gabriella didn't answer, Merrilee nodded. "Until Brad does something to earn your distrust, you should let nature take its course and see where it leads, Gabriella. Otherwise, you might miss the best things in life because you're too afraid worrying about what might go wrong."

CHAPTER NINETEEN

BRAD WAS MORE THAN READY to blow off some steam by the time Friday rolled around. The first cutting of hay had been completed, covered and stored before a thunderstorm struck. Luck was with them, but that was the least of his troubles.

On Monday afternoon Charlie had relayed the message that illness had struck the herd grazing north of the ranch. Calves were down and it was spreading fast.

Brad had loaded up the truck with medicine and all the necessary supplies then headed out, not getting home until well after dark and worried sick because they couldn't afford to lose a single animal.

On Tuesday morning the cows and calves in the north were showing improvement but another group showed signs of the illness. And because the cattle were spread out over the range, it took him and the members of his crew not haying the rest of the week to get the herd medicated. The animals had a mild infection, like a human getting a virus, but it wasn't something the cattle could rid themselves of on their own. Once weak and unable to eat, the infection could have easily wiped out his entire herd in a matter of days.

Since Monday he'd eaten, slept and worked with the hands, sorting out the sickest of the animals to take to the barns to be kept in isolation and watched over—feeding, watering and caring for them like children.

They'd managed to save all but three of the calves. Still, losing those three had hit hard and made him feel as though he'd failed.

When Chance mentioned his intent to go to the Wild Honey Saloon Friday night, Brad invited himself along. A man could only take so much.

Chance nudged him and Brad looked up to see Liam headed their way, holding Carly's hand and glaring at the men checking out his fiancée.

But it was who trailed behind the happy couple that had Brad gritting his teeth and beggin' God for mercy. There was no mistaking that white-blond hair. Thankfully Crystal was nowhere in sight.

Several long, low whistles filled the air, audible despite the jukebox and noise of the crowded bar and Brad could see why. He clenched his hand on the cue stick he was holding. Gabriella looked as though she wore little more than a rubber band around her hips.

He'd ventured out to get *away* from her, since working like a dog all week hadn't managed to keep his mind off her. He didn't want to spend the evening with her, especially not with her dressed the way she was.

"How long do you suppose her legs are?" Chance murmured.

Brad and every man in the room had a good view given the shortness of her so-called skirt. "Long enough."

And then some.

"What's wrong with you?"

"I can't escape from her," he muttered. "Do you know she was on the phone with her assistant today and the entire time all they talked about were thongs." He wouldn't admit to being in the bathroom listening to Gabriella's voice drift through the vent, or how he'd gotten back into the tub for a cold shower before it was over.

Chance laughed. "And your problem with that is?"

What could Brad say when any excuse would reveal his fantasies for Zane's daughter?

"Mind if we join you?" Carly asked, polite as always even though Liam had simply pulled out a chair at the table closest to where they stood.

"Have a seat." Chance flashed one of his ready smiles. "You can cheer me on while I kick Brad's butt. He's...not on his game tonight."

Brad stayed quiet, trying hard not to swallow his tongue when he got an up-close look at Gabriella's outfit. He thought of the telephone ad from years ago about wanting to reach out and touch someone. He wanted to touch *her*. Now. Bad.

"We talked Gabriella into joining us." Carly fiddled with the pendant dangling from her necklace. "No sense in her staying home on a Friday night, right?"

"And in case you're wondering, Crystal decided a *saloon* wasn't to her taste," Liam said in a low voice only Brad and Chance could hear.

"Hi," Gabriella said. "I hope you don't mind. I don't want to intrude."

"You're not. I told Gabriella we wouldn't dream of missing out on her Honey debut." Liam shot a pointed look at Brad and Chance, who still stood holding the pool cues but not playing.

Brad couldn't unglue his tongue from the roof of his mouth, especially when Gabriella sat and crossed her legs. It defied all known laws of nature, but the skirt got shorter.

"Well, I appreciate it. My mother is practicing for an

audition," Gabriella said to no one in particular. "Every time she screamed I dropped something."

Her tentative smile kicked him in the chest. Thankfully she turned her attention to the bar's decor.

A hundred or so lantern lights—a mix of old and new—hung from the ceiling. The walls were covered in antique signs, some from the state's mines, some with ornery statements on them about cowboys and horses. Higher up on shelves were small, empty barrels and mining pans and an assortment of artifacts covering two hundred years of history.

"What do you think? Eclectic, huh?" Carly asked.

It was a dive. But it was the closest place where they could kick back without driving into Helena.

Brad forced his attention to the pool game in progress to no avail. Chance won the game as a local band took the stage. The band consisted of kids with more brass than talent. Thankfully the noise kept conversation at the table to a minimum—until they played a slow song.

"Oh, I love this," Carly cried, immediately turning to Liam and batting her eyelashes.

He groaned but stood and led her to the dance floor. Chance glanced between Gabriella and Brad, then shrugged before jackknifing off the chair and heading toward a blonde seated at the bar.

Brad remained where he was, unsure of what to do. Holding Gabriella would only stir up trouble. The moment he spotted George Abbott moving toward Gabriella, however, Brad stood. "You want to dance?"

Gabriella glanced at him in surprise, hesitated briefly, then rose, meeting him eye-to-eye. "Lead the way."

THEY HAD MADE EXACTLY six sways in time with the music before Gabriella broke the silence. "Liam told me about the herd being sick. I'm sorry."

"They're better now. That's all that matters."

More people were pairing up and the dance floor was getting crowded. Someone bumped into Gabriella and as a result she stepped on Brad's foot. "Oh, sorry."

"No problem."

The couple appeared to be pretty drunk and when a collision seemed unavoidable, Brad executed a quick turn so that they bumped into him—which was like hitting a brick wall. He didn't budge from the impact but the protective gesture wasn't lost on her. He could give a caveman a run for his money at times but she'd be lying if she said Brad's action wasn't a total tummy-tightening moment. How could he be such a contrast of hard and soft? Protective and unrelenting but caring and…vulnerable?

Dancing closer now, his lips settled near her ear and with every sway of his body against hers, it got a little harder to breathe.

One glance into his eyes and—yep, right there it was. He had been a perfect gentlemen but his eyes gave him away. She wasn't the only one feeling this way.

Merrilee's questions about whether Brad had given Gabriella reason to distrust him or whether she was holding her feelings for Zane against Brad played over in her mind. And the answer?

She had to admit that maybe Merrilee was right.

But where did it leave Gabriella?

She shook her head and the move brushed her cheek against the tantalizing shadow on his jaw. An immediate shiver ran through her.

The things that drew her to Brad were not the things

her mother or Alicia or any of her friends would consider prize qualities in a man. He wasn't white-collar, wasn't smooth and sophisticated.

Brad didn't drop a couple hundred dollars on a haircut, wear Armani or vacation in exotic locations. But he worked hard and he'd proven—more than once—that he could be trusted. There, she'd said it. That it didn't mean she wasn't wary. It would still be fairly easy for him to make her life so miserable at the house, she would leave.

She was confused. Tempted. Wary.

How many times could she open herself up only to get hurt and walk away semi-whole? Where could they go when neither of them was prepared for more? There were times when she wasn't even sure if Brad *liked* her. She wasn't a woman foolish enough to believe sex and desire equated to an emotion like caring or love.

"I have a question for you," she said.

His Adam's apple moved up and down as he swallowed. Did he pull her a little closer?

"What is it?" A muscle spasmed in his jaw, the deep green of his eyes sharpening. His arm around her waist squeezed tighter.

"Don't laugh. What's your five-year plan? Where do you see yourself in five years if—" she forced herself to say it "—hypothetically, everything works out exactly as you want it with the ranch."

His chest brushed hers as he inhaled. "If everything works out, I see myself ranching. It's who I am and all I ever want to do."

"What else? Do you want a family? Children?"

"Isn't that what most men want?"

She almost laughed at the response until she realized he was serious. Because he *was* serious. Maybe that was another difference between Montana and California men. At least the ones she knew. Brad valued family—a contrast to all the stories she heard of men fathering children only to leave.

Like Zane?

Once again she reminded herself that she couldn't hold Brad responsible for Zane's actions.

"What about you?" Brad asked. "Where do you see yourself in five years? If, hypothetically, things go the way you want them to?"

She couldn't look him in the eyes now. "You know what I want."

Her words emerged as the last strains of music sounded. The band immediately started a much faster song.

Brad released her and stepped back, and she suddenly found herself missing the warmth of his body.

"You thirsty? I need a drink."

She nodded. He escorted her off the dance floor with a gentle hold on her elbow, the subject dropped.

Throughout the rest of the evening she was surrounded by McKennas—or future McKennas. Carly and Liam were adorable in their coupleness, Chance an incorrigible bad boy, the opposite of Brad in all his quiet, sexy watchfulness and steadfast presence.

The brothers ribbed each other and told stories about their years running wild and being ornery and Zane's responses.

Instead of being jealous and upset Gabriella actually laughed along with them and enjoyed the tales for what they were. She even added a few funny memories of her own, of when she and Crystal had gone on trips and when Crystal had taken her to a carnival along the beach that she'd first visited with Zane.

Gabriella had wanted to have her face painted but was scared. To show she shouldn't be afraid, Crystal had let the artist paint her own face. Only the paint hadn't come off as easily as the guy said it would and she had gone on set the next day sporting black zebra stripes across her nose and cheeks.

Relating that story and laughing along with everyone about Crystal's response, it dawned on Gabriella that Zane was right. She'd had her mother growing up and, while not perfect, Crystal had loved Gabriella. Brad, Liam and Chance had needed someone like that. Somehow she couldn't unearth any of the resentment she'd felt when she first arrived on the ranch. She did feel a certain amount of guilt. If she'd pressed Zane and demanded to be a part of his life, he wouldn't have turned her down. Part of the responsibility for their separation was definitely hers to bear.

As for the ranch… For a moment when she'd danced with Brad, she'd forgotten everything else. Was this what it would be like if she stayed? If she didn't sell and made them all part of her life?

That was ridiculous. Wasn't it?

The night wound down, the band packed up and the stories continued until a sudden lull mushroomed over the table. Gabriella was shocked to see Chance's nostrils flaring as he blinked rapidly. Liam slapped Chance on the shoulder in an unmistakable show of support.

Finally, Chance lifted his glass. "You'll be missed, old man. To Zane."

Brad, Liam and Carly lifted their glasses, as well. "To Zane."

Gabriella was slower and very aware that Brad watched her, waited. A man was dead, and his life meant something to these people. And now, thanks to the list she had yet to complete, he'd finally come to mean something to her other than the father who'd given her away. "To Zane."

Gabriella remained lost in her thoughts and quiet while Brad drove them to the ranch. Once he'd parked, he helped her out of the jacked-up truck. "Thanks," she said when her heels touched ground.

They walked to the porch side by side, not touching. He opened the door but caught her arm before she stepped over the threshold

"Gabriella, I didn't tell you but…you look pretty tonight."

"As opposed to the other nights?"

"No, I meant—crap."

She laughed and placed her hand on his chest, the beat of his heart strong and firm beneath her fingers, the light from the kitchen revealing his reddening ears. "I'm teasing you. I know what you meant. Thank you, Brad. I had a nice time tonight. I liked hearing the stories about Zane."

Brad looked at her hand, then made eye contact. Once again Gabriella was treated to a blazing glance full of desire.

"When I saw you walk in, I admit I expected the fun to be over. But it turned out to be a nice night, didn't it?"

Gabriella waited, for what she wasn't sure—or maybe she knew but wasn't ready to admit it—then removed her hand. "Good night."

"Night. Sweet dreams."

She made it up the stairs but didn't remember climbing them. That was how strong her reaction to him was. She grabbed her pajamas and locked herself in the bathroom to wash her face, feeling like a schoolgirl who had gotten her first kiss.

It had taken a bit of time to grasp the enormity of holding the water rights to this and other ranches but now she did. Poor Merrilee worked so hard in her garden to put food on the table. If they had to pay to have water hauled in...

And the Second Chance—on the way to the bar they'd passed it and Carly had explained what a wonderful place it was, how it hosted so many disabled families. Gabriella couldn't bear the thought of putting them—any of them—out of business.

Surely there was a way around it? Some clause that could be included in the contract that would keep the buyer from withholding water?

You know how the legal system works. If there was a foolproof way of doing that, Brad wouldn't be worried.

Which brought her back to square one with no solution in sight. In the end, they would all hate her. And she and Brad would never be more than they were now.

She needed time to think, time for a creative idea to accomplish the impossible to occur to her. Because after hearing all their stories tonight she couldn't stand the thought of hurting them. Yet equally abhorrent was the thought of coming here, disrupting her life and career, only to fail Molly in the end.

BRAD WATCHED THE LITTLE band of material around Gabriella's hips sway all the way up the stairs. The moment he heard the bathroom door click closed, he exhaled hard.

"That's quite a telling reaction from a man who

stands to lose his livelihood," Crystal said from the dark shadows of the adjacent living room.

Brad felt as though he'd been caught with his pants down. "You're up late."

Dread coiled in his stomach like a rattler shaking its tail. Tonight had turned out much better than he'd ever thought it could. But Crystal's tension-filled presence shot his good feeling to smithereens. The woman was hell in heels and she made no secret what she thought of him. "Beautiful night outside. Maybe some fresh air would help your headache."

"I don't have a headache."

"Oh." He let his gaze shift slightly to the wrinkles formed by her knitted eyebrows and her hand shot to her forehead, her fingertips smoothing the area before she caught herself and lowered her arm to her side.

"I won't keep you," she said. "I simply wanted to say—loud and clear—that you need to stay away from Gabriella."

"That's kind of hard to do when she's living in my house."

"You heard me."

"Why?" He wasn't all that surprised by the demand but he wanted Crystal to state her reasoning for the order. Just so they were clear.

"She doesn't need someone like you. You have no business inheriting anything of Zane's but I'd rather see you have it than for Gabriella to think, even for a moment, that she's meant for a place like this."

That sneer. She'd be a pretty woman if she'd get that haughty, rich-bitch expression off her face. "I'm going to let those comments slide because I can tell you love your daughter. But don't disrespect *this place*," he ordered, aware that she'd paled in response to his growl, "and expect to stay under its roof."

Squaring her shoulders, Crystal moved forward, not stopping until she stood head to chest with Brad.

"I can tell you want her. It's written all over your face when you look at her. I know why, too."

"It's not because of the land she stands to inherit." He wasn't about to let her get away with accusing him of that, too.

All this time he'd held back. Minding his manners because he thought that's what Zane would have wanted. But Zane would want Gabriella to be happy. Maybe if Brad could show her how, she could be happy here. Was that possible? Or a pipe dream?

He heard Gabriella upstairs—water running, gentle thumps. He never thought he would say this but he liked having her in the house—even though he had everything to lose.

And everything to gain?

He was tired of swallowing his pride to keep peace. Tired of pretending. Maybe Crystal hadn't said anything he hadn't already told himself but her snooty attitude pissed him off enough to want to go upstairs and kiss Gabriella senseless for no other reason than because worrying about the future and five-year plans would fly out the window the moment they did.

He and Gabriella might be opposites in nearly every way but them getting together made perfect sense. Crystal and the will and a slew of other reasons stood in his way—unless he came up with a plan to settle things. Somehow.

"Gabriella is talented. She's smart and determined. She's meant to achieve outstanding things."

"I agree."

"So you'll do the right thing for her? Stay away from her? Because I'm telling you right now—I didn't lose my daughter to him, and I certainly won't lose her to you."

Staring into Crystal's face—seeing the bitterness and the love—Brad faced the facts. Any dealings, any life he might have with Gabriella would include Crystal, who had made Zane's life hell and kept her daughter from knowing her own father. Brad didn't doubt Crystal would make her son-in-law's life a living hell.

So was that his decision? Marriage?

With Gabriella it couldn't be anything else. He didn't want anything else.

Even though he might have matured with age, inside him was a rebellious teenage boy now hell-bent on proving Crystal wrong. "We'll see about that. Good night, *ma'am.*"

CHAPTER TWENTY

SATURDAY AFTERNOON GABRIELLA had her earbuds in, listening to Pink as she dug in the garden, when something alerted her to the fact she was being watched. She looked around and tried not to gape at the sight of Brad seated on a huge horse.

He leaned forward in the saddle, one forearm braced across the expanse of the horse's back, the other resting on it. He looked relaxed and comfortable and decidedly sexy in a raw, totally alpha kind of way, even though the terrifying animal she remembered from the second stall in the barn kept shifting its weight beneath him. The fact that Brad calmed the horse's movements by simply tightening his strong thighs around the animal's girth didn't go unnoticed.

"Been shopping?" he asked once she'd plucked out the earbuds. His gaze took in the dirt, flowers, plants and even the gloves on her hands.

Her fingers flexed instinctively. The sunflower design on her gardening gloves looked a bit cheesy but her fake nails couldn't handle any more damage. As it stood, she'd resigned herself to the fact that while she was here, the nails had to go. "A little." She shaded her eyes. "I decided to try my hand at planting something so I drove into town to McKenna Feed. Oh, before I forget, Chance sent a box for you. It's on the kitchen table."

"Thanks."

She avoided looking at him when she stepped toward the open passenger door of the truck to gather the last of the plants that hadn't fit in the rear bed. Those that had made the trip to the ranch back there had gotten windblown and a little wilted. Fortunately, water had perked them up. *Un*fortunately, she'd added the water before planting them, which meant her gloves were now soaked. *A newbie mistake.*

Brad dismounted. "Gabriella, come here."

With a beast that size nearby? "I'm fine here." She carefully righted an overturned leaf lettuce and warily eyed the animal.

"You know you want to go to the falls. You don't want to miss seeing it."

When had he moved behind her? "Find another way. I'm not in the mood to do that today."

"I can get you in the mood."

The husky timber of his voice had sexy images popping into her brain and she remembered what he'd said that night on the swing.

She'd been the one teasing him lately, flirting, for the hell of it. Because it was so easy. And, yeah, she thought his ears turning dark red was ridiculously sweet. But shouldn't *get you in the mood* have been her line?

"Come here, sweetheart."

Sweetheart? She rolled her eyes but her heart picked up speed at the endearment. "Laying it on kinda thick, aren't you?"

His mouth lifted at the corners in a genuine smile. "You can do this. Let me help you."

"I petted one the other night. And I've been feeding Spot. That's enough."

"That was the first step. This is the second. Trust

me. I won't let anything happen to you. Can't you play along and do what I say?"

"I could. But why would I want to?"

The cream-colored hat Brad wore highlighted his sun-darkened skin and the green of his eyes watching her so closely. She was playing with fire, coated in dirt and more than a little sweat—women her size didn't glow—her heart pounding in her chest.

She wasn't sure if it was her or him, but something had changed between them. She felt it. The air was charged with it. He was a manly guy who liked to take care of his woman and know he was needed. She liked that about him, if she was perfectly honest. In the business world she had to be strong and tough and outspoken, take charge and make sure things were done. But that didn't mean she wanted a guy she had to direct in bed. With Brad, she knew that *so* would not be an issue.

In her experience most men were turned off by women as strong as she was, which led to a rather boring—*Don't you mean non-existent?*—love life. Dates were few and far between, because men in L.A. wanted women devoted entirely to them, not a career.

And Brad wants a home and family, kids. What's the difference?

"The falls are unbelievably beautiful," Brad drawled. "Since you've been here you've oohed and ahhed over the sky and trees and rocks. You're really going to miss seeing the main attraction because of one little thing?"

"It's hardly little." Catching the double entendre, she winced. There was no mistaking the glint in his eyes now. Nor the way he leaned in a little more.

"Back to that trust issue again. You've got it bad, don't you?"

Trust was fragile, elusive.

What if Brad really was different? What if he could be trusted? Zane had trusted Brad with the running of the ranch. So did Brad's brothers. He had obviously earned that confidence over the years. But having been lied to by her mother, abandoned by her father, cheated on by a boyfriend…

"The water is clear and dark blue," he said softly. "Like your eyes. The snow caps reflect off the surface, the falls are still rushing with the spring thaw and this time of year everything is green and lush and beautiful."

His gaze lowered to her lips when he said the word *lush* and by the time *beautiful* emerged, she was struggling to not throw herself against him and kiss him with every pent-up need she had.

"You don't strike me as a woman who runs from a challenge. Or do you?"

Maybe he didn't intend for things to go further but his words *were* a challenge. Holding his gaze and praying her mother wasn't inside near a window, Gabriella raised her face and kissed him full-on.

A kiss might be just a kiss. But standing in the open door of the old truck, this embrace was hot and gritty and borderline frantic. Their tongues rubbed together, their breaths mingled and somewhere along the way his hands grasped her behind and lifted her so that her hips rested on the edge of the bench seat. Brad stood between her legs, pressing her into the cushion. Pressing her into him.

The material of her shorts was thin and no barrier against his touch, the feel of his body against her. His hands gripped her, hard and firm, melded her against the very heat of him, until he gained control of the kiss and possessed her in a way that left her gasping for air and seeing stars.

This was no shy cowboy.

Brad varied the angles and depth, the pressure and finesse, used his lips and tongue and teeth to nibble with enough *bite* to send a red-hot jab of passion streaking through her that made her think hot and dirty and out in the open wouldn't necessarily be so bad.

His fingers drifted to her sides, tried to maneuver beneath the tight, form-fitting tank top. When the clingy material proved too difficult, he slid his hands along the outside of the material up, until he cupped both her breasts in his oversize palms.

Gabriella tore her mouth loose from his to draw a breath, barely managing to squelch a moan as he rasped his thumbs over the pebbled tips of her breasts. Good, good, good. Hot, hot, *hot*.

A loud thump sounded on the far end of the truck bed.

"Men coming in," Charlie called out.

Brad dropped his hands and stepped back so abruptly Gabriella nearly fell off the seat.

Her chest heaving for air, she glanced out the rear window to see Charlie, his face averted, marching toward a truck pulling a trailer down the lane to the barn. "Brad—"

"Finish planting your stuff. When you're done, come see me."

That sounded like an order. "Why?"

"Because we need to set some things straight."

AN HOUR LATER, WHEN BRAD returned from a short ride to check on a well, he saw that Gabriella had finished her planting spree. An idea formed. One she'd hate but would cut through the defenses she built up every time she came within a few feet of a horse.

Spying her talking to Charlie near the corral beside the barn doors, he guided Major through the rear opening to emerge within a few feet of Gabriella.

Hoping his plan worked, Brad wrapped a thick arm around her waist and lifted her onto the horse, onto his lap, ignoring her shriek of surprise. "What are you—Put me down!"

Major sidestepped several times and shook his head but Brad stayed in total control. *"Stop."* He said it soft and low, but she heeded it immediately. He knew the result was mostly out of fear of what the animal would do but he didn't care. "Throw your leg over the horn."

"Put me *down*."

He wasn't a cruel man. But Gabriella wasn't making any progress on conquering her fear and more than anything he wanted her to trust him. Needed her to trust him. Sometimes trust could be built over time but he'd learned from Zane that sometimes, trust had to come about the hard way—by being thrown into a situation. "Put your leg over the horn." He tightened his grip on her waist, holding her securely so she would understand nothing was going to happen.

Gabriella stiffened her legs and attempted to slide off but Brad put Major in motion.

"S-stop. Brad, please." Her nails dug into his arm. "What are you doing?"

"Can't be too comfortable sittin' the way you are. Toss your leg over the saddle and settle down in front of me. I've got you, Gabriella. We're going to ride up the road a bit toward Liam's and come back. That's all."

She glared at him, her lower lip trembling. "I thought we'd c-come to a-an agreement. Getting along."

"We are."

"I hate you right now."

"I don't doubt you do." Aware too many eyes were upon them, he managed to keep from pressing a kiss to her stubborn mouth. "You'll thank me in the end. I promise you that. Lift your leg over the horn."

Carefully, clutching his arm so tightly that she nearly broke the skin, Gabriella shifted her leg up and over. "Why are you doing this? I don't understand why you care whether or not I ride a horse."

"I care," he said, unable to admit more. He didn't want to be that guy laughed at by the hot girl he'd asked out. Not again. But admitting more wasn't going to be easy despite the surprise make-out session at the truck.

Major's slow pace and the call of the birds in the trees filled the silence as he searched for words to talk to her the way a man should. She was probably used to pretty words. Clearing his throat, he inhaled the scent of her hair. "I didn't expect to like you. You surprised me, Gabriella." His words were met with silence so he added, "Just relax."

"You're insane if you think I can relax on this thing."

"Chance is the insane one," he said, trying to make conversation since she hadn't responded to his admission of *like*.

You sounded like a teenager admitting his first crush. No man says they like *someone.*

"Why do you say that?"

"He's into extreme sports. Some of the things he does makes my hair stand on end."

Shifting the reins into the hand attached to the arm around her, he raised his other hand and pointed overhead.

"Look at that."

She grabbed his arm and yanked it back into position, her fingers gripping his so that his palm rested below her breast.

Well, all right, then. Now they were getting somewhere. Almost. She was stiff as a board. "Take a deep breath, Gabriella. Feel how the horse is moving? Tune in and go with the flow."

"I'd rather walk."

Her hair caught in his whiskers when he adjusted his head next to hers to better hear her. "Tell me about Molly."

"What do you want to know?"

"What was she like?"

"Nice. Funny and smart. Loyal. I sound like I'm describing a beloved pet but Moll— What you saw was what you got and I loved her for it."

"You trusted her."

"Implicitly. She's the only person who never, ever let me down. We shared everything. Molly was like a sister to me. That friend you could call no matter what time of day and she'd drop everything to listen."

"Zane said you two had fun in Europe that summer you were sixteen. He got quite a few gray hairs hearing about how you snuck away to see U2."

She leaned her head against his shoulder and tilted her face toward his long enough to actually smile. "I still have the T-shirt."

The horse tossed its head impatiently, used to a faster pace, but Brad didn't give Major his lead. Getting Gabriella on the horse was enough for today.

"Do you always go this slow?"

"Not quite."

"But you are for me?"

"Until you know I would do everything in my power to keep you safe, we'll take it a step at a time."

"Because of Zane."

"Because of you, Gabriella."

They topped the rise where Liam's driveway veered to the left and Brad swung the horse around to make the return ride.

Gabriella had to adjust her weight with the downward slope of the land but she leaned into him as she should and didn't comment on the slide of his thumb up and down on her side. She was tall and thin but solid, and he liked the thought that she could handle him.

"Why can't we ride together to the falls?"

The fact that she wouldn't mind riding double wasn't lost on him. "It's too far. We'd injure the horse." And it would kill him. He was getting as tense as Major but for an altogether different reason.

"I could hike part of the way."

"Too far. Gabriella, why did you kiss me?"

"Are you complaining?"

"No, definitely not."

"I suppose you're feeling guilty again because of Zane."

He should. But he didn't. "I've been thinking about what you said. I don't think Zane wanted you here because of guilt. I think he's trying to make up for what he didn't give you growing up."

"That's the same thing."

"Not necessarily."

"Why are you defending him? It's wrong, coming from you. You don't want me here but you want to have sex with me. Do you think I don't know that?"

They rode in silence. Nearing the barn and the area where he'd snatched her up in front of him, Brad brushed his lips against her hair. "I want to be with you. But that's not all. That's not *why*. Sometimes a man simply makes peace with the hand he's dealt."

"And that means what?"

He walked Major over to the ramp they used to load cattle for transport and tightened his grip on her waist to lower her, aware that the ranch hands who had been there earlier weren't around. "It means, I'm not minding you being here anymore." Leaning low, he kept his hold on her long enough to brush a soft kiss over her lips. "I've made my peace with that."

CHAPTER TWENTY-ONE

BRAD'S WORDS STAYED WITH Gabriella the rest of the day. So much so Crystal had sent her worried looks and followed Gabriella around the house, repeatedly asking what was wrong. She had gone to bed early to get away from her mother, even though she knew she'd be staring at the ceiling once more.

What exactly did making peace with her being there mean? That Brad was ready for them to take the next step? Was she reading too much into his words?

She mulled over the questions and doubts and feelings a long time before finally saying a prayer for peace and falling asleep. She imagined she was on the horse in front of Brad again. This time the gentle sway of the horse coincided with the meandering of Brad's strong hands, and his order to shift her leg over the saddle was to reposition so that she faced him. He kissed her and showed her exactly how possible the impossible was.

Gabriella awoke, her cheeks hot, her body uncomfortable. What a dream.

She climbed out of bed to go to the bathroom, her gaze drawn to Brad's open bedroom door.

On her way back, his door was still open. Gabriella peeked over the stair railing. The lights were on in the kitchen.

She was halfway down the stairs when her mind asked, *What are you doing, Ella?*

The kitchen was empty but a peek out the window revealed light coming from the barn. At this hour? It could only mean one thing.

Heart thumping, she hurried to her room and pulled a jogging suit over her pajamas, found shoes. Then she was out the door and running toward the structure.

Sure enough Brad stood with his elbows braced against the gate of the largest stall, the sound of heavy panting and grunts loud in the quiet barn. When he heard her enter he turned.

"You're in time. I was going to wake you but didn't want to leave yet."

Despite her earlier upset with him Gabriella couldn't help but smile as she approached. Inside the stall, Pikipsi was on her side in the straw bed, laboring through a contraction.

The sight stopped Gabriella cold. The animal was massive and frightening but at the moment she was helpless and in pain. Who couldn't feel empathy for that? "Is she okay? Shouldn't you call a vet?"

"She's doing fine. The vet's on alert but this isn't my first foaling."

"You sound so calm."

He smiled at her, his craggy face softening. "I might not know a lot about people and relationships, but I know animals."

When Pikipsi let out a low groan, Gabriella's eyes prickled with tears and a sickening twist of her stomach had her wrapping her arms around herself. Swallowing, she studied the barn, breathing through her mouth.

Brad drew her in front of him and put his arms around her.

"I'm still mad at you about today," she whispered.

"I know." He breathed the words into her ear and Gabriella shivered.

Minutes passed, the silence broken only by Pikipsi.

"She'll be fine, Gabriella. Relax." He shifted so that he could massage her shoulders and back and she welcomed the relief.

She took only quick peeks at the scene in the stall. It was gross and nasty, heartbreaking, yet totally fascinating. Bracing herself for another look, she gaped. "There's a hoof."

Brad's deep chuckle filled her ear. "Let's pray there are four of them."

Gabriella closed her eyes several times during the process but couldn't help but laugh when it was all over. "That's amazing. I mean, it was thoroughly disgusting, but look at her."

"She's a little beauty. That blaze on her forehead matches her socks. She's marked up really nice and distinguishable."

His excitement was contagious. He grinned like a proud daddy, going on about how beautiful the colt was. His words reminded her of his plans—ranching, family, kids.

She'd spent the past hour or so in his arms, secure in his embrace. But it was temporary. All of this was temporary. As soon as the three months were over or until Alicia had an unmanageable crisis…

The only thing Gabriella knew for certain was that she would miss this place. This man.

Pikipsi was on her feet with a roll of her massive body, towering over the tiny colt and doing her motherly duties of sniffing and cleaning.

"So, what do you say? You want to name it?"

"In exchange for learning to ride? No."

Brad's gaze narrowed, a sexy grin quirking his lips in a smile she found way too tantalizing. "I owe you for today. It was a low trick to pull you on the horse. But I had to prove that you could handle it. And you did. How about you ride with me every day, let me teach you so we can go see the falls? In exchange, you can name her. Look at her, Gabriella. She'll grow fast. She could be your horse when you come back to visit."

Come back to visit? Longing rocketed through her. Oh, that was sneaky. "You admitted *you owe me*."

Brad lifted his hand and stroked her hair away from her cheek. "Do you like being afraid?"

She hated it. Hated knowing when push came to shove, the beautiful animal in the stall now taking such gentle care of her baby terrified her.

"Look at them, Gabriella. See how gentle she is? How motherly? How can you call either of them beasts?"

Maybe the colt wasn't one now but it would grow up to be one. Then again, Gabriella had never had a horse, and as a little girl with a cowboy daddy she'd always wanted one. Until that fateful day, she'd been horse crazy, with posters of them on her wall, on the covers of her notebooks.

Did she dare try again? Let Brad help her? Fear hammered at her insides. "Fine."

"What was that?" He dipped his head as though to hear her better.

"I said *fine*. I'll do it. And you can't change whatever I name her."

"Can I make a suggestion?"

"No. Whatever I decide goes." She poked a finger into his chest. "Even if I name it something weird like— like Elvis Stardust Picklesymer."

He snagged her finger and lifted it to his mouth,

brushing his lips over her knuckle. "Deal. We'll start after we both get some sleep."

The images from her dream flashed through her head. Apparently Brad was able to decipher them—or at least the heat that rushed into her face as a result.

He exhaled, the sound rough. *"Gabriella."*

She tilted her head to the side and wet her lower lip, liking how his gaze followed the movement and immediately glittered with heat.

"You look at me like that but you don't want to want me, do you?" she asked.

"We have a lot standing in the way."

"Only if we let it," she said, surprising herself.

"I can't take advantage if you're not planning on staying."

Meaning if she were, he'd want more?

She wasn't brave enough to ask that question. Wasn't today full of surprises, though. "Most men would take whatever is offered. They'd think it the perfect setup."

In a quick move Brad lowered his head, captured her mouth and kissed her like a man about to face a firing squad.

All she could do was hold on and feel. She'd *never* responded to anyone this way. Ever.

Then as quickly as the kiss had begun, it was over.

He tore himself away, his breath sounding ragged. The look in his eyes one of suppressed longing.

"Why did you stop?"

Taking one last long taste, he pulled away. "Because I want more than sex with you."

"Because of Zane." She sighed.

"Because I can't look at you and not wonder what it would be like. What *we* would be like."

It was a nice thought but their lives were too different. And it made her think Brad was more of a romantic than she was. "Temporary things aren't all bad," she whispered. "Think of a cold. You're sick, yeah, but you get to stay home, sleep in, watch television. Sometimes temporary is good."

"Maybe I'm not most men, but I won't treat you—Zane's daughter or not—like that."

His sense of honor ran deep. No, he wasn't most men.

"Gabriella, I want a woman who isn't so ready to settle that she gives up something bigger."

Bigger? Meaning what? More? With him? But that wasn't possible. Didn't he see that?

CHAPTER TWENTY-TWO

No mention of attending church had been made this week but when Brad came downstairs the following morning, Gabriella was ready.

Crystal decided to stay home, but made a point that she'd expect their return immediately following the services. He noticed that Gabriella quickly agreed and frowned at the way she allowed Crystal to control her. He'd thought they could eat at the diner in town, just the two of them. Instead he would bring her straight home. Although, maybe they could begin her riding lessons.

Liam had to work but Carly and Riley were sitting in Zane's pew. Chance was a no-show, and Brad wasn't surprised. A pretty day like today meant Chance was out climbing, even though his ribs hadn't yet healed from his last injury. Would he ever conquer whatever demon drove him, Brad wondered? And if so, at what cost?

After the service was over, Gabriella invited Carly and Riley to the ranch to see the colt and came up with the idea of an impromptu picnic. Sunday was the only day he had any time to spend quality time with Gabriella but he wasn't about to protest the invitation since it was obvious Carly and Gabriella got along. He might not know much about women but he knew enough that Gabriella needed someone to talk to after losing Molly. And any friendship she formed here was a good thing.

They'd stopped at Frank's Grocery on the way home to pick up fried chicken and egg salad for sandwiches. While Carly and Gabriella prepared a basket, Brad wandered into the den, relieved to see Chance there working on the books rather than climbing. "Missed you today."

"Overslept and thought I'd get this done."

"How'd we do this week?"

Chance had a pen in his hand and waved it in the air. "We did fine. Great, actually. But I hope you're not planning on eating much over the next twenty years. Taking this much out of the accounts leaves you with nothing to work with. Adding in two more mouths to feed doesn't help expenses, either."

"Neither one of them eat much," Brad said.

"No, I imagine not. But you could at least have Crystal paying for her keep. Telling her she had to might be a good way of getting rid of her. No luck with Crystal convincing Gabriella to leave?"

"No." And he refused to admit why he was fine with that.

"What's it like being under the same roof as Zane's ex?"

He thought of his conversations with Crystal and frowned. "She sticks to Gabriella like glue when I'm around but keeps to herself and reads screenplays otherwise. I think she's afraid to get dirty or risk some sun—she never moves beyond the porch."

"So you're not getting any alone time with Gabriella?"

"Some," Brad admitted, knowing Chance had spent enough time with them at the Honey to be perfectly aware of his growing feelings.

Laughter filtered in from the kitchen, and Brad

smiled in response. Carly and Gabriella were having fun, whatever they were doing.

"It's picnic time. The girls want Riley to see the colt. I talked to Liam on the way home. He's going to swing by to eat then head out on patrol again. You coming?"

"I finished as you came in the door."

Chance followed Brad to the kitchen but Brad stopped in his tracks when he spotted Gabriella opening one of the many delivery boxes she'd received yesterday. She held up a negligee for Carly to see.

"Whoa," Chance murmured as Gabriella fitted the top to her chest to show Carly.

"Watch yourself," Brad warned.

"Advice you should probably take. You know she's not in this for the long haul, right?"

Right. Crystal's interference had made him angry enough to entertain some foolish thoughts about the future, but no matter how interested he was, no matter how rational and logical it would be for him and Gabriella to get together, could he survive putting himself in a no-win situation?

Gabriella had sent his blood pressure soaring last night in the barn. But he wanted the next fifty years to be spent with a house full of kids and grandkids on his knee. He wanted a marriage that turned this house into a home, not some Hollywood-style fling. Unlike Chance, he wasn't a serial dater. He was the guy who asked a woman out only when he really thought they might have a future together. And Gabriella?

Set aside geographical locations and their different takes on Zane, Crystal, vegetarianism and quite a few other things, and Brad saw... Well, he saw that with Gabriella. He saw the possibility of a future. Wanted it as much as he wanted his next breath.

"You're not holding back because of Zane, are you?" Chance asked. "Because if you really care for her, you know he wouldn't have a problem with you being with her."

In the beginning Brad had believed the opposite, but after some soul-searching he knew Chance's words were true.

"I confess I love delivery day," Gabriella said to Carly as she dug inside another box. "It's like Christmas. Here it is. This one is perfect for you and looks to be the right size. Take it."

"Seriously?" Carly asked.

"That's guaranteed to give Liam a heart attack," Chance teased, giving away their presence.

Carly blushed from her neck to her hairline but Gabriella simply laughed.

"I smell chicken," Chance said, nudging Brad out of the way to enter the kitchen. He rubbed his hands together in anticipation. "What's this I hear about a picnic?"

"Almost ready," Gabriella said. "We got a bit sidetracked."

"I can see why," Chance said, poking a finger into the box and coming out with a leopard-print thong.

Gabriella found whatever it was she was looking for and held it up. "Here it is. I know redheads don't often like to wear pink, Carly, but what about this one? I love it. It's one of my all-time favorites."

Gabriella held up a negligee by the tiny straps. The bright pink material was silky in texture and left little to the imagination. Combined with her hair, Gabriella looked like a piece of cotton candy—his favorite indulgence at the state fair.

"Oh, that's beautiful, but I don't know about the pink. I like this one better, I think," Carly said.

"I know someone who likes it," Chance murmured, staring at Brad and drawing the others' attention to him.

Bold as ever, Gabriella gave him a smile that socked him in the gut.

The sound of Crystal's heels on the stairs broke the tension in the room. Flashing him another smile, Gabriella tossed the garment in the box and she and Carly grabbed drinks from the fridge.

He needed some air—or a cold shower. "I'm going to go check on the colt. You got a name for it yet?"

"I think so."

"Good." Naming the colt meant she intended to stick to the agreement. Learn to ride.

Come back to visit?

He didn't know which would be worse—never seeing Gabriella again, or seeing her enough to always want more. Brad suddenly understood why Zane had all those pictures.

BY MIDAFTERNOON EVERYONE was stuffed. Gabriella and Carly sat on a blanket beneath a shade tree near the McKenna cemetery, watching as Brad, Chance and Riley walked Liam to his patrol car. The sun was shining, clouds dotted the sky like white marshmallows, and the fresh scent of grass and pine and wildflowers tinged the air.

Down below, Pikipsi was in the corral with her baby, and Gabriella couldn't take her eyes off the colt as it ran and jumped and played.

"Gabriella?"

She glanced at Carly and found the other woman staring at her, a too-serious expression on her face considering how nice the afternoon had been. "Something wrong?"

"You tell me. You seem awfully intense."

"Just thinking."

"About Brad?"

Gabriella didn't answer because there wasn't really a need to.

"Gabriella, I like you. A lot. This afternoon was more fun than I ever thought it could be so soon after Zane's death. But something is obviously going on between you and Brad and, as much as I like you, I'm going to be really angry if you hurt him."

"I don't want to hurt him."

Carly shifted onto her knees to load the remains of lunch into the picnic basket and cooler. "Good. Because Brad's their rock now that Zane is gone. Yet as strong as he is, sometimes I wonder if he's not the most vulnerable."

"What do you mean?"

"You already know how much this ranch means to him. If you take the ranch *and* break his heart...I'm not sure he could recover from that."

Gabriella grabbed the paper plates and put them in the small trash bag they'd brought. "Nothing's happened between us. We've kissed. That's all."

Carly seemed disbelieving, but didn't call Gabriella on it. "It's enough. Look, you're part of this family. Whether you stay or go, that's a fact. But before anything beyond a few kisses happens, consider all the ramifications and the impact your actions are going to have on Brad."

Gabriella shoved herself to her feet, the basket in her hand. "I will."

"Good. Because today was fun. Wouldn't it be nice if it was the norm?"

Gabriella watched as Carly made the trek to the house. Riley saw her coming and ran up the sloping hill toward her, his little face smiling from ear to ear. Such an endearing sight, like something from a movie.

What would it be a like? Sunday afternoon picnics with family, children—Carly's and hers playing together.

Gabriella turned her head away from the pretty picture of Riley running into Carly's arms and her dropping the basket to pick up Riley and swing him around.

Gabriella's gaze landed on Zane's headstone. "What have you done?"

AFTER EVERYONE HAD LEFT, Brad was in the barn saddling Star Bright when Gabriella appeared, dressed to ride as promised.

He tried to be content with the fact she had shown up without complaint, but all he could focus on once they were astride the horse was the way she squirmed. The breeze carried the scent of her hair to him, filling his lungs. "Take the reins."

"What? No. I don't need to hold them." She fisted her hands to avoid holding the leather.

"I'm right here with you. Nothing is going to happen."

"What are you going to do?"

"Relax and enjoy the ride. Sunday's my day of rest. Let me rest, would you?"

Obviously reluctant, she opened her palms and allowed him to show her the correct way of guiding the horse.

With his hands free Brad found himself at a loss as

to where to put them. Finally he settled them on her waist, his pinky fingers sliding into the seam of where her hips and thighs met.

He heard her shaky inhale. As quickly, his mind focused on how she felt, his thumbs flexed and his hands slid up to brush the underside of her breasts.

Apparently he was a masochist. How else could he explain shutting her down the other night but being unable to stop himself from touching her?

As they ambled along, he took in his surroundings. The blue sky stretching on above their heads, the green valley and the mountains ahead of them. Fresh air, a beautiful woman. He felt a sense of contentment and excitement he hadn't felt for a long time.

"You're so quiet it's making me nervous. Say something," she said.

"What do you want to talk about? Five-year plans?"

"No."

"When's your mother leaving?"

A laugh bubbled out of her chest. "I don't know. What is that?" She held the reins tightly but lifted a finger to point at the hay almost ready to cut. "Tell me about haying. Why did everyone get in a panic when it looked like it would rain?"

He squeezed her waist a little tighter—yep, he was definitely a masochist—then he taught her a little more about ranching.

CHAPTER TWENTY-THREE

WHEN THEY RETURNED TO the barn, Brad stopped alongside the corral. "Time for your next lesson."

"What do you mean?" Gabriella asked, her heart skipping a beat.

"I'm going to get off. You're going to stay on and keep riding."

"What? No. No way." She tried to throw her leg over the pommel but he held her in place.

"I'll lead you. Real slow. Just stay seated."

The thudding in her chest became so fast and strong she felt ill. "I don't want to do this. We've done enough for today."

"You trust me, Gabriella. Hold on to that a little harder."

Instead of helping her off the way any nice guy would do, he grasped the bridle and began walking the perimeter of the corral.

Air was hard to come by. Gabriella closed her eyes and gripped the saddle horn until her fingers ached. The horse's constant shifting, every clump of its hooves, made it seem as though she would fly off face-first.

It was a long way down.

By the time Brad made the circle twice, her legs ached from trying to keep her balance.

"Keep going." He fastened a long rope to the horse's bridle.

"What?"

"I'll hold on to the lead but you are to keep going. Understand?"

"Brad—"

"You can do this. I have you, see?" He showed her how he gripped the rope. "All you have to do is guide her."

They made several more painstakingly slow trips around the corral.

"I'm doing it," Gabriella breathed, her head pounding due to the stress and sheer terror pumping through her with every beat of her heart. "I'm actually doing it."

"It's not me." He grinned at her, causing her heart to race even more. He was so sexy, big lug that he was.

"You ready to try it without me holding the lead?"

She immediately shook her head.

"Come on, sweetheart. Make one circle the same as you've been doing. I'll be right here waiting for you."

She glanced around and wished she hadn't. The men were returning from the weekend and had gathered to watch. Her nerves were pulled taut but her pride kicked in. She hated being led around like a little girl or stuck riding double because everyone now knew she was too scared to do it on her own. "Okay. Okay." She scrounged for courage. "I'll do it."

"Thatta girl. You ready?"

She clenched her jaw and nodded. She might not have any teeth left to grind once the circle was made but she was going to face her fear, one way or the other.

Brad handed her the lead to hold along with the reins and stepped away from the horse. She gulped a deep breath, encouraged by his nods of approval and the words of encouragement from her audience.

With a little nudge, the horse began to walk. At this

rate it would be midnight before they completed the circuit but Gabriella didn't dare go faster.

They made it to the one-sixteenth point, the eighth. Nearly to the halfway mark, Gabriella felt a little braver and urged Star Bright to pick up the pace a tad. The horse responded immediately and she bounced a bit out of rhythm until she found her seat.

"That's it. Keep going," Brad called.

Smiling, *so* proud of herself, she approached the three-quarter mark when a loud *bang* rang out. Star Bright whinnied and shifted sideways into the middle of the corral. Gabriella panicked, unsure of what to do and pulled on the reins hard, desperate to stop.

In response Star Bright reared and Gabriella went flying through the air. In the blink of an eye the ground raced toward her and she landed hard.

"Gabriella!" Brad skidded to a stop next to her.

Gabriella moaned and tried to catch her breath, shaking so hard she felt like a human earthquake.

"Are you all right?"

All right? "No." This was stupid. What was she thinking, letting him talk her into getting on a horse? Riding by herself? She could have been trampled, broken her neck.

"You sound okay."

She rolled over, every part of her body aching from humiliation if not pain.

"What are you gonna to do?" Charlie asked, his voice grim.

"Anything broken?" Brad demanded.

It took a moment for her to catch her breath and assess. "I don't think so."

"Good. Charlie, bring her over here."

Since Gabriella was the only *her* there other than Star

Bright, she looked up and saw Charlie leading the horse toward them. "What are you doing? Keep her away."

"It's not her fault you couldn't hold your seat."

"*She* threw *me* off!"

"You pulled the reins too hard and hurt her mouth. You lost control. Added to the noise, she got scared and reared."

She stared at Brad, incredulous. "You're defending the *horse?* Are you serious?"

He tugged her to her feet and refused to let go. "You're getting back on."

"Not bloody likely."

One minute she was on her feet and the next she was on the back of a trembling Star Bright. Curses streamed from her lips and she called Brad every creative name she could think of, earning chuckles from the men.

"You done yet? Because you're making it worse. Star Bright needs reassurance from you that you're not going to hurt her. Cussin' me out isn't doing it."

"It makes me feel good."

"Gabriella—"

"I want off *now.*"

"Don't you dare move."

She couldn't do this. As much as she wanted to be brave and strong and one of those gung-ho women, she wasn't. Not when it came to this. "Brad, please," she said in a bare whisper. "Let me *down.*"

"You're going to stay on that horse and ride her around the corral one more time if I have to tie you to the saddle. Now calm down and get going or we'll be here all night."

They all watched her. The men muttered to themselves and shook their heads and she hated seeing them look at her that way. Chance had entered the corral and approached them, covered in grease.

"Gabriella, I'm sorry," Chance said. "I was trying to get Zane's tractor running and it backfired."

"She's fine," Brad insisted.

"I hate you," she said to Brad. "Let me down."

"Use that hate to get you around the circle. One time, Gabriella. One time and you can get off."

"When I get my inheritance, I'm going to sell it to *piss you off* for doing this to me," she added meanly, too angry to guard her words.

His expression tightened but he didn't call her on her threat. "All night, Gabriella. Get going and don't jump off or I'll put you right back on."

She knew what he was doing. Everyone had heard the saying but who knew people took it literally? She couldn't move, couldn't breathe. She *hurt*.

"If you don't do this now, you'll be afraid forever. You that much of a coward, sweetheart?"

Gabriella glared at Brad, ignored Chance and the others, but gave Star Bright a gentle nudge.

She made no effort to go to the outside edge. Instead she prodded the horse around the center of the corral in a short circle. When she'd made it within a few feet of where Brad waited, she stopped the horse, slid off and tried not to limp as she walked to the gate. "I'm not your damned sweetheart."

Crystal greeted Gabriella when she stomped into the house. "Gabriella, what happened to you?"

"The horse threw me."

"*What?* Are you all right? Where's Brad?"

Gabriella climbed the stairs slowly, feeling each and every one of them. "I don't know. I don't care. He left me on the horse alone and then said it was my fault because she threw me."

"That, my dear, is a typical man. Oh, thank God you weren't seriously injured."

For all her flaws, her mother's concern was evident. The tender tone reminded Gabriella of her childhood, living in a condo and playing on the sidewalk. With every stubbed toe, skinned knee and boo-boo, her mother had been there, kissing them to make them better.

"I want to make sure you're okay." Crystal followed Gabriella.

Had these stairs always been this steep?

"Oh, darling, haven't you had enough? I understand why you wanted to come, why you wanted to know more about your father. But are you finally ready to go home?"

Gabriella wanted to say yes. She opened her mouth but the word wouldn't come no matter how much she tried to force it out. "I'm not a quitter. I *can't* quit."

"You know I've always tried to be supportive of your ideas," her mother said in a chiding tone, "but I think it's best if we *leave*. Molly would understand and you would still have the hundred thousand. And my offer stands to back you on the rest of what you need."

It was about more than the money now. Even more than getting to know Zane. Brad had embarrassed her; maybe pride was a sin but she had plenty of it.

Maybe that was his goal. Maybe he wanted her to leave and by shoving her back on that horse he'd hoped to accomplish his goal. Maybe in the beginning he'd tolerated her. Maybe he'd come to *make peace with it,* but now that she was getting closer to inheriting, maybe he was willing to do anything to keep that from happening.

She couldn't give up now. She was four and a half weeks away from owning a piece of land worth a million dollars.

This is for you, Moll. Every last bruise, every name I called him. I'm going to make our dream come true, I promise you.

Finally she made it to the top of the stairs and headed into the bathroom. She wanted a hot bath with her scented soaps and she planned to stay there all evening. Fighting with Brad, fighting with her mother—yeah, not how she wanted to spend her day.

"I'll do that," her mother said, shooing Gabriella away and turning on the tap to fill the tub. "What scent?"

"That one." Her arm hurt when she lifted it to point.

In seconds the air smelled of rosemary, juniper, lavender, lemon and wintergreen, all scents that promoted relaxation.

Gabriella sat on the toilet seat and tried to toe her shoes off.

"Let me." Crystal dropped to her knees.

"Mom, don't."

"Oh, hush. Gabriella, I don't care about my clothes. Haven't you figured out by now that I'm here for you?" She pulled off Gabriella's shoes. "Because I love you? I don't care about a little dirt. Not when my baby is hurt."

"I love you, too."

Crystal got the second shoe and sock off and stood to help remove Gabriella's jeans.

"Ow."

"I'm sorry."

"It's okay. My muscles are getting stiff. Thanks. I'll get the rest," Gabriella murmured.

Crystal turned and checked the water temperature. "A little warm but I think you need it that way. When I was injured on the set I spent hours in the tub. It will help."

"Thanks, Mom."

"You're welcome. Gabriella, I know you don't want to hear this, but I hope what happened today makes you reconsider staying."

"I have to stay but you don't. You can leave anytime you want."

"Oh, Gabriella. I couldn't leave you back then, what makes you think I could leave you now?" Her mother opened the bathroom door but made no effort to leave. "I suppose this is as good a time as any to tell you that I contacted Richard Meredith. Remember him? He played Dr. Felix in *Sands of Time?*"

"Vaguely." She didn't have a clue. Nor did she care. The water called to her.

"He's in real estate now and doing quite well despite the economy. I told him about your inheritance. He said if you sign with him he can almost guarantee you ten percent more than the listing price."

Almost guarantee, huh? "Mom—"

"If you are determined to stay here, you need to put the wheels in motion, Gabriella. That's all I'm saying."

"I know. But right now all I want is a bath. Everything else will have to wait."

"Just say you'll call him. He was quite excited at the prospect. According to him, he has several European clients wanting a piece of the Wild West."

"Fine. I will." What else could she say?

CHAPTER TWENTY-FOUR

THE MOMENT BRAD ENTERED the den that evening Gabriella glared at him. "Close the door."

He complied, one thick eyebrow lifting high on his forehead. "How do you feel?"

"How do you think I feel? Like I hit the ground at twenty miles an hour. I hurt all over, which means I definitely won't be getting any sleep and it's your fault. So do you know what that means?"

"No."

"You get to be miserable with me." She held up a deck of cards. "Blackjack?"

Brad walked over to a chest and grabbed a bottle of lotion. "Use this. It'll help. If you run out, look around. There are tubes stashed all over the house."

"What is it? It'll probably turn me blue or green or splotchy. You think I haven't noticed that you *like* torturing me?"

"Gabriella, I'm sorry about today but you had to get back on."

"No, I didn't, and you had no right to force me."

He stepped close and snagged her elbows in his hands. He ran his hands up and down her arms, finally settling on her shoulders at the base of her neck where he began to massage. She melted in an instant, barely managing to keep her mouth shut so he wouldn't hear her sound of pleasure.

"Be honest. Are you really sorry I did?" He lowered his head until his nose touched hers. "Even though you were afraid, you *rode* her. By yourself. Doesn't that feel good?"

She stared at him, torn between wanting to hit him for putting her on the horse and wanting to hit him for being right about how she felt. That was how confused she was. Soaking in the tub until she resembled a prune had given her plenty of time to acknowledge the significance of what he'd done—of what she'd done. But it didn't make the act any less acceptable to her, not in the mood she was in. "I still hate you. And don't grin at me like that, damn it."

Even as she said the words, her pulse thrummed in her ears, drowning out everything around them. She saw his smile widen and oh, how it made her heart squeeze.

"Some folks say love and hate go hand in hand." His calloused fingertip brushed her lower lip before he stepped away. "Use the lotion. It'll help."

"You're playing cards with me."

"Gabriella, if I do anything with you, it won't be playing cards."

She hadn't expected so blunt an admission. In response she loosened the belt of her robe and opened it to reveal her tight tank and boy shorts. "You owe me." She tossed him the tube. "Consider it punishment."

It was an underhanded move. Hot guy, a girl, a private room. Brad wanted her and she knew it.

"Gabriella—"

"I can handle it if you can."

"Sweetheart, I dream about handling you."

She had to be honest. Guys who put it on the line

that way were the best thing since body glue and high heels.

Her ex Samuel had cheated on her with his twenty-year-old secretary-porn star. Gabriella had caught them in his office where he'd tied the girl up—using the tie Gabriella had bought him for his birthday.

So she knew a thing or two about regrets.

This wouldn't be one. She'd gotten to know Brad well enough to like what she saw. Living with someone had a way of making quick work of the getting-to-know-you phase.

Sitting in that tub had given her lots of time to think. One of Molly's regrets had been that she hadn't found a nice guy and had those kids she wanted. And Gabriella admitted how lonely it was to work all day helping other people find their romantic side, then go home to her empty apartment.

The fact Brad had forced her on a horse today? She couldn't qualify her feelings as love or hate. More somewhere in between. Something strong and fierce. He'd known how important it was to her that she didn't fail but when she couldn't find the courage in herself, he'd done the only thing that *made* her find it.

His gaze remained fixed on her mouth for a long moment. But when their eyes locked, he brushed his lips over hers once, twice, before settling firmly and parting her mouth with a bold stroke of his tongue that made her toes curl into the carpet. His hands settled on her shoulders and neck once more, smoothed down her back. She flinched.

"You really are sore."

Gabriella drew his lower lip between hers and sucked on it. "Kiss it and make me better."

"Where?"

"My, um, side and…ass." She said it deliberately, her last shot to get even with him.

With a twinkle of amusement sparkling in his eyes, Brad pressed another kiss to her lips. "Lie down. Face-down."

"Kinky," she said with a grin. She couldn't think straight due to lack of oxygen as she moved to the old leather couch and lowered herself to the surface. She glanced over her shoulder and while she couldn't see Brad clearly, she felt him watching her. She was a strong woman, bold. Take-charge. But here? Now?

Here she was a woman heart-thumpingly attracted to the wrong kind of man. And she wouldn't walk away from the experience whole. Not when her pulse jumped looking at him even though she was still ticked off about today. It didn't make any sense. But then…love never did, did it?

She managed to squelch a gasp at the thought but before she had time to recover her composure from her mind-blowing revelation, his hand caressed her back and she heard the sound of the lotion cap being flipped up.

What kind of man was he? Considerate enough to warm the lotion or insensitive enough not to care? Maybe that should be her deciding factor.

The liquid squirted—but not on her.

He worked the hand-warmed lotion into her sore muscles. She pressed her face into the softness of the cushion and moaned.

"Good or bad?"

"Good." Definitely good. And the way she was so aware of his denim-clad legs beside her?

The next few minutes consisted of nothing but her melting as he massaged her, paying extra attention to her lower back after he lifted the tank top out of his way. Eventually he moved lower still and she stifled a short scream of pleasure-pain when he palmed both cheeks outside her shorts and squeezed. Who knew her behind could be an erogenous zone?

Brad moved on to her legs but returned to her bruised behind several times, his breathing getting rough and ragged, matching her own.

He leaned low over the bruised area, pressing a sweet, soft kiss to each cheek before sliding his lips up her back to her ear and ordering her to roll over.

BRAD'S HANDS SHOOK as he helped Gabriella turn. She'd gone from being tense and tender to relaxing beneath his ministrations. Now she stared at him with a drowsy, seductive expression that rocked him clear to his soul. No matter how many times he ordered himself to leave, to let her go, he couldn't force himself to do it. Not again.

He leaned over and took her mouth in a kiss so hot he thought he'd combust. Her hands pulled at his shirt and he sat up long enough to yank it over his head.

Gabriella reached for him but, given their positions, she could only touch his chest and stomach. She trailed one fingertip down the line of hair disappearing into his pants, her lips parting, every breath a pant that made him hunger for her more.

His hand slipped under her top and covered her ribs, moving up, tugging the material along until she was bare. He stroked his thumb over her pebbled tip and relished her gasp before he covered her with his mouth. Gabriella arched her back and sought more. His entire body was on fire with need for her.

"Brad?" Her hands pulled at him, tried to move him over her.

Gentling his caress to one last tantalizing lick, he shifted his attention to her other breast, nuzzling the tip, playing peekaboo with the material of her top. "Take it off."

Gabriella stilled but she didn't disobey his request. The moment the material was over her face he lowered his head again and kissed her, sucking her into his mouth while sliding his hand down her side and between her legs.

She issued a sharp, needy whimper. *"Brad."*

"You're sure?" He was. Right then he knew what he had to do.

She swallowed audibly and nodded.

He kissed her mouth in approval, nipped the skin of her neck and removed her underwear. That done, he began to explore her body like a man starved, touching, tasting. He parted her legs with his hand, stroked her until Gabriella's eyes closed and she gripped his arm. Seeing her that way, so vulnerable, so beautiful…

Not taking any chances, he continued stroking her, alternating his caresses, the depth of them, until she arched and gasped and came with a barely muffled cry that had him grinding his teeth to keep from making a fool of himself.

He found his wallet and pulled a recent addition from the folds, then quickly shucked what was left of his clothes. Knowing the couch wouldn't accommodate his frame, he plucked Gabriella from the cushions and settled her on his lap, his heart galloping out of control when she took over and positioned herself.

"Mmm. That feels good."

That it did. Her body welcomed him home and Brad

helped her establish a slow pace that rocked her to the point of interest once more, until she arched against him, clutching at his shoulders.

Before long the tension became too much and he took her gasps in his mouth, her body gripping him so tightly she sent him over the edge until all that existed was the knowledge he didn't ever want to let her go.

CHAPTER TWENTY-FIVE

BRAD WAS ALREADY UP and out of the house when Gabriella awoke the next morning. She could hear his voice outside the bedroom window, talking to Charlie about the tractor and what Chance had done to fix it.

Gabriella shifted and winced when the movement brought immediate pain. Warm from a hot bath and then massaged, she hadn't been all that sore last night by the time she and Brad had snuck upstairs. But today?

She forced herself to sit on the edge of the bed by sheer will, then limped her way to the shower. Thank goodness her mother liked to sleep in. At seven o'clock in the morning, Gabriella knew her presence in Brad's room wouldn't be discovered.

Half an hour later Gabriella emerged from the steam-filled room to spy Brad on his way up the stairs. In his hand was one of her protein shakes.

"Good morning."

She smiled at him, aware of the way he looked at her in the too-short towel. "That for me?"

"It sure as hell isn't for me," he said with a slow grin. "You okay?"

"Yeah."

He leaned a hand against the door frame and lowered his head, kissing her until she loosened her grip on the towel and wrapped her arms around him. She heard a low thump as he set the glass on a nearby table and laughed softly when the towel fell to the floor in a damp heap. "Oops."

"Door's locked. Men are gone. Sally won't be here for another hour."

"My mother will sleep for a while longer thanks to her sleeping pills. But I'm very, very sore," she said with a deliberate pout.

"Best way to get over that is to work it out. Need another massage?"

"I thought you'd never offer."

"I'LL HOLD," GABRIELLA said to Alicia on the phone the following Wednesday. "Go take care of that."

Every day since their night in the den, Brad had insisted she ride Star Bright, and as of that morning, Gabriella had swung herself into the saddle and found her seat all on her own. The horse had proven to be amazingly gentle and steady, patient with Gabriella and her mistakes.

After their rides, she'd fallen into the habit of feeding Star Bright a carrot and currying the horse, discovering the process more relaxing than she'd dreamed possible. It was amazing, considering how terrified she'd been.

While her mother slept in, called her friends to whine about her daughter's stubbornness at staying in Montana, read and practiced the scripts of potential roles, Gabriella spent the time with Merrilee in her garden, tending to the potted plants beginning to grow on the porch, or working. Once the house was quiet at night, Gabriella would sneak into Brad's room and make love with him, then sleep amazingly well in his arms.

She carried her dessert plate into the kitchen and gazed out the window above the sink. The faded red barn had character, the lush green pastures and valley leading up to the mountains in the distance a beauty unmatched. Something here had untied the knot in her stomach and allowed her to relax in a way she hadn't been able to in ages. Better than a beach or a spa ever could.

So was that something nature, or Brad?

"Hello? You still there? Gabriella? I'm back. Did you hang up?"

Alicia's voice pulled Gabriella to the present. "No, I'm here. Sorry, I was daydreaming."

"About your cowboy?"

She glanced into the living room and saw that Crystal was engrossed in a soap opera, miming the words and trying to put a little more drama into the melodrama. "He's not mine," she said, lowering her voice.

"Ooh, you're defensive. And the only reason you'd be defensive is if there *is* something going on. Spill. Have you slept together?"

"Alicia."

"So you have. Was he good?"

"Stop it. I refuse to discuss—"

"So there's something to *discuss?* I am so jealous. Now for the big question—what are you going to do when the time is up? This is a fling, right?"

Leave it to Alicia to get straight to the point. "Of course it is."

"You don't sound so sure."

"I am. What else could it be?" Brad had intimated that he wanted more, but he knew where Gabriella stood on the matter and hadn't said anything since. That meant he'd accepted her decision and changed his mind on taking advantage of the situation, right? So the only thing left to do was take it a day at a time. Lots of adults had relationships like that. Busy lives, busy schedules—long distance. *Welcome to twenty-first century romance.*

She closed her eyes and forced a laugh. A fling. She hated the term, what it stood for, but the truth was the truth. Much like her mother had with Zane, Gabriella had begun a fling with Brad. Maybe she was insane. "I'm not discussing this."

Maybe, if she was forced to hang on to the land for a while, she and Brad could continue as they were. Maybe she could make a few return trips throughout the year. Or not. But if Brad was open to the idea, long distance relationships sometimes worked.

But that's not a fling.

True. And where would it lead in the end? She couldn't possibly give up her life in California. And Brad was a family-oriented kind of guy who would eventually want more and not be satisfied with what she could give him. The three-month deadline would be a natural end to their relationship.

But Brad aside, could *she* handle a casual friendship with him knowing it would lead nowhere?

Shouldn't you have thought about all this before doing something you couldn't change?

"You know, I've paid attention over the past couple years. When you date and it means nothing, you gush. But when you get quiet, like with Sam before we found out what a jerk he is? That's when you're getting serious. This is serious?"

She inhaled, unable to deny the truth. She'd already admitted her love for him to herself. What more proof did she need to know she was over her head? "It's complicated."

It was the only answer to give. Her stay in Montana was way more complicated than she'd ever anticipated. While her instincts were to run and run fast, she couldn't. She had to see this through.

IT WASN'T UNTIL A BRIGHT sunny Friday morning ten days later—nine weeks into her stay—that Brad sprang the news on Gabriella that he'd chosen that day to leave for the waterfall.

Since getting together they'd quickly fallen into an unspoken agreement of not discussing the future. He worked the ranch, she worked her business, and whenever they could be together they would ride or sleep or make love.

But after showering together in the wee hours of the morning and dressing for the day, Gabriella wasn't prepared to find Chance in the kitchen with Brad when she descended the stairs. Liam was there, as well. "Good morning."

A chorus of replies came at her.

"What's going on?"

The kitchen table was covered with duffle bags of what appeared to be food, two sleeping bags, a tent and other odds and ends. The pit of her stomach tightened. "Have I mentioned I don't like surprises?"

Her comment drew a smirk from the typically non-smiling Liam. "Looks like today's not your day, then."

Charlie knocked once on the door to the porch and stepped in without waiting for an invitation. "Horses are ready to go when you are."

Oh, no. This was why Brad had told her to dress comfortably. She'd thought he'd planned another riding lesson and picnic or something.

"Charlie, would you load the horses? Gabriella and I will be out in a little bit."

"I need to get to work. Thanks for the coffee," Liam said. "Gabriella, try to enjoy yourself."

"Um…thanks." But how was that possible, riding as far as they were going to?

"I'll be back here tonight and plan to stick around," Chance added, looking at her. "Dooley's covering things at the store, so I'll keep an eye on your mother."

"Thank you. But maybe we should wait. I have to gather the eggs," Gabriella said, scrambling for an excuse. "Merrilee will be expecting me."

"I'll do that." Chance smiled. "Brad said they need some work done around the house, so I'll tackle that. Don't worry about them."

"But…she's planning on hoeing the corn tomorrow. There's too much for her to do alone."

Both of them looked surprised at her statement. As though they didn't expect her to know or care about such things.

"I'll give her a hand." Chance lifted his chin toward the refrigerator. "Better hurry up and eat before you miss out on the opportunity. Brad's an eat-in-the-saddle kind of guy."

"Chance brought you some riding boots. Go grab two pairs of jeans and some tops. Leave a note for your mother, too," Brad instructed. "Tell her we'll see her on Wednesday."

Wednesday? Today was Friday. Was he serious?

She watched as Chance left the kitchen, focusing on him rather than the man about to make her life miserable in *so* many ways.

Riding to Liam's cabin or around the ranch for an hour wasn't enough to prepare her for the ride to the waterfall, that much she knew.

Brad stood and pulled her close, dropping a kiss on

her forehead before giving her an encouraging smile. "Gabriella, do you trust me?"

"Yes, but—"

"No buts. You're going to be fine. I won't let anything happen to you." His eyes were warm with concern, soft with caring. Had they been anything else maybe she could have argued going this particular weekend rather than the few remaining, but she couldn't.

And being able to go away with him? Where they didn't have to hide and sneak?

She wanted to do this. Had to do this. Not only for herself but for him. If Brad wanted her to see the falls and to spend the time with him, she'd go and face her mother's wrath later. "Where's the paper?"

CHAPTER TWENTY-SIX

IF HE WASN'T SURE OF his feelings for Gabriella before the trip started, by the end of the first day Brad knew she was a keeper. She hadn't complained. Not once. And after a day in the saddle when she'd never spent more than an hour or two at a time in one, he knew she had to be hurting.

That's why he'd pulled her from her horse onto his, cradling her against him to give her a break. He knew how much pain she was in when she didn't complain about that, either.

An hour later at the base of the mountain he drew the horses to a halt at the campsite he and Zane had always used when they made this trip. "Think you can stand?"

All he received as a response was a nod.

In short order, Brad unsaddled the horses and got set for the night. Soon the tent was erected and a fire going. Gabriella hobbled along and did what she could to help but she was visibly exhausted, a fact proven when she climbed into the tent and fell asleep without supper, so tired insomnia wasn't an issue.

Sitting by the fire, Brad stared into the tent and watched the play of light across Gabriella's face. Seconds passed and one thing became more and more clear. He tilted his head back and stared up at the stars. "I hope you're right about this, Zane."

Because it was clear that the ranch wasn't the only thing he stood to lose.

THE NEXT MORNING GABRIELLA was barely awake when Brad encouraged her onto Star Bright. She'd eaten breakfast, thankful for his thoughtfulness in bringing a cooler. On the way to the falls she was able to dine on egg salad and cheese sandwiches he'd packed for her, but once they were there, a cook fire would become a necessity, and for more than simply coffee.

Brad had taken Star Bright's reins and was leading the horse up a steep incline. Gabriella held on for dear life and kept a running prayer in her head Finally they topped the ridge and traveled deeper into a wooded area. The sound of water blended in with the background noises of birds and a determined woodpecker, the repetitive clomp of the hooves, but the roar grew in intensity so she knew they were very close.

Brad turned in the saddle and gave her a smile that warmed her heart.

"Are we there?"

The rush of water over rocks was so loud she had to raise her voice to be heard but a thicket of trees surrounded them. Where was it?

"Keep going. Straight ahead. I'm right behind you."

Excited for the first time since they'd begun this journey, Gabriella put Star Bright into motion, aware the sun was going down because her slower than slow speed meant the ride had taken longer than planned.

She had to duck to avoid branches, shove them out of the way, but there it was. A white wall of water crashing into a pool so blue it made the famed Montana sky pale in comparison.

To say it was picturesque was horribly unfair. It was…heaven on earth. Tall pines stood guard over the lake, the mountain from which the water gushed the master of them all. There were snowcaps in the distance, the valley beside the lake a lush green dotted with wildflowers of all colors.

"I've never seen you speechless."

A laugh bubbled out of her chest. "That's because it's never happened. It's— That's—"

"Special," Brad finished when she couldn't find the words.

Special, majestic. The best gift her father had to offer her. A symbol of the love he hadn't been able to express?

Tears pricked her eyes and she blinked to clear them away. She was tired, *exhausted*. That was the source of her emotions because she wasn't the weepy sort.

But seeing this did indeed give her a better understanding of why Zane loved the Circle M. Why he'd protected it so fiercely.

So why did he give it to you?

They might not have talked often but if Zane kept tabs on her, then he knew how stressful her life was, probably knew she needed people she could trust, a place to escape to.

"You going to sit on that horse all day or get off and explore?" Brad asked, a smile in his voice.

Gabriella swung her leg over the saddle and slid to the ground, her aches and pains present, but not as distracting as the jumbled mess of her mind.

She had a million-dollar deal with Alicia. But how would she ever be able to give this up?

BRAD BUILT A FIRE and set up camp before the sun sank behind the mountain.

Gabriella picked her way around the edge of the lake, stopping every few minutes to stare at the waterfall. He wished he'd brought a camera. Then he remembered the all-in-one phone she was constantly on and snagged it.

The buttons were self explanatory and he took a picture of her staring at the falls, one of her kneeling on the edge peering into the water, one of her walking, head down and lost in thought, back to him. "Something wrong?" he asked after he'd set her phone aside.

"No. Just thinking."

He wanted to ask what about but knew better than to broach the subject.

"What's for dinner?"

"Vegetable soup."

"You really put some thought into this adventure of ours."

"I did," he admitted. "Merrilee helped with the menu." And feeding her along the way was important to Gabriella having strength for…other things.

"What else did you bring?"

The throaty tone in her voice couldn't be ignored and gave him insight that they were on the same wavelength. "I might have dug into some of those boxes you left lying around the house."

She glanced at the lake, a frown pulling at her lips. "How cold is the water?"

"Cold. But I brought that lotion that claims to heat things up. If you're interested."

Gabriella undid the buttons of her blouse, one by one. "I'm game if you are. Bring it on, cowboy."

Brad couldn't do anything but sit and watch as Gabriella performed an impulsive striptease. She pulled off her boots, shucked her shirt and unbuckled the belt of her jeans.

"Don't just sit there. You're coming in with me." She tilted her head toward the waterfall. "It's like a big shower, isn't it?"

"Yeah. But I don't like cold showers."

She tilted her head to the side. "That lotion works both ways, you know. What if I promise to heat you up?"

They didn't last two minutes in the water. Once she figured out exactly how cold a melted snowcap was, they rinsed off the trail dust and got out, laughing and shivering as they ran to the fire for warmth.

"Your teeth are chattering."

Brad drew her beneath the sleeping bag with him and began to rub his hands up and down her length, leaving her gasping. She didn't remember ever having so much fun with someone, and she was a little surprised to discover this side of Brad. Or that it appealed so much.

She felt freer, more comfortable with him, than she had with anyone in her entire life. At the same time there was an edge, a hunger, she couldn't deny. One that grew every time he touched her, rather than waned.

Despite the goose bumps, her body warmed at his touch. She held him close as he slathered the lotion on her and began to rub a little more slowly. Before long they were both slick, her hands trailing down his broad chest to his hip and the hard length of him.

"Gabriella."

Teasing him and drawing groans and shuddering inhalations, she rolled on protection and plastered herself to his front, her body tingling from the lotion and his touch. She found a rhythm immediately, sat on his lap and held on to his shoulders while he guided her with his hands.

Whatever happened, whatever the future held, she was thankful to have this time. To be in this place. Here. Like this.

ON SUNDAY MORNING GABRIELLA surprised Brad with Merrilee's secret weapon—biscuits baked over the fire.

He had been so good to choose food she could eat, even bringing eggs along, so Gabriella decided to show him what she'd learned.

Her treat went over well with Brad, who raved about his breakfast. Maybe Merrilee was on to something with her comment about the way to a good man's heart.

Gabriella and Brad explored the area a little, spent a lot of time in the tent and fell asleep in each other's arms, staring up at the star-studded sky.

On Monday morning, Brad decided to surprise her—but it had nothing to do with breakfast and everything to do with creativity. He kissed her awake, touched her until she squirmed then dared her to climb aboard his horse with him and let him show her how much fun riding could be.

She'd thought him insane but a part of her was intrigued. She rose to the challenge and followed him outside.

But as Gabriella held on to his broad shoulders and stared at the waterfall in a daze, she knew she would never, ever be the same.

THEY LEFT FOR HOME ON TUESDAY.

When Gabriella had begun thinking of the ranch house as home, she wasn't sure. But after spending Sunday and Monday camping at the lake, making love in the tent, braving the falls several times for the brief minutes they could tolerate the cold and simply being with Brad, her thoughts were heavy as they loaded up the horses and climbed into their saddles.

She told herself not to look back. The entire time they'd been together Brad hadn't once said a word to indicate his feelings were more than physical. She was a big girl. They had had a good time. Chemistry couldn't make up for the two very different lives they led.

Could it?

Still, as they guided their horses out of the clearing, she did look back.

And she did wonder.

That night their passion was even more intense. The moment dinner was over Brad stood and drew Gabriella to her feet and they stumbled toward the tent, pulling at clothes and kissing as though they'd never see each other again. As though it was the end.

Molly had always said Gabriella had a sixth sense about such things. Before she shut her eyes for the night, Gabriella prayed hard that Molly was wrong.

CHAPTER TWENTY-SEVEN

BRAD FROWNED AS THEY made it to the ranch house and the men were nowhere to be seen, Chance included. The door was open, the screen door revealing Crystal on the other side as though she'd been watching for their return.

She stepped onto the porch, a coffee cup in her hand. The pinched look on her carefully made-up features alerted him to the fact she'd had days to stew in her anger. This wasn't going to be pretty.

"Hey, Mom. We're back."

"So I see." Crystal was dressed in black. A high collar framed her head with dramatic flare, a wide belt cinched her waist and she wore a wrap of some kind despite the fact the temperature was in the low eighties.

"I'm sorry I didn't wake you when we left but the trip was a surprise to me, too. Brad didn't want me to worry about it."

"But it was okay for me to worry? I've been calling you to check on you. I've been worried sick. Do you know all the things that pop into a mother's head when her child doesn't respond for *days?*"

Brad remained silent but he could tell Gabriella was feeling the weight of Crystal's words. To be honest, he was, too. Her love and concern for Gabriella was genuine.

"I forgot to charge my phone the, uh, night before we left. Then we were out of range. I'm sorry."

"What if something had happened to you?"

"Brad would have protected me."

"And if something had happened to him? You would have been out there unprotected and— Gabriella, I didn't raise you to be so irresponsible."

Gabriella dismounted and dug into the saddlebag she'd taken with her. Brad hated to see the phone make a return because once it did...

"Mom, it's done. I'm here now as you can see. We're both fine."

Crystal clearly wasn't mollified. "Yes, well, I'm not the only one who has been frantic to get in touch with you."

"Alicia?" Gabriella looked at her mother. "What's wrong?"

"She wouldn't give me details, only that it had something to do with the Lewis-Tate event. She seemed very upset."

"Oh, no. That's our biggest client right now," Gabriella said to Brad. "I have to call her."

"I'll see to the horses." He slid off Major and began to unload the items that needed to go into the house. He needed to radio Chance to find out where the men were, ride out and check on things himself.

"How dare you take off with my daughter like that," Crystal said the moment Gabriella was out of earshot. "If anything had happened to her—"

"I'd die before I'd let that happen," Brad said with brutal honesty, despite what it revealed about his emotions. It would be public knowledge soon enough. Seeing as how they'd made the trip to the falls alone, people would talk and he didn't want anyone talking about Gabriella that way.

He led the horses to the barn. Unsaddling them and leaving them in the corral with an extra treat didn't take long. He made his way to the house and gathered the items he'd left on the porch, noting Crystal hadn't bothered to carry in any of them, not even the name-brand bag of Gabriella's. *Left to the hired help.*

Inside, he dumped the lot of it on a bench at the base of the stairs and headed straight for the coffeepot. Gabriella was a heavy coffee drinker and he hadn't packed enough to see them through, slacking off on his portion this morning so she'd get her fix. Now to take care of his, he thought, pleased to see that Crystal was domestic enough to see that a fresh pot brewed.

Down the hall, the door to Zane's office opened and Brad recognized Gabriella's footsteps followed by the click of Crystal's heels.

"What are you going to do?" Crystal asked.

Brad sipped and waited for the women to enter the kitchen. Gabriella's expression tightened his gut. "What's wrong?"

"We have a very high profile, very vocal client who isn't pleased that he planned his events through me but I'm not there to execute them. He refuses to work with Alicia, and says if I'm not there to handle his engagement activities as planned, he wants a refund and will let everyone know we performed what he's calling a bait and switch." She closed her eyes and rubbed her palm against her forehead. "I can't lose this account."

"It's just one guy," Brad said.

A weak laugh escaped Gabriella. "It's a three-million-dollar event that takes place in one day."

Three million dollars in a single day? "A wedding?"

he asked, unable to comprehend spending that kind of money on anything but the land where they stood.

"A proposal. The wedding will most likely top ten to fifteen million, and if I keep him as a client—"

"You could be planning it." This world of extremes astounded him. Some people had too much money and no sense. A three-million-dollar engagement? Ten- to fifteen-million-dollar wedding? And then what? A twenty-million-dollar honeymoon?

"Exactly. The commission would go a long way to filling in the financial cracks of opening a second location."

Brad gripped the mug in his hand a little tighter. She was still talking about a second location? Even after the past five days?

"The only thing I can think of is that nowhere in Zane's will does it state that I have to be on the ranch twenty-four hours a day, only that I had to stay here, sleep here. If I catch a red-eye to L.A., do the event and fly home before midnight…"

Brad nodded, willing to accept almost anything if it meant Gabriella wasn't leaving for long. Crystal's hovering presence and peeved attitude wasn't lost on him but he chose to ignore it for the time being. If he had his way, ignoring Crystal was something he needed to learn how to do. Still, he would prefer to be having this conversation with Gabriella alone.

"That sounds like a wonderful plan. While you're there you can drop off the contract to Richard. He shipped it here while you were gone. All it needs is your signature."

"Who's Richard?" Brad asked, the knot in his gut growing bigger once more.

"Richard is one of the best real estate brokers on the

West Coast," Crystal said. "He's going to be handling the sale of Gabriella's inheritance."

"You've already contacted some real estate guy?"

"Richard isn't *some real estate guy*," Crystal argued. "He has contacts willing to pay *more* than the estimated million."

"Mother, please. Shut *up*."

More? He had yet to finalize scraping together a number close to the estimated value. He could never come up with more. "You agreed to this?"

Gabriella swallowed audibly. "Yes."

"When?"

"*Before*. I agreed to talk to him before we…left."

A spark of hope flared to life. "And now?"

If Gabriella said she'd changed her mind, if she said she loved him, if she said she'd *stay*— All she had to do was say the words.

But seconds ticked by and Brad stared at her, waiting, hoping and praying for a compromise. Nothing. If she would only say the words. Tell him she loved him, that she wouldn't sell them out. Somehow he'd come up with an answer.

But that didn't happen and it wasn't going to.

"Mom, why don't you go pack?"

"Of course."

Crystal flashed Brad a parting smile. "Welcome home." She'd gotten her way and she knew it.

"You never once considered holding on to your inheritance, did you?"

"Brad…"

The earth shifted on its axis because of the guilty expression Gabriella wore. "The whole time you've been here… Even when you were sleeping in my bed?"

"I have to sell."

"No, you damn well *don't*."

Gabriella glanced toward the stairs before she moved closer to him.

"You are unbelievable," he said. "You've made friends here, settled in better than I ever thought you could. It was all an act, wasn't it?"

"No. Brad, I love it here."

"Then why the hell are you so willing to be rid of it? Does money mean that much to you?"

"Brad, listen to me. It's not what it looks like."

"You sure about that? Because it looks to me like you used me and Zane's list to pass your time here but you never once took your eyes off the million-dollar prize. How much more is Richard going to get you?"

Gabriella closed her eyes briefly before inhaling and staring at Brad full-on. "I'm not sure. And before my mother finds some shocking way to blurt it out, you need to know something. Alicia and I agreed on a partnership in exchange for her covering the three months that I'm here. The deal was I'd get the money, expand the business and we'd each run a location of *Premiere Vue* in exchange for her working seven days a week. I have a signed agreement with her. If I don't do this, she still gets half the business."

"I don't imagine expanding a business comes cheap—especially in Hollywood."

"Exactly."

"Friends don't come cheap, either, Gabriella. Good friends, people you can count on when you need them. How are you going to look the Browns or anyone else in the face after you do this? Or does that even register with you when you have three-million-dollar engagements to plan for people who won't be married in six months?"

"If there was another way…"

But there wasn't. Not one she'd ever consider because it would mean getting less money.

And that was his answer.

He yanked his hat firmly on his head. "You are your mother's daughter, aren't you?"

He watched Gabriella flinch with the impact of his words but he hardened his heart to the sight. Obviously what had taken place between them meant nothing to her, whereas he'd fallen like a boy with his first girl. How could she do this? How was he going to stand being under the same roof with her for the remainder of her stay? It would be hell. If Gabriella cared for him at all, she wouldn't dream of selling. "Zane said once that Crystal wanted to rough it with him to pass the time in that airport. Is that why you were with me? Did Hollywood want some country while you were here?"

"No." Gabriella lifted her chin, her face flushing as her eyes glinted with embarrassment. But she should be embarrassed. So should he. He's the one who should have known better.

"Then why, damn it?" The words came out low and rough and bitter though he tried to hold them back. To have some pride and dignity when he had none left. He felt used, like a male prostitute, worth some cash and a good time but nothing more.

"Gabriella, do not respond to that," Crystal said from the stairs. "Brad obviously thought seducing you would work to his advantage. He's the one who should be made to feel ashamed and embarrassed of his actions, not you."

Brad didn't deny the claim, though he knew he should. He didn't care what Gabriella thought. Not now.

With one last glare at Crystal, Brad gathered up what

was left of his pride and headed outside. Atop Major, he charged down the road, cutting across the field away from them all.

What a fool. Taking her to the waterfall had been a mistake. Like Zane, he'd gambled and lost. He'd hoped Gabriella would see the beauty and the land would endear itself to her, make it so she couldn't bear to part with it. But he didn't doubt all she'd seen were more dollar signs.

And he'd played right into her hands instead of doing everything in his power to send her away the way he should have done from the start. Asking him to rub lotion on her? Sleeping with him? She'd known what she was doing.

He needed to call Chance and Liam. Needed to call the attorney.

Come hell or high water, they weren't going to go down without a fight.

CHAPTER TWENTY-EIGHT

GABRIELLA STARED AFTER Brad's retreating form for a long time, waiting, wishing he'd turn around and come back. He didn't. He kept going, disappearing from view.

In fantasies and old Westerns, cowboys rode off into the sunset *with* the damsel. They didn't leave her behind. But what else had she expected from him? She'd known he wouldn't take the news well.

"Come inside, Gabriella. You must be exhausted. You can rest after you pack. I'll call the airport and make the arrangements."

Gabriella turned toward her mother and noted Crystal's overbearing satisfaction. It was in her mother's expression, her stance.

She and Brad had had such a wonderful time at the waterfall, on the journey, long though it was. But Brad's expression had been easy to read. Anger and disappointment, bitterness. Hurt. But at no point in time did she see any sign of love. Not once had Brad complained about her leaving—and didn't that say a lot about their relationship?

Maybe what they both needed was some breathing room, time to think and figure things out. *If there is anything to figure out.*

"Oh, I knew this would happen. Men think of themselves and anything they want first." Crystal's words cut deep and Gabriella was rendered speechless from the pain.

Brad wanted the land. So was that the sole reason he had slept with her? Had she ignored her earlier cynicism about his reasons for saying he wanted to be more when she was right all along?

She cared for Brad, deeply, but under the circumstances who wouldn't be suspicious? The look on his face…

Like some bad movie cliché, Brad was desperate to save the ranch. Desperate enough to sleep with her, pretend, in order to get what he wanted?

In her heart of hearts, she knew it was unfair to doubt him given her own questionable actions, but how could she not? Love was about trust and how could she ever know if Brad wanted her, truly, deeply cared for her, or if he wanted a piece of property?

The pain of the realization took the breath right out of her lungs.

"Gabriella, I can't stand seeing you like this. You need to dig deep. Be the strong, wise woman I raised you to be. Your father always put this ranch first, and Brad is a product of his upbringing. A boy who came from nothing who doesn't want to lose the gift he's been given. I don't want to hurt you, I swear it, but you had to have considered the possibility that his motives were deceptive."

Gabriella couldn't look at her mother. Crystal was oftentimes manipulative and would use every opportunity to further her cause—that of getting Gabriella back to California—but facts were facts. Right now she needed that bluntness, that slap in the face capable of rendering perspective.

"It's human nature to find yourself attracted to him.

But Brad's not the man for you. You see that, don't you?"

"Why? Because he works hard and gets dirty and isn't some rich producer from Hollywood?" Gabriella argued for the sake of arguing. She wanted to fight, wanted to strike at…everyone.

"*You know I'm right.* Brad riding off like that proves it. It's the perfect example of your future, him leaving you stuck here in this Godforsaken place, giving up *everything* for him. And for what? I don't see him standing here at your side."

She hated it when her mother made sense. Maybe Brad had thrown the accusation at her about her using him but the first to accuse was typically the one guilty of the crime. Samuel had accused her of cheating when all along he'd been the one cheating on her. The same concept applied here.

Maybe she'd gotten swept up in the romance of it all, the fantasy. Like her business, she'd put a romantic spin on being here, living with him. Flirting with him. But peel away the layers and Brad's readiness to accuse her then abandon her said all she needed to know.

"Let's go inside. You can sign the papers Richard sent while I help you pack."

Inside the kitchen Gabriella gazed at the scarred and scratched furnishings, the worn wood, the house smelling of lemon polish letting her know Sally had come and gone. "I don't want you to come back," she said, watching as her mother's expression tightened. "Pack everything you brought. I'm returning alone."

"Gabriella—"

"Enough, Mom. The truth is out in the open for everyone to see. You don't need to be here any longer."

Looking uncertain, Crystal lifted her chin. "I don't

mind coming back with you to finish this. Uri is…upset with me."

Despite the brevity of the description, Gabriella understood perfectly well why and knew her mother was up to her old tricks. "Who was the guy?"

"An old friend. A producer. We had a few drinks and one thing led to another… It didn't mean anything."

Of course it didn't. Because nothing was sacred to her mother. Not wedding vows, not trust, nothing.

By bringing Gabriella here, Zane had given her something far more valuable than land or water rights. He'd given her a new way of viewing life, a sense of peace, belonging. Showed her how responsibility and love and respect for others went hand in hand.

Zane had visited the parents of his long-dead wife. He'd played Santa. He'd performed tasks simply because he'd loved. And in tackling his list—even the simplistic things—he'd taught Gabriella to love, to give. To see things in a new light that wasn't jaded by Hollywood's so-called morals where so long as you weren't caught nothing mattered.

They entered Gabriella's bedroom. Crystal immediately moved to the closet to pull out Gabriella's suitcases but Gabriella stared around the room, finally crossing to the bedside table where Zane kept one of the few pictures taken of him and her together.

When she'd first slept in the room she'd turned the photo facedown, too angry to look at it. Now…the photo would go home with her.

"Gabriell— Oh." Crystal looked at the photo.

Gabriella wasn't sure what it was that broke through her mother's facade but something did. It began with a flash of insecurity, a crack in the veneer Crystal had worked so hard to perfect.

"He's not here to argue with you anymore. Are you still upset because I had to get to know him better?"

The sunlight shining through the window revealed the slight show of gray at Crystal's roots. "No, I suppose not. I knew it might happen one day. I'd…hoped it wouldn't."

"How did he find out about me? You said he'd proposed to you. How did it happen?"

"Zane flew to California because he said he had to know there hadn't been any consequences." Her mother's face deepened with guilty color. "I had planned— When I found out I was pregnant, I was going to take care of things on my own."

Realization dawned with a sick twist to her stomach. Aborted? She'd almost been *aborted?*

"I changed my mind, Gabriella. I couldn't do it. They showed me a picture of you and…I couldn't. When Zane arrived later that week, I was terribly ill with morning sickness. He was sweet. He fixed me soup and took care of me and for a while I thought maybe it could work between us."

"But?"

"Exactly what I told you. We were too different, Gabriella. He hated the things I loved."

"And vice versa."

"Yes. I wanted to stay in California and he refused to consider staying here. No woman wants to be second. It was bad enough Zane still mourned his dead wife but I had to compete with the ranch, too? No. I know I can be selfish but that wasn't something I was willing to compromise on. So we discussed other options. Since a single man running a ranch wasn't the best father material, he agreed to my raising you. It wasn't until you were older that he wanted more."

Gabriella closed her eyes, pain shooting deep into her heart. Zane *had* wanted her, finally Crystal admitted it. She wasn't sure why it was a milestone but it was. "Keep going. There's something you aren't saying."

Crystal tried to take Gabriella in her arms but Gabriella moved away, hugging the photo to her chest.

"I was afraid. You know how the business is and sometimes I felt so alone and I didn't— I couldn't lose you."

"From the sound of it you didn't *want* me."

"I did. I panicked at first but once I realized— Gabriella, you can accuse me a lot of things but not loving you isn't one of them. Zane would come to visit. He'd never stay longer than a few days because he always had to get back here," she said bitterly. "But that was acceptable and doable. When you were older, every time he visited all you talked about was seeing him again. Staying here with him. It scared me and I knew I'd lose you."

"That's no excuse."

"I know. But things were different then. When you were young we were so close and I wanted *our* life, not his. If he'd been willing to sell out and stay in California, put me first?"

"His roots were deeper than yours, Mom. Look at you now. You're fifty-two and you're trying to act like some starlet breaking onto the scene."

"I like my life," Crystal stated simply. "And while I'm not proud of some of my actions, I make no excuse for that."

"That's fine for you. But that isn't my life."

"Of course it is. Places like this are for vacation, Gabriella. They're pretty to look at and explore but they're not for people like us. That summer, when Zane brought you here and you were almost *killed?* That's when I knew I had to do something to protect you, to keep you from wanting to stay here permanently."

"So you told him he had to come to us or not see me at all."

"He was so frightened by what had almost happened, he readily agreed, Gabriella. I didn't coerce him, if that's what you're thinking. I'm not proud of some of the things I've done, but I did them to protect you, because I thought they were best for you. Right now is another example. You don't belong here, but I can see you faltering because of Brad. Can't you see history repeating itself? You're me. Brad is Zane. You have to leave while you still can."

Gabriella tried to ward off the truth of her mother's comparison. Hadn't she thought the same thing herself? There was one glaring exception, however. "Maybe I am you. In a sense," Gabriella was careful to add. "And maybe Brad is like Zane but you're missing something important and that is how much I care for Brad. We're not you and Zane. It wasn't just sex. Not to me."

Crystal's eyes filled with tears, genuine ones. "Then I feel sorry for you, because that man will never look at you and not see the piece of property you'll soon own. Can you live with that for the rest of your life?"

GABRIELLA FELL ASLEEP on the downstairs couch waiting for Brad to return before she and Crystal had to leave for the airport.

He didn't.

So she'd gone to L.A. on the red-eye, soothed the massive ego of her client and watched as the couple kissed and laughed and celebrated their five-star engagement.

If she were a betting woman, she'd give them six months as Brad said. No doubt the wedding preparations would last longer than the marriage.

It had taken everything in her to get on the plane for her return flight. Because throughout the day when she'd get a moment she'd called the house and Brad's cell only to be ignored.

Now here it was, after midnight, and Brad wasn't home. She'd done a lot of pacing, a lot of mumbling, showered, and even made a list of things she wanted to clear up between them when he finally returned. The list was in her pocket, carefully folded and ready at a moment's notice.

Gabriella sat up on the couch and swung her legs to the floor, stretching out the kinks and holding her neck because of the taut muscles.

Fine, he didn't want to come to her? She'd go to him. One way or another they had to settle this and she had to know the truth.

Gabriella passed a mirror on the way to the kitchen and groaned at her reflection. She fluffed up her hair, pinched her cheeks and forced a smile in a sad attempt to erase her sleepless nights. Whatever. It would have to do. She was not her mother, who would go upstairs and throw on some war paint before letting herself be seen.

She pulled on her shoes and left the house. Brad had to be in the barn, or the bunkhouse or—she had no idea.

The barn was quiet, empty. Star Bright came trotting to the fence and nickered softly.

Gabriella petted the horse and rubbed her soft nose, amazed at her actions after having been afraid so long. "Where is he, girl?"

"Miss?"

Gabriella turned and spotted Charlie standing a few feet away.

"You all right?"

"Yes. Just restless."

Charlie nodded. "Seems to be a lot of that going around. If you're looking for Brad, he ain't here."

Her stomach knotted into a hard lump of unease. "Do you know where he is?"

"Said he was heading out to the west corner along the ridge. He's probably staying in a line shack out there."

"Oh. I see. I guess I'll talk to him tomorrow—er, this evening, then."

"He won't be back for a while. Maybe not for a week or more."

A *week?* He was that desperate to avoid her?

"Is it true? You're selling us out?"

She didn't need to explain herself to anyone, but Charlie was a nice man. "When I came here I planned to sell the moment the land was mine. But now…it's a little more personal."

"So you ain't going to sell?"

"Charlie, your guess is as good as mine. I need cash, and a lot of it," she stated bluntly. "But I know people like Merrilee and Barney are involved and it's not such an easy decision. Life is rarely easy, is it?"

"No, miss. It rarely is."

Looking at the man, she'd guess not. Charlie wore his years on his face. "I've been trying to come up with an alternative to selling. Maybe I can get a mortgage to finance the expansion of my business."

Charlie shoved his finger beneath the rim of his hat to scratch his balding head. "What happens if the business fails? You might not want to think of something bad happening to it, but if it does it does, that means we still got to be prepared for the fallout. The bank would take the land and not think twice about it. Especially that piece."

As much as she didn't want to agree, it was true. Being the savvy businesswoman she was, why hadn't she considered that aspect of her hastily thought-up plan? No one wanted to think of a business failing but it was something she had to consider.

What a mess. As bad as it was recovering from Molly's passing, life had been simpler before learning of her inheritance. The weight of the consequences from her actions was a heavy one to carry.

"In all my years of working here, I never seen Brad so angry before. Now I understand why."

A rough huff left her chest. *Brad* was angry? So was she. Her father had put her in an impossible situation. He'd given her access to her and Molly's dream only to attach a heavy emotional burden.

Brad should be standing where Charlie was, thanking her because Crystal was gone. Thankful that Gabriella was open to discuss options given the state of their relationship and what he'd said to her.

Gabriella realized she was Zane McKenna's daughter after all. Because no matter how angry Brad was with her, he'd done his job well. She'd learned to love this ranch, too. It needed to be watched over, protected. And only one man could do that. She couldn't take that away from Brad—nor could she be with him when she would always question the source of their relationship.

Her father had walked away from her out of love, because he'd wanted to do what was best for her.

Now, it was up to her to make the same decision.

CHAPTER TWENTY-NINE

ON SATURDAY MORNING Brad dismounted, bone-deep exhausted from working hard enough for three men in an attempt to fall into his cot in one of the line shacks out on the range and sleep peacefully. Didn't happen.

This morning he'd woken up to discover his anger with Gabriella had diminished, waning to the point of bitter acceptance. Zane had taken a gamble but he'd known the risks when he'd left his daughter that plot of land. Whatever happened, he had understood the consequences. And since he had believed Brad could triumph regardless of the result, he had to find a way to do that.

Storing up water reserves and finding a back-up system would take time and a hell of a lot of money he and his brothers didn't have. But they could do it somehow. Their very lives depended upon it.

Chance's truck was parked outside the house when Brad approached and he noticed Zane's old truck nearby. Gabriella's car was gone.

Good. Maybe he could get in, have his weekly meeting with Chance to go over the books and expenses for the ranch and the store and get out before Gabriella returned from wherever she was. "Chance?"

"Hey, didn't think you were coming. Where you been?" Chance called from the den.

Brad headed toward the stairs and ignored his brother's question. "Give me five minutes to shower."

He took the steps two at a time and was back downstairs in seven. Chance had coffee waiting for him. "Thanks."

"No problem. Figured you might need it."

Brad sipped the too-hot coffee, appreciative that it was fresh and strong and black. "How have things been this week? Picking up?"

"That's it? *How have things been?*"

He didn't want to get into it. "I needed to get away. Have Gabriella and her mother been giving you a hard time?"

Chance stared at him in confusion. "Look around, Brad. See anything missing?"

For the first time he realized all of Gabriella's stuff was gone. The negligees, the lotions. Everything.

"They're gone. Crystal left the same day you did. Gabriella came back like you said she would but she packed up and pulled out the day after."

Brad couldn't think straight. "She's gone?"

"If you'd have taken a radio with you, you might know these things."

All he knew was that it was a good thing he was sitting down. "I noticed her car was gone but I thought— I thought she was in town or something. She only had a couple weeks left to get her inheritance."

The screen door opened then banged closed.

"Anybody home?" Liam called on his way down the hall. "Sorry we're late. Had to cover a few hours for someone."

"Brad didn't know Gabriella was gone," Chance called out.

The silence in the room was broken only by the steady *ticking* of the old mantle clock.

Liam entered the room and made himself at home. "Good to see you're back."

Brad didn't acknowledge his brother's words. "I don't get it. Why stay all this time and leave when she's so close to getting the deed?"

Liam swung his foot to the floor and sat forward on the couch. "Gabriella stopped by Carly's on her way out of town. They had some kind of girl pow-wow and ever since then Carly's been muttering under her breath about how stupid men are. You could ask her."

"You haven't?"

"I'm not about to poke that snake's den."

To be honest Brad didn't want to, either. "Guess we need to call the bank and tell them to transfer the funds?"

"I already did," Chance said.

"Losing a hundred grand is going to make for a long year but we dodged a bullet," Liam said. "Whatever happened to change her mind, Gabriella did us a favor by leaving."

That she had. But why, when she was halfway to her goal?

"Strange thing, though." Chance rubbed his hand over his mouth and stared at Brad with a thoughtful expression.

"What?" Brad asked.

"I had the bank transfer the money the day after she left, since the will was broken by her not sleeping here."

"So?"

Chance pointed to the computer screen. "It's in the account."

Brad's stomach twisted into a hard knot. "What?"

"No way," Liam murmured.

Chance nodded. "When you came downstairs I was about to call Joe Kinney at home and see if he could log into the bank records to check it out for us."

Seconds later Chance was on the phone, while Brad paced and Liam fidgeted.

"Thanks. Yeah, I'll tell him." Chance hung up.

"Well?"

"Joe said he's been expecting our call and that we need to ask Carly."

"Carly?" Liam demanded, standing and visibly befuddled.

"Apparently the girls are in cahoots about something," Chance informed them.

Brad didn't wait for his brothers as he hurried to the kitchen. The moment Carly's gaze met his, he knew Chance's statement was true. Normally warm and friendly, this time his sweet little future sister-in-law glared at him. "What's going on?"

Carly was mixing up a batch of cookies. "Took you long enough. I can't believe you're only now getting around to asking."

"Caroline," Liam said, the use of her given name revealing his frustration with being kept in the dark.

"The money is still in the account, right?"

"Yeah," Brad said. "Why is it still there?"

"Let's see, Brad, *why* do you think? I mean, really. Gabriella had a chance at inheriting a massive amount of property worth *a lot* of money. Instead, she left and voided the terms of the will. You guys sent her money, but she didn't accept it. Do you really not understand *why?*"

Brad waited, unable to breathe because of the band around his chest, squeezing. He didn't dare hope.

"Men really are blind when it comes to women, aren't they?" She gave a disgusted sigh.

She walked to her purse and pulled out an envelope that she slapped against Brad's chest. He caught it instinctively.

"For the record, I *hate* being compared to my mother, too," Carly drawled sharply. "And if you can't get it through that thick skull of yours that Gabriella is in love with you and *do something* about it, I'm going to bop you upside the head even if I have to get a chair to stand on in order to do it."

"She said that? That she loves me?"

For the first time since her rant began, Carly faltered. "No, but—"

She had a bit of a romantic streak a mile wide and no doubt she was seeing what she wanted to see.

"Open the letter. What's it say?" Chance demanded.

They gathered around Brad but he needed some space and some air to come to terms with whatever was going on. Was it possible? Was Carly right?

But what about Crystal? Gabriella's life in California?

"Don't just stand there, hurry up and read it so we know what's going on," Liam ordered.

Brad didn't look at them. Carrying his letter, he went out to the porch and sat in Gabriella's spot on the swing.

I wrote a list of things I wanted to talk to you about but it's really quite simple. If you're reading this, it's because I'm giving up something big because I want something bigger.
—G
P.S. It wasn't because I wanted to rough it. Keep the money. Use it to keep my father's dream alive.

The screen door opened and his family emerged from the house, but all Brad could do was stare at the paper in front of him. He'd gotten what he'd wanted. She was gone. The land, the money. "It's ours," he said, aware they waited for a response from him. "It's all ours."

Because she wanted something bigger.

Did that mean what he thought that meant? What about Gabriella's dream? Molly's?

He had to clear his throat twice to speak. "I have to go."

"Where?"

The knot in his stomach tightened but he kept walking, hurrying to his truck. "California."

"Wait." Four hours later, Brad grabbed Alicia's arm to stop her as she left the store.

She reacted instantly and before Brad knew what hit him, Alicia had nailed him in the chest, no doubt going for the throat, and taken him down to his knees.

"What the hell. You stupid cowboy, what are you doing here? Haven't you done enough?"

Brad wheezed, thankful Alicia released him the moment she recognized him. "Where is she?"

"Like I'd tell you." She took a step as though to walk away and, despite the danger, he reached out again, this time clutching her purse. "I need to see her."

Alicia glared at him, one eyebrow raised high as he got to his feet.

"There a problem over there?" a man called from down the alley where he was carting boxes to a Dumpster.

"No, Carl. Only a moron on the loose."

Brad watched as she waved the man to return to his

work then crossed her arms over her chest. The guy kept watching.

"You have five seconds to convince me. Go."

"Alicia…"

"Three."

"I love her," he blurted, shocked to hear himself say it out loud. And to the wrong woman, no less. Brad swore at himself and paced away to the brick building across the alley.

"You told her she acts like her *mother*."

Did every woman have issues with that? "I was angry. I realize now I was wrong."

"And?"

And what? "I need to see Gabriella. Where is she? I went to her apartment but she's not there."

"She's not here, either."

Holding on to his patience took more willpower than he thought he possessed.

"You really love her?"

"I'm here, aren't I?"

Alicia lifted her chin and regarded him with a superior stare. "I guess you are. Come with me."

GABRIELLA SMILED and held her arms out to accept the engagement gift from a sixtyish Hollywood producer and the twenty-something starlet on his arm. Gabriella put the gift with the others on the beautifully decorated table as promised, then continued on her mission to check with the caterers.

The hotel ballroom was draped in mini white lights, with touches of soft pink here and there. The cake was three tiers, the flowers imported, the invitees the hottest stars and movers and shakers in the business.

After returning from Montana, she'd thrown herself

into her work, even more so than before Molly's death. Alicia hadn't been pleased by her sudden reappearance so close to the end goal, nor had she liked the fact Gabriella had refused the hundred grand.

But it was the right thing to do, the only thing to do in her opinion. She'd promised Alicia she would find a way to open up a second location and give Alicia the partnership as agreed. Things between them had been tense but Alicia had managed to set her feelings aside and accept Gabriella's decision.

Then again, Alicia's acceptance might have been based on how Gabriella, upset and nearly incoherent, had appeared on her doorstep in the middle of the night after she'd landed in L.A.

Gabriella was observing the wait staff when a disturbance at the entrance drew her attention. She turned to see Alicia talking with the event manager and head of security.

Gabriella sighed. Another gate crasher? Ever since the movie *Wedding Crashers,* it had become an even bigger game to fans of Hollywood's elite. But with Alicia at the door, Gabriella knew the matter would be handled.

Still, seconds later murmurs arose from the crowd and Gabriella turned in time to see a dark-haired man rapidly making his way across the room. The crowd parted and for the first time she caught a glimpse of Brad.

Dressed in jeans, boots, a black button-down shirt and a black hat he looked rough and dangerous and the sight of him took her breath away. What was he doing here? *Here?*

His ears were a dull burgundy because everyone stared. The moment he got within range of her, Brad reached out, took her face in his hands and kissed her until all she could do was hold on.

A combination of gasps, chuckles and *ahs* emerged from the crowd.

When he let her up for air, Gabriella struggled to concentrate. "What— What are you doing here?"

"I came for you."

"Why? You got what you wanted, you got all of it."

"What I *thought* I wanted. I want the land, Gabriella, we need it, you know that. But more than anything I want *you*. I'm not leaving without you."

"Not leaving without— You *left* me when you rode off into the sunset without me."

"I know. But I'm here now."

"Oh, so that's supposed to make me feel better?"

"Gabriella, I want something bigger, too. Why would I be here if I didn't have something more important on my mind? I braved a plane for you. I got my ass grabbed by two *guys* trying to get here to you," he added, drawing another laugh from those close enough to hear his words. "I'm sorry. Do you hear me?"

Brad pressed another short kiss to her lips, their noses touching. "I was a blind, terrified fool, but I'm here begging you to forgive me. Come home with me, be with me. *Marry* me. We'll keep your father's dream alive together. And Molly's. We'll figure out a way to make them both happen."

It sounded wonderful, like a fairy tale. But how could they do both? What about her life here?

"I know there's a lot to figure out but we'll do it. You worked from your computer the past couple of months. What if you made that more permanent? You can fly here when you need to. I'm not asking you to give up everything, just compromise so we can be together."

"Why?"

The red in his face got a little darker. "You know why."

"Say it." She had to hear him say it. Before she let down her guard completely and allowed herself to believe, she had to hear him say the words.

"I love you, Gabriella McKenna."

McKenna, not Thompson. She smiled at his declaration, aware that the guests had moved closer them. To bear witness. Not that it mattered. All that mattered was Brad. "I love you, too. I have since that day you made me pet Pikipsi."

A slow, sexy smile curved his lips. "And?"

"You'll compromise, too? On everything?"

"Like what?"

"Cut back on red meat?"

"We'll discuss it."

"Recycle?"

"With pleasure."

She tilted her head to one side and lowered her voice. "We'll get to ride double again?"

His eyes darkened with a promising gleam. "As soon as I can find a horse."

The knot in her stomach loosened by slow degrees. "Did you sleep with me to get the land?"

"I slept with you because I wanted you. Still do. I want you more than I ever thought possible considering the first time I saw you I wanted to strangle you. Now answer the question, woman."

She laughed at his tough-man expression. Beneath the frown, she saw so much more. "Yes, I'll marry you."

The moment she agreed, Brad gave her the sweetest, hottest kiss imaginable. He gathered her into his arms, drew her to her very tip-toes and kissed her to the point of oblivion.

The crowd broke into applause she barely heard because of the way her pulse sounded in her ears.

The moment Brad ended the kiss, Gabriella searched the room, finding Alicia standing nearby, tears in her eyes as she smiled and gave her a thumbs-up. The bride-to-be looked at her aging, forty-years-her-senior husband, a wistful look on her very perfect face, and more than one producer and director pulled out a cell phone to make a call, whispering about treatments and screenplays.

"We're going to wind up a Lifetime movie," she whispered.

"That wouldn't be so bad."

She looked at Brad in surprise. "I can't believe you said that."

"Sweetheart—" he dropped his voice to a low, sexy murmur "—you know good and well these yahoos could to learn a thing or two from us cowboys."

* * * * *

COMING NEXT MONTH

Available November 8, 2011

You can find more information on upcoming
Harlequin® titles, free excerpts and more at
www.HarlequinInsideRomance.com.

HSRCNM1011

REQUEST YOUR FREE BOOKS!
2 FREE NOVELS PLUS 2 FREE GIFTS!

Harlequin

Super Romance

Exciting, emotional, unexpected!

HSR11

Harlequin® Special Edition® is thrilled to present a new installment in USA TODAY *bestselling author RaeAnne Thayne's reader-favorite miniseries,* THE COWBOYS OF COLD CREEK.

Join the excitement as we meet the Bowmans—four siblings who lost their parents but keep family ties alive in Pine Gulch. First up is Trace. Only two things get under this rugged lawman's skin: beautiful women and secrets. And in Rebecca Parsons, he finds both!

Read on for a sneak peek of CHRISTMAS IN COLD CREEK. *Available November 2011 from Harlequin® Special Edition®.*

On impulse, he unfolded himself from the bar stool. "Need a hand?"

"Thank you! I…" She lifted her gaze from the floor to his jeans and then raised her eyes. When she identified him her hazel eyes turned from grateful to unfriendly and cold, as if he'd somehow thrown the broken glasses at her head.

He also thought he saw a glimmer of panic in those interesting depths, which instantly stirred his curiosity like cream swirling through coffee.

"I've got it, Officer. Thank you." Her voice was several degrees colder than the whirl of sleet outside the windows.

Despite her protests, he knelt down beside her and began to pick up shards of broken glass. "No problem. Those trays can be slippery."

This close, he picked up the scent of her, something fresh and flowery that made him think of a mountain meadow on a July afternoon. She had a soft, lush mouth and for one brief, insane moment, he wanted to push aside that stray lock of hair slipping from her ponytail and taste her. Apparently he needed to spend a lot less time working and a great deal *more* time recreating with the opposite sex if he could have sudden random fantasies about a woman he wasn't even inclined to like, pretty or not.

"I'm Trace Bowman. You must be new in town."

She didn't answer immediately and he could almost see the wheels turning in her head. Why the hesitancy? And why that little hint of unease he could see clouding the edge of her gaze? His presence was obviously making her uncomfortable and Trace couldn't help wondering why.

"Yes. We've been here a few weeks."

"Well, I'm just up the road about four lots, in the white house with the cedar shake roof, if you or your daughter need anything." He smiled at her as he picked up the last shard of glass and set it on her tray.

Definitely a story there, he thought as she hurried away. He just might need to dig a little into her background to find out why someone with fine clothes and nice jewelry, and who so obviously didn't have experience as a waitress, would be here slinging hash at The Gulch. Was she running away from someone? A bad marriage?

So…Rebecca Parsons. Not Becky. An intriguing woman. It had been a long time since one of those had crossed his path here in Pine Gulch.

Trace won't rest until he finds out Rebecca's secret, but will he still have that same attraction to her once he does? Find out in CHRISTMAS IN COLD CREEK. Available November 2011 from Harlequin® Special Edition®.

Harlequin®
Super Romance®

*Discover a fresh, heartfelt new romance
from acclaimed author*

Sarah Mayberry

Businessman Flynn Randall's life is
complicated. So he doesn't need the
distraction of fun, spontaneous Mel Porter.
But he can't stop thinking about her. Maybe
he can handle one more complication....

All They Need

LONGER
BOOK
Same Price!

*Available November 8, 2011,
wherever books are sold!*

HSR71742

ROMANTIC
SUSPENSE

CARLA CASSIDY
Cowboy's Triplet Trouble

Jake Johnson, the eldest of his triplet brothers, is stunned
when Grace Sinclair turns up on his family's ranch declaring
Jake's younger and irresponsible brother as the father of her
triplets. When Grace's life is threatened, Jake finds himself
fighting a powerful attraction and a need to protect. But as
the threats hit closer to home, Jake begins to wonder
if someone on the ranch is out to kill Grace....

A brand-new Top Secret Deliveries story!

TOP SECRET
DELIVERIES

Available in November wherever books are sold!

www.Harlequin.com

HRS27751